STOLEN

DJINN DOMINION: BOOK 1

CHRISTINE POPE

DARK VALENTINE PRESS

STOLEN

ISBN: 978-1-946435-12-5

Copyright © 2018 by Christine Pope

Published by Dark Valentine Press

Cover design by Lou Harper

Print formatting by Indie Author Services

ONE

Leila Donovan was running. It felt as though all she'd done for the past two months was run—hiding in warehouses, sleeping in abandoned cars, that one strange, brief period when she and the rest of her little group of survivors had taken refuge in the steam tunnels under Caltech.

But then their hiding place had been discovered, and they'd had to run again. So many lost that day to their strangely beautiful but implacable pursuers.

Djinn.

No one had known who they were at first, although Leila had her suspicions. Her mother's family came from Iran and brought their folk tales with them. The terrible beings Leila spied just as the deadly fever began to spread, wiping out everyone she'd known and loved, matched a little too closely the genies of legend that her grandparents had spoken of when they told her bedtime stories. She'd tried to convince herself that it was crazy to think those people she'd seen could be djinn, that these murderous men—and a few women—who looked like supermodels on a rampage had to be something else, but deep down she'd known she wasn't crazy, impossible as the truth appeared on the surface. Besides, the world had gone mad anyway...did the addition of some djinn really make the situation that much worse?

They'd killed Tyrell, the nominal leader of the group who'd hidden underneath Caltech, and Allan. And Macy, and Jack, and Taylor and Emily and Jared. Leila made it a point to remember their names, to murmur them to herself every night before she went to sleep. They shouldn't be forgotten, swept away like the countless millions who were already dead.

Billions, actually. From what Leila had read on the internet before it crashed, and had seen on the local TV stations before they stopped broadcasting, the Heat's mortality rate had been more than ninety-nine percent. How she'd managed to survive, she had no idea. Some strange immunity hidden within her, something that made her and the rest of the people in her group of survivors one in a million, or maybe even more than that. Math had never been her strong suit, and it wasn't as though she'd had time to stop and try to puzzle her way through the numbers.

And now it didn't matter, because they were all dead. Every person who'd shared a space on the floor of the steam tunnels under Caltech was gone. Only Leila was left. How she'd managed that particular feat, she had no idea. It wasn't training or physical superiority, or Tyrell, an ex-Marine who'd once played semi-pro football, would have been the one to survive. Leila was only a waitress and wannabe actress whose world had gone sideways. Maybe it was sheer dumb luck that had kept her alive this long, but she had a feeling that her luck was going to run out in the very near future.

Her heart pounded in her chest and she panted as she ran, wishing she could take the time to drink from the bottle of water that even now smacked into her leg with every stride she took. But there wasn't any time. She would quench her thirst when she found refuge again.

If she found it. It seemed that no matter where she went, her hiding places were discovered. How that was even possible, she didn't know. But she'd come to realize that, once all of her companions had been killed, it was no longer packs of djinn who hunted her.

No, it was just one man who pursued her.

Not a man, a djinn, she reminded herself, dodging around a corner and into a deserted department store. She'd been lurking in the Lincoln Heights area just north of the 5 Freeway for the past few days, stealing what she could from the empty *mercados* and taco shops. The power had been out for nearly two months now, so she didn't dare eat anything that couldn't last without refrigeration. Stale taco shells weren't exactly nourishing, but they were better than starving to death. The freeze-dried food they'd pillaged from a camping store in Pasadena was now long gone. Her hunger had become her only companion, an endless, gnawing ache inside. She could try to ignore it, but it was always there, waiting to weaken her, make her a victim like the companions she'd lost.

Inside the grubby store where she'd taken refuge, the light was dim, barely filtering through the dirty plate-glass windows and the bars that covered them. A shape loomed up at her in the darkness, and she almost let out a frightened little scream before she realized the threatening figure was only a mannequin, one that stared at her with flat, disinterested glass eyes.

The horrible thing about the djinn was that you couldn't hear them pursuing you. They didn't run on foot, but moved through the air, diving to strike like giant birds of prey, or appeared out of nowhere, materializing on the street in an uncanny way that would be frightening enough even if you didn't know why they were chasing you. Why the one that had been tracking her for the past few days had zeroed in on her particularly, Leila didn't know. He was tall and dark-haired, with swarthy skin and black eyes that seemed as if they would bore right through her if she stayed in one place long enough to let them. Handsome, of course, just like they all were. Not that it mattered. They might look like gods on the outside, but inwardly, they were devils straight from hell.

She paused, half-crouched, next to a rack of sweatshirts with various sports team logos screen-printed on them. Those teams were gone now, along with everything else. Maybe somewhere a pro football star had the necessary immunity to survive the Heat, but Leila thought the odds of that happening were pretty low. And even if he had survived, there was no guarantee he would have been able to evade the djinn, who seemed intent on erasing every last man, woman, and child on earth.

Over the past few weeks, she'd learned how to mask her breathing, to take quick, shallow pants that couldn't be overheard even when she'd exerted herself, as she had now. At least, she hoped they couldn't be overheard. She didn't know how sharp the djinns' senses actually were, but she thought they couldn't be too much better than a human's, or else she would have been caught by now.

Why did she keep running? She didn't even know anymore. There didn't seem much left to live for, and yet something within her refused to give up, wouldn't let her stop and turn toward her pursuer, throw open her arms and lift her head to the sky so he might easily slit her throat…if that was even what he had planned for her. She'd seen people blasted by fire, or torn limb from limb by an unseen wind. She'd seen the earth open up and swallow them whole, seen deluges of water appear from pipes and fire hydrants that should have been long dry and sweep their hapless victims away to drown in unnatural floods.

Compared to any of those unfortunate endings, a slit throat seemed pretty mild. And yet she'd continued to run and hide, some instinct within her preventing her from simply giving up. Life—even her current hunted existence—still seemed better than the alternative.

Having caught her breath, Leila figured it was

a good time to move on. She hadn't detected any sounds of pursuit. Maybe the djinn who'd been following her so relentlessly hadn't seen her slip into this shabby store, with its knockoff purses and cheap T-shirts and shelves of useless made-in-China crap.

She looked around, habit born of the past few months of scavenging, scanning the racks of clothes and the display cases, searching for anything that might be of some use. There wasn't much here; what she really needed was a gun store, or at least an outdoor supply shop where she could get a knife and a pistol to replace the ones she'd lost when she'd had to flee her last hiding place, in the basement of a falling-down Craftsman house on the outskirts of Highland Park. The area had begun to get updated and renovated during the past few years, but gentrification hadn't yet found that house. Its deep basement had made it a perfect hidey hole, though.

Or at least, it was perfect until the djinn found her again this morning. Good thing she'd at least been dressed when he came poking around, or she would have had to run from him barefoot.

All her things had been left behind, though, the .45 Tyrell had taught her to shoot, the hunting knife, the travel toothbrush and tiny tube of toothpaste, her underwear and spare jeans and everything she'd held on to through these desperate weeks. Those things could be replaced—it was pretty easy to get what you needed in a place the size of L.A. when most of the population had dropped dead—but the real trick was being able to forage without having your every footstep dogged by an otherworldly pursuer. It was stupid to mourn items that had so little intrinsic value, but she did mourn them, their loss magnified by the much larger losses she'd already suffered.

Leila pulled in a breath and began to inch toward the rear of the store. From there she hoped to go to the loading dock, and hopefully the alley; she'd roamed around the area enough and done enough scrounging that she'd gotten a halfway decent idea of how these places were laid out.

One careful footstep, then another, the rubber soles of her hiking boots making no sound on the scuffed linoleum floor. The back of her neck tingled, but that was just nerves. She hadn't heard or seen anything to tell her the djinn was anywhere nearby.

Past the dressing rooms, then through a door that opened on a short hallway. To one side was a small room with the door standing open, probably the store manager's office, judging by the shabby desk and equally shabby chair behind it, and the ancient computer that sat on the scarred metal desk.

The lighting here was dim, but not so dim that Leila couldn't see the small pile of gray ash sitting on the seat of the office chair. She swallowed and forced herself to keep going. By now she was used to the sight, but those unobtrusive heaps of pale ash only reminded her of all those who'd perished in the fever known as the Heat, evoking images of the unseen millions who'd suffered a similar fate.

It was a tidy disease, she had to admit. A day or so of a burning fever—hence the name of the sickness—and then the victims' bodies burned so fiercely, they were reduced to those small piles of ash. No worries about millions of rotting bodies and all the disease those corpses would have brought with them. Now the world was clean, scoured.

Except for those few pesky humans who'd been immune to the disease.

Leila hoped with all her heart that her parents had survived, but she had no way to know for sure. When the Heat had first begun to flare up among the population, she'd been preoccupied, consumed with prepping for what was supposed to be her big break, an audition for a television pilot. True, she'd already had another such "break" the year before, with a pilot that went nowhere, but she'd convinced herself that this one would be it, that a producer somewhere would have to pick it up, even while she had to admit deep down that the jokes weren't all that funny and the characters not much more than a cliché.

At any rate, she hadn't been paying attention to the news, and she'd banned herself from the computer, knowing she needed to concentrate on the audition. And the Heat had spread so quickly, there wasn't time to recover. Or rather, when she'd gone to the audition and found the studio shuttered and no one there, not even a sign on the door, she'd begun to realize it was too late. She turned on the radio in her car and heard warnings to stay home and stay out of contact with others, heard that a dusk-to-dawn curfew had been instituted. Fear struck her then, and she'd picked up her cell phone to call her parents in Orange County, but she couldn't get through, couldn't get anything except a fast busy signal. Panicked, she went home, thinking she'd grab a few things and then head south…and that was when she saw her first djinn, striding down the street outside the little bungalow in Highland Park she'd shared with her roommate Tracey.

Leila had thought for one wild second that they must be filming a movie or TV show in her neighborhood, even though she hadn't gotten any of the customary notices that usually preceded such an event. But what else could it be when an impossibly good-looking man in Middle Eastern–looking robes went walking down the middle of the street in a Los Angeles suburb?

The illusion had held until the djinn encountered one of her neighbors, an older man Leila knew on sight but whose name she'd never learned. The man had seemed panicked, flushed with fever. He'd gone up to the djinn in his delirium, probably trying to ask for help.

Fire had flared from the djinn's fingertips, and a second later, Leila's neighbor was gone, a charred, blackened corpse lying where he'd stood only a moment before. A scream had risen in her throat, but she'd clapped her hands over her mouth, made herself remain quiet as the djinn continued his slow, purposeful progress down the street. And then, body shaking, she'd grabbed her phone, intending to call 9-1-1.

But all she heard was that same fast busy signal, telling her the iPhone she'd spent so much money on was now basically useless. With trembling fingers, she shoved the phone in her purse, then tiptoed into her bedroom and quickly changed out of the skirt and blouse she was wearing and into jeans and a T-shirt and her favorite pair of running shoes. She still didn't know what the hell was going on, but she knew it was better not to face it while wearing a short skirt and a pair of high heels.

Still shaking, she'd slipped out through the backyard and into the alley beyond. Some instinct had told her that trying to take her car would make her an obvious target, that she needed to stick to the alleys and yards and side streets until she could figure out what was going on.

She'd been running ever since. What else could she do?

It was very dark back here, only a little bit of daylight from the front of the store reaching this employees-only hallway. Leila put out a hand to feel the wall, letting the solid, reassuring surface beneath her fingertips guide her to the back door. She reached out, allowed her fingers to drift until she found the doorknob. At least with the electricity out, she didn't have to worry about setting off any alarms.

Blessed daylight leaked in as she opened the door a crack and peeked outside. Yes, there was the alley she'd hoped for, crowded with Dumpsters that would never get emptied, a small breeze blowing several pages from a discarded newspaper idly along the pavement with a ghostly crackling sound that made the hair stand up on the back of her neck. The smell of rotting garbage lingered on the air, just another of L.A.'s ghosts.

Still, the place looked deserted. Partway down the alley was an abandoned Ford Explorer, parked at an odd angle. No doubt if she looked inside, she'd see the remains of the SUV's owner in a neat pile on the driver's seat. Unfortunately, tempting as the vehicle looked, Leila knew she couldn't take it. The minute the engine started up—if it would even start at all, considering it had now been sitting there for the greater part of two months— every djinn in the area would descend at once.

She cracked the door just wide enough to slip out into the alley, then shut it quietly behind her. A quick glance around told her that she was still alone. From back here where she stood, it was hard to get her bearings, but she thought if she went to her left, she should be headed west, which was the direction she wanted to go. After losing the last of her companions, she hadn't known what to do, but she thought that it seemed best to go downtown, to try to lose herself in the maze of L.A.'s streets. There had to be hundreds of viable hiding places there.

To be safe, she looked upward, but the skies were clear, much clearer than they would have been if all of the city's inhabitants had still been alive, choking the streets and freeways with their cars. This week, the hot, dry Santa Ana winds had blown, making it much warmer than it should have been in mid-November, even in Southern California. No fires, though, thank God; Leila supposed with all the people gone, there were far fewer ways for a fire to get started—no stray sparks from a lawnmower or an engine backfiring, no carelessly tossed cigarette butts from car windows.

Anyway, she didn't see any sign of the djinn, whether here in the alley or in the sky above her, and so she decided it was safe enough to hurry down to her left, where she spotted a street thick with more abandoned vehicles. Even if it hadn't been for the djinn, she still didn't know whether stealing a car would even work; so many streets were so choked with cars, they wouldn't have been passable anyway. Maybe a motorcycle could have gotten though, but she didn't know how to drive one. Going by foot was infinitely easier and safer.

When she got to the end of the alley, she paused again, looking up and down the street. The only movement she could see was a couple of pigeons waddling down the sidewalk. What they were foraging on these days, Leila had no idea, but they seemed fat and happy enough, and no worry of hers.

Time to go.

She eased out onto the street, hugging the wall of the storefront next to her and wishing that it had an awning or some other kind of overhang, just so she wouldn't feel so exposed. Since there was none, all she could do was hurry forward, her feet taking her closer and closer to downtown with every step. She didn't know the area by heart, but she did know that if she could cut over to Main Street, she could follow it through the semi-industrial area on the west side of the 5 Freeway all the way to downtown. It would be slow going, but there were enough buildings and warehouses in between here and her destination that she should be able to hide from time to time, whenever she started to feel hinky.

A shadow passed overhead, one far too large to be a pigeon. Leila glanced up and saw the djinn descending toward her out of nowhere, the cobalt silk of his garments fluttering in the breeze, silent as death.

The terror that exploded in her chest was so intense, she didn't even have time to utter a curse. Instead, she took off running, even as her gut told her that there was no way she could outrun him now, not when he was so close.

But she had to try.

A burst of speed took her to the opening of another alley, and she zigged down there, praying it would be enough of a feint to throw him off but knowing it wouldn't. Her heart pounded and her breath came in quick, terrified pants, but her feet still moved, pounding into the pavement, achieving a burst of speed that took her another hundred feet into the alleyway.

Now she did hear footsteps behind her, a strong, purposeful stride that echoed off the walls of the buildings to either side as his boots touched the asphalt. She didn't dare look behind her, though, didn't dare do anything that might slow her down.

A wall was coming toward her. Leila pulled in a gulp of air and looked from side to side. No, this wasn't possible. The alley couldn't be a dead end. It had to branch off to one side or another. But as she approached that wall, with its markings of angular graffiti and daubs of pigeon droppings, she realized that the alley did in fact end here. There was no escape, no way out.

Stiff with terror, she forced herself to turn. Her hands clenched into fists, broken nails digging into her palms.

The djinn stood there before her. The same breeze that had sent the newspaper rustling down the alley before now caught at his robes, causing them to ripple gently. This close, Leila could see the gold border woven into the fabric. It glinted in the afternoon sunshine, shimmering like the gold bracelets her grandmother had smuggled in her clothing when she escaped Iran after the Shah fell.

A step closer, then another. The djinn's heavy dark hair ruffled in the breeze as well, touching his fine, wide cheekbones, causing one lock to fall over his brow.

Now the wall was at her back, the rough cinderblock seeming to bite through the T-shirt she wore. Although the day was warm enough, she thought she'd never been this cold, her entire body trapped in a sort of frozen terror.

He paused about a foot away from her, coal-black eyes scanning her entire person, top to bottom and back again, until he stopped and held her gaze for a long moment.

A shudder went through her. Would it have been better or worse if he wasn't so unbelievably handsome? It wasn't really fair for a destroyer of worlds to look like a male model.

Then he spoke. His voice was deep but soft, with a faint accent she couldn't quite place. "Why," he asked, "are you so afraid?"

Perfect English. Leila didn't know why she hadn't been expecting that. She swallowed, her throat so dry and tight, she wasn't sure she'd be able to force the words out. She replied, the syllables not much more than a whisper, "Because you're going to kill me."

His eyes widened slightly, the straight heavy brows lifting in surprise. "Kill you? Why would you think such a thing?"

Despite her terror, she couldn't help but experience a flutter of annoyance. Was he messing with her? Trying to lull her with gentle words, when they both knew exactly how this little scene was going to end? Another swallow, and she said, "Oh, I don't know. Because your people have been murdering mine for the past two months?"

The djinn frowned then. "Yes, some of them have. But I am not one of those who have pursued the remnants of mankind. I have far better plans for you, Leila Donovan."

He knew her name. How the hell did he know her name? Maybe the djinn were all-knowing, but she didn't think that was the reason. Otherwise, he would have found her far more easily than this…unless he'd simply been toying with her the whole time.

Her fists squeezed tighter, the roughness of her ragged nails biting into her palms. "What kind of plans?"

Very gently, he reached out and unclenched her hands. His fingers were warm and strong, possibly warmer than a normal man's should be, and although his touch was light enough, Leila could feel the coiled power in him. She wanted to pull away but held herself still, fearing what he might do if she attempted to struggle at all.

To her relief, he let go of her a moment later. That relief was short-lived, however, because instead of stepping away, he came even closer and cupped her face in his hands. Her breath caught, and she wished more than ever that she could run from him, run before he did anything else. A faint scent of sandalwood came from his clothing, or possibly from his hair. She could see the stubble dark on his cheeks and chin, the heavy long lashes that framed his night-black eyes.

"You have nothing to fear, Leila Donovan," he said, and bent and pressed his mouth against hers.

This wasn't happening. How could this be happening? A djinn…kissing her? She wanted to tear herself from his embrace, but found she somehow couldn't. A warm heat was rising inside her, one she didn't want to acknowledge but was impossible to ignore.

Desire.

No. She couldn't possibly want him. He was a djinn. He was a murderer, no matter what he might have said to her a moment earlier. Was he just perverted enough that he took pleasure in romancing his victims before he killed them?

That thought was enough for her to regain herself, to wrench herself away from him so suddenly, his hands held empty air for a moment. Then he seemed to register what was happening, saw how she was poised to flee.

"Oh, I don't think so," he said.

One hand reached out and caught her by the arm, and the next thing she knew, she was being pulled close to him, was pressed against the heavy muscles of his bare chest. She began to struggle in his grip, but it was too late. Darkness closed in around them, and the alley was gone.

TWO

MALIK AL-MAZIN HAD EXPECTED LEILA TO struggle. How could she not, when she'd spent the last few weeks watching as everyone around her was killed one by one? Clearly, she hadn't believed him when he told her he meant her no harm, and he could not blame her for that. They needed to talk, but there were far better places for such a discussion than a dingy alley, one that stank of the garbage that had been rotting there ever since the world ended.

They reappeared in the house he had taken for his own, the one that overlooked the wide sweep of the Pacific Ocean. The sound of the surf far below echoed in the house, soothing to him, for he was an elemental of the water, and its presence gave him strength.

However, Leila appeared far from soothed. As soon as solid ground rested beneath their feet once more, she pulled herself from his grasp and took a few steps away from him, looking around at her new surroundings with a mixture of shock and consternation.

"What—?" she began, then shook her head. A few dirty strands of hair, come loose from the ponytail she wore at the back of her neck, fell around her face. "What is this place?"

"My home," he said easily. His home for now, at any rate. He knew he would not be allowed to stay here indefinitely, not when the others of his kind had already made the area the humans called "Bel-Air" their home here on earth. But he'd requested that he have some time alone with Leila while she came to terms with her new life, and the elders had agreed. Only until the turn of the year, though, which meant he had little more than a month to make her understand that her survival depended on becoming his partner in eternity.

He had thought a month would be more than sufficient. Looking at Leila now, however, and recalling how she had managed to resist the glamour he'd tried to cast on her, Malik wondered if a month would be enough after all.

"Your home," she repeated, looking around once again, still with that wary expression in her dark blue eyes, that same tension in all her limbs, making her appear as a wild animal ready to bolt.

Unfortunately for her, there was no place she could go and manage to evade him.

"Yes," he said.

"This looks like a regular human house," she returned. "Or at least, a regular human house from *The Real Housewives of Beverly Hills.* But you're a djinn."

Malik didn't know who these "real housewives" might be, although he assumed they must be characters from a book or a magazine or a television program. "It is a human house," he admitted. "I believe it was built for someone who was on your people's television, although I do not recall his name. But it is mine now."

Her chin went up, challenging. "Did you kill him?"

"Oh, no," Malik replied. "He was dead long before the sickness swept through your population. Those who lived here after him—the fever claimed them, although they were not here when they perished. Besides, as I told you earlier, I have killed no one."

She seemed to ponder this statement for a moment, as though deciding whether to argue with him further. To his relief, she did not challenge his words, but instead was silent as she threaded her way through the living room's furniture and stood in front of the wall of windows that made up one side of the room. Below the bluff where the house was situated, the Pacific thundered, breaking on a beach that was empty as far as the eye could see, pale sand uninterrupted by a single soul, human or djinn.

One hand pressed against the glass, not looking at him, she uttered a single word. "Why?"

He should have known she would ask him this, and he intended to tell her the truth, or at least as much of it as he deemed necessary. However, he also knew that she needed a bit of time to recover from the life she'd been living these past few months. They would have plenty of time to talk.

"That is…a long story," he replied. "We will speak, and share some food, but first, perhaps you would like to bathe?"

At once she turned from the window, all tension once again. He could practically smell the adrenaline coursing through her veins. Or perhaps what he smelled was something else entirely; for all her beauty, she was quite unkempt, smudges of dirt on her face, her hair and body badly in need of washing. Malik would not fault her for her current condition, since she had been living an existence which did not allow for the niceties of hot baths and regular changes of clothes, but now that she was here, there was no excuse for her dirty, bedraggled appearance.

"You needn't fear me," he said easily. "I will stay far away while you bathe and change."

"Change into what?" Mouth twisting, she went on, "I must have left my luggage at the Ritz-Carlton."

He assumed she was making a joke. Voice calm, he replied, "Things will be provided for you."

"And I'm supposed to trust you?" she asked with a short, bitter laugh.

"Yes. Believe me," he added, as her delicate jaw set in a hard line, "if I had wanted to cause you any kind of harm, there is nothing you could have done to stop me." Her eyes flared with sudden alarm, and he said in his most soothing tones, "Please…let me show you to your room."

For a moment, she lingered by the window, clearly loath to believe anything he had to say, not wanting to go someplace where he might corner her. But it seemed that her need to cleanse herself overrode her caution, for after that initial hesitation, she seemed to shrug and then came toward him, although he noted how she stayed just out of arm's reach.

He didn't speak, but only turned and went

toward the graceful spiral staircase that led to the home's second floor. Leila followed a few paces behind, still silent, although he'd noted the way her eyes darted this way and that, taking in the home's details, the indoor atrium with the trees that reached twenty feet and more to almost touch the ceiling, the quiet murmur of the fountain nearly hidden by the luxuriant foliage that surrounded it. Indeed, he'd chosen this house because it had water both inside and out, making the space more welcoming to him than any of the other homes he had inspected.

With any luck, Leila would come to love it, too…at least for the time they'd be allowed to stay here.

The spiral staircase brought them to a large landing, one decorated with more plants, along with vases of Ming ware that were almost as old as he was. On the other side of the landing was a sort of study area, with a priceless desk of inlaid wood and several welcoming chairs. A set of double doors opened onto that area, revealing the master suite. Malik had determined that it should be Leila's—at least until such time as she accepted him, and they were able to share one room.

She stepped inside, eyes wide and almost fearful, although this time it seemed as if that fear was a sort of awe at her surroundings, rather than unease due to his presence. The room was beautiful and large, with a fireplace on one wall, topped by a flat-screen television. All the other walls, except the one behind the bed, had windows of plate glass like the ones downstairs, affording an unhindered view of the ocean.

"I—" She turned toward him. "You can't expect me to stay here."

"Is there something wrong with this room?" he asked, giving their surroundings a quick glance. As far as he could tell, everything seemed to be in order. The house had been very clean when he took it over—he didn't know where its current owners had been when the Dying struck, but they apparently had not been home—and it had been a simple matter to use his djinn abilities to flick away any stray dust that might settle over the course of time.

"No, there's nothing wrong with it, but —" Once again she broke off, then crossed her arms and looked away from him. Voice barely above a mutter, she said, "This whole situation is impossible."

"I see nothing impossible about it," he returned calmly. "This is your room now. You are safe, even though you appear disinclined to believe me. In the bathroom you will find all the toiletries you need, and in the closet there is a variety of clothing to choose from. You may meet me downstairs when you are done."

Having delivered this information, he gave her a slight bow, then retreated and closed the bedroom doors behind him.

As he descended the staircase, he wondered how long it would take for her to overcome her shock before she began to explore her new suite.

Was she dreaming? This had to be a dream. How else could she explain her surroundings? This home was so opulent, Leila knew she hadn't seen anything like it outside the pages of one of the lifestyle magazines her mother tended to leave lying around her house.

But when she walked over to the bed and gently touched the silk damask duvet that covered it, the smooth fabric felt real enough against her fingertips. The same for the burled maple night-stand, and the remote for the television she found in the top drawer.

This was real. She didn't know what Malik wanted from her, but—

Oh, you know exactly what he wants, she told herself as she headed into the bathroom. *Why else would he have kissed you back there?*

Good question. Maybe he had every intention of raping her, but he was too fastidious to touch her in her current filthy condition. She'd hated to live like that, but her options for bathing had been pretty limited. Much as she hated to even let the thought cross her mind, she couldn't really blame Malik for wanting her to wash up; she wouldn't have wanted to touch her, either, if their roles had somehow been reversed.

A shiver went through her. Once she was presentable, would Malik try to force himself on her? Maybe it would be better to remain a filthy wreck.

No, Leila couldn't quite allow herself to do that. No matter how strange the situation, the idea of getting clean, *really* clean, for the first time in almost two months was one she couldn't ignore.

The bathroom was just as elegant as the bedroom, with marble counters and floor, and an enormous walk-in shower, and a whirlpool tub in a little plant-filled grotto off to one side, again with windows all around that afforded more of those jaw-dropping views of the Pacific Ocean. Leila wasn't sure she liked the idea of getting undressed in such a fishbowl, but she tried to reassure herself that there wasn't anyone left to see in.

No one except Malik, that is. She'd seen the

way he could hover in the air and supposed he could do the same thing here so he could get a peep at her naked body. For some reason, though, that didn't seem like the kind of maneuver he would pull. His manner toward her had been gracious, almost courtly, but she supposed that could have all been an act to get her to let down her guard.

There had been many times during the last few weeks when she'd thought she would cheerfully kill for a hot shower. Was she really going to let the possibility of a djinn Peeping Tom keep her from getting clean for the first time since the Heat had swept over the world?

Well, when she put it that way....

A door in one wall opened onto a closet roughly the size of her bedroom in the small pre-Depression bungalow she'd shared with Tracey. The racks in the closet weren't full, but they still held an impressive collection of clothing. More importantly, there was a fluffy white robe hanging from a hook on one side. Leila quickly peeled herself out of her dirty clothes and looked around for a hamper, but saw none. Oh, well, she'd leave the clothes on the floor for now. A quick inspection of the built-in drawers in the closet revealed a variety of undergarments, all silky and brand-new. At least Malik wasn't expecting her to go commando. She didn't quite want to contemplate how he knew her size, because that would seem to indicate he'd been watching her for some time. That realization only made a creepy-crawly sensation move down her back, even as she wondered why he'd singled her out among the others who'd managed to survive the heat.

She was too dirty to want to put on the robe, but she did hold it in front of her as she hurried over to the shower enclosure, which was so large, it had a bench built into it, and banks of shower heads on facing walls. After taking a quick glance at the windows and reassuring herself that nothing was out there except some seagulls, she dropped the robe and climbed into the shower. A few touches to the controls, and a blessed wave of hot water emerged from the shower heads installed on the walls.

How this all worked, when there hadn't been electricity or running water since the Heat claimed most of the world's population, Leila didn't know. Possibly Malik was powering it somehow. Maybe that was something djinn could do.

Djinn. She poured some of the high-end shampoo she found on a shelf in the shower into her palm, then worked it into her hair. Ah, that felt good. It was better to think about how blissful it was to get clean, to lather her hair not once, not twice, but three times altogether, washing away all the grime that had collected over the past few weeks, than to dwell on the puzzle of the djinn who currently had her captive. She didn't want to think about that. Better to focus on how, ever since she'd fled her house, she'd had to let her hair go until she couldn't stand it anymore, and even then only rinsing it with cold water and shampoo from a travel-size bottle she'd carried in her pack. However, that makeshift solution wasn't the same as standing here and feeling the blast from all those shower heads rinse the last of the dirt and oil from her long dark hair. In fact, it was so squeaky-clean that she knew she needed to follow up with conditioner, but that wasn't a problem, since it had been provided as well.

However, she had to give the conditioner time to work its magic. That was all right, because now she could concentrate on using body wash and a loofa to scrub every inch of her body, getting rid of all the accumulated dirt. The warm water beat on her, soothing, better than a massage. Once upon a time she might have shaken her head at the waste of using so many shower heads, but now she could only be glad of their presence, glad of the way they so efficiently blasted away the grime. Besides, water conservation wasn't really a problem with ninety-nine percent of the population now dead, was it?

That thought drew her back to the djinn who waited for her downstairs. Before this afternoon, she would never have believed that the murderous elementals had any interest in humans, other than killing them for sport, but apparently they must, or why else would Malik have kissed her? And if that was the case, why hadn't any of the djinn her group had encountered tried to sexually assault the women, rather than killing them outright? Leila hated to think of the situation in such bald terms, but it was a question that needed to be asked.

She doubted she'd have the courage to question Malik about it, though. Normally, she didn't have too much trouble speaking her mind, but a being like Malik al-Mazin was completely outside her experience. She had no idea how he would react to—to almost anything, actually.

At last her hair was clean and conditioned, her body scrubbed pink and clean. With some reluctance, she turned off the water, then climbed out of the shower enclosure and immediately grabbed a couple of the big fluffy cream-colored towels that hung within arm's reach. Once one was firmly fastened around her body and the other around her hair, she went back into the closet and shut the door, then turned on the crystal chandelier that hung overhead.

It glittered like a miniature crown of diamonds, sending little sparkles around the chamber, dancing off the custom cedar cabinetry and the full-length mirror, framed in gilt, that hung on one side of the closet. Leila went to the drawers where she'd spied the underwear, removed the towel she was wearing, and put on a pink silk bra and bikini panties. No plain cotton underwear here, that was obvious. Well, if Malik was expecting to see her in it, he was going to be sorely disappointed.

No jeans or T-shirts, either. After a moment's deliberation, Leila put on a flowy red silk skirt with gold embroidery in a wide band around the bottom and a cream-colored knit top with elbow-length sleeves. The day had been warm for mid-November, thanks to the Santa Ana winds, and she didn't think she needed anything more than that, even this close to the coast. Some gold sandals, and a pair of dangly gold earrings she found in another drawer, one filled with baubles so extravagant, they surely must be costume jewelry…although Leila feared they weren't, that all those green and red and blue stones weren't glass at all, but emeralds and rubies and sapphires.

The earrings were the only jewelry she put on,

just because she always felt naked without earrings. Then she went back out to the dressing area and towel-dried her hair, working some serum she found in a drawer in the vanity into it.

Makeup? Leila hesitated as she looked at the contents of another drawer, this one filled with expensive cosmetics, all sealed and brand-new, the kind she vowed she'd buy one day when she got her dream part in a movie or TV series and could finally afford something more than the drugstore stuff. Now, however, the thought of playing with the makeup didn't seem nearly as appealing as it once might have. Instead, she brushed on some mascara and some warm-tinted lip gloss, and ignored the blush and the eyeshadow and the eyeliner. Who was she trying to impress, anyway? It wasn't as though she was going to an audition.

Except...maybe she was. Maybe this whole thing was some kind of weird tryout, to see if Malik really wanted her after all. No, that couldn't be right. He'd already kissed her, even when she was dirty and stinky, with greasy hair pulled back in a too-tight ponytail.

A strange tingle went through her at the thought of that kiss. She couldn't have enjoyed it, and yet now the memory made her all flushed and warm, wanting more.

Maybe you're going crazy, she thought as she

made herself leave the bathroom, then pass through the bedroom and on to the landing and down the stairs. *All the strain has finally made you snap.*

That was actually a more comforting notion than trying to believe she wanted Malik in any way.

To her surprise, she didn't see him when she got to the ground floor. She'd assumed that he would be waiting for her in the living room, although she had to admit the house was vast, and she'd seen only a small portion of it. He could be in another wing altogether, although she didn't know why he would play mind games with her and force her to go hunting for him, unless through some perverse djinn need to show his dominance.

But then she realized that a soft breeze, faintly scented with salt, was blowing through the room. One of the windows wasn't a window at all, but a French door that opened out onto a brick walk-way. It stood ajar, letting in the sea breeze. Leila went out through the door, pausing for a moment to admire the waterfall just outside, which plunged into a large pool populated by equally large koi. They swam unconcernedly through the water, flashes of copper and white and pale gold.

The breeze was stronger now, blowing through

her damp hair. She hurried down the path, out of the shadow of the house, so the sun could touch her, warm her. It was now dropping toward the west, although there were still a few hours to go before it set altogether.

A large pool shimmered blue-green before her. Around it was a large brick-paved area, with an ostentatiously oversized grouping of patio furniture off to one side, obviously meant to accommodate outdoor partiers. There was no one here now, though, and the whole place looked rather forlorn.

Leila stopped by the pool and looked around, still seeing no sign of Malik. But a smaller path wound away from one side of the pool, and she followed it as it took her up a gentle rise, and then to a cozy flagstone patio under a spreading tree, surrounded by plants and flowers. In the middle of the patio was a small round table with a bottle of white wine protected by a silvery metal cooler. A pair of glasses sat next to it.

Standing beside the table was Malik. His rich blue silken robes rippled in the breeze, the gold border shimmering brighter than ever in the sun. He was looking away from her, his gaze apparently fixed on the ocean and its empty horizon, but as soon as she began to approach, he turned, a smile showing off his white teeth.

"Leila," he said. "I thought you might like some refreshment."

How long had it been since she'd had a glass of wine? More than a month; it wasn't that she hadn't drunk any alcohol after the Heat destroyed the world, because sometimes she'd needed something to blunt the pain of her current existence. Unfortunately, bottles of wine weren't all that practical to cart around during the apocalypse. She'd settled for a flat canteen of Jack Daniels, which provided the needed kick in a pinch but still tasted like ass to her. Wine would be nectar of the gods after that rotgut.

On the other hand, all she'd eaten today was a protein bar some eight hours earlier. True, she'd learned to live with her hunger, ignore it as best she could, but it was still there, lurking. She knew it probably wasn't wise to refuse the djinn's offer of wine, but she'd have to be careful. Tiny sips only.

"Sure," she said cautiously, and waited a few paces away as he picked up the bottle and poured some pale, straw-colored wine into one of the glasses. He extended it toward her, and she had no choice but to come closer so she could take it from him. His fingers brushed against hers and she shivered, even though that touch was warm enough.

If he noticed her reaction, he apparently chose

not to say anything about it. He only poured his own glass, then said, "You are looking very well."

"I guess that's what happens when you wash off six weeks' worth of dirt."

A flash of that white smile. His teeth were perfect, but perfect in a natural sort of way. They didn't have that unnaturally flat and filed-off look you got with caps or implants. And, spending most of her time around actors and other people in the industry, or the well-heeled patrons of the expensive restaurant where she'd once worked, Leila had seen her share of the best cosmetic dentistry had to offer.

"That must have been difficult for you," he said.

Difficult? Was he joking? To mask her anger, Leila lifted the glass of wine to her lips and took a small sip. A *very* small sip, although she would have preferred a healthy swallow. "Which part?" she asked, her voice clear, cold. "Watching everyone die around me, or spending the better part of two months like a hunted animal, never getting enough to eat, never having a chance to shower, always worrying that one injury, one illness, was going to be the thing that finished me off, that allowed one of you djinn to finally catch up with me?"

To his credit, Malik winced slightly. He drank

some of his wine as well, a noticeably larger swallow than the one she'd taken. "I am very sorry you had to go through that. It was not my intention that you had to spend so much time 'like a hunted animal,' to use your words. But you were so clever in evading pursuit, so good at keeping yourself hidden, that it was impossible for me to catch up with you until today."

"You're saying I would have been better off if I'd allowed myself to be caught?" Leila asked, not bothering to hide the disbelief in her tone.

"Yes," Malik replied his dark eyes meeting hers in a forthright way she hadn't been expecting, "because I never meant you any ill, and the other djinn knew to leave you alone. Did you never wonder why you were the only one of your group to survive?"

Of course she'd wondered that, every time one of them was felled by a djinn, until at last she was the only one left. Dark comprehension dawning, she stared up at him, at the handsome, regular features, features that looked like those of a man but which she knew weren't. "You—you were protecting me that whole time?" And again she asked the question she'd first uttered in the living room of this huge, elaborate house. "Why?"

He hesitated, then set his glass down on the

granite surface of the table next to him. "Perhaps you should sit down."

Leila didn't want to sit down. She wanted to run far, far away from this place, from this inhumanly handsome man who was now watching her with caution, and possibly a little regret. But because she knew that wasn't possible, she made herself sit down and fold her hands on the tabletop. "All right, I'm sitting. Are you going to tell me now why you were protecting me, instead of killing me off the way your people have the rest of mankind?"

"Not all of you," he said, and an enigmatic smile touched his lips. "Some few remain, those who were Chosen."

She could almost see the capital letter he gave that word, meaning it must have some special significance to him, to the rest of the djinn. "Chosen for what?"

He didn't answer right away, but instead took his glass of wine and sipped at it again. "Chosen to be kept safe, as you have been. Chosen to be with us."

A cold trickle worked its way down her spine, even though the sun beat down on them warmly enough. "I don't understand," she said…although she feared she did.

From the way one eyebrow lifted as he calmly

regarded her, he apparently saw that she'd guessed at the truth. "We could not save all of you. From those who were immune, we chose the ones who would be our partners going forward."

"So you chose me for your…partner."

"Yes."

Leila lifted her wine and gulped far too much of it. Suddenly sour, it caught in the back of her throat, made her cough. "Why couldn't you save everyone? If you djinn are as powerful as I think you are, there must have been something you could have done. The Heat—"

Malik raised a hand. "You misunderstand me, Leila. The djinn caused the Heat, as you call the sickness that took so many. In their eyes, it was time for the world to be cleansed, for it to be returned to them. But no matter how deadly the disease, there are always some who will be immune to it. That is how we selected our Chosen."

The horror which enveloped her as she sat there, staring at her djinn captor, was so great that Leila didn't know if she could force her shaking limbs to move. But she had to. She had to move. How else could she get away from this monster?

Somehow, she forced herself to stand. Malik rose as well, watching her with concerned dark eyes. "Leila, you must understand. I—"

"I don't need to understand anything!" she flung at him. "You—you're *murderers,* all of you. Genocidal maniacs. I thought it was bad before, but—"

"Leila—"

His voice was pleading, but she didn't want to hear anything more that he had to say. Even though she knew such flight must be futile, she turned and ran from him, sandals slapping on the brick walkway. With every step she expected to see his shadow hovering over her, or to have him appear on the path in front of her, blocking her way.

But he did none of those things. She was allowed to run into the house, to pound her way up the stairs, to flee into the bedroom that had been given to her and lock the door. That flimsy lock wouldn't have kept out a determined human, let alone a djinn, but the door remained shut. Malik didn't come to break it down. He didn't knock.

For the moment, it seemed he was content to leave her alone with her fury and her sorrow.

THREE

THE WINE WAS SOUR ON HIS TONGUE, BUT Malik made himself finish what he had poured in his glass, mostly because by doing so he kept himself from running after Leila. Then, because he did not want it to go to waste—and because his kind had a far greater capacity for alcohol than their human counterparts—he poured himself more from the open bottle of chardonnay, although he did not touch Leila's glass. The wine she had left behind would have to be thrown away.

He sat and watched the shifting colors of the waves. Far out from shore, he caught the glint of smooth, silvery-gray backs, leaping out of the water. Dolphins, joyful as ever. Perhaps more so now that their waters would no longer be polluted by the bilge of fishing vessels, or spills from the oil derricks off shore. He could not know for sure, because his people, for all their talents, did not have the gift of speaking to animals.

Unfortunately, he was far less joyful than the dolphins. Leila's reaction hadn't been completely unexpected, and yet he'd hoped, in his heart of hearts, that she might have been able to stay long enough to listen to the whole story, to learn how not all of the djinn were the genocidal murderers she thought them. Many, true, but definitely not all.

He recalled how his people had gathered before the palace of the elders, under the strange, shifting skies of the otherworld, the djinns' place of exile once the earth was taken from them so many millennia ago and given over to men to rule…and to ruin. The arguments had surged back and forth, until at last, Ibram, eldest of the elders, held up a hand and said, "We have heard all your arguments. The world shall be ours again, by means of the sickness that has been wrought here and now only waits to be released. But for those who would not see mankind perish, we have a small solution. From those whom the sickness does not touch—for we know there will be a few —you shall each choose one to save, one mortal who will be your partner for eternity. Choose wisely, though, for these mortals will share your long life, will have the same unending health and beauty. And for those of you who are not among the thousand who wish to see humanity survive, you have free rein to hunt down those survivors who are not Chosen. But," Ibram went on, directing a severe dark gaze toward the most bloodthirsty among the crowd, "if you should raise a hand against any Chosen, then your own life will be forfeit. This is the word of the elders, and it will not be gainsaid."

There had been those who grumbled at these strictures, but Malik had not been among them. Indeed, his own heart was troubled, for while he did not quite agree with the utter destruction of human-kind, he also did not know whether he had the fortitude to take a mortal as his own and be forced to share the rest of his life with her.

Until he had seen Leila Donovan, Omar al-Tariq's choice.

Yes, she was beautiful. But her beauty was not what had drawn him to her...not at first, anyway. The world had many beautiful women, even among those who would be Immune. No, as soon as he had heard that Omar al-Tariq had chosen his partner for eternity, Malik was troubled. He feared that al-Tariq was motivated far more by a desire to inflict pain and suffering than he was by a need to protect one of humanity's few immune specimens. This worry did not come merely from a dislike of the other djinn, but instead was based on stories some of Malik's past lovers had told him, revealing that those who had become intimate with Omar always seemed to suffer some kind of heartbreak, for his delight did not come from the physical act of love. No, he seemed to prefer to play with their thoughts and hopes and wishes, toying with them, making them believe he loved them when he most decidedly did not.

Malik's own sister Fatima had briefly flirted with Omar al-Tariq, but, God be thanked, the relationship did not proceed very far before Fatima took al-Tariq's measure and ended their liaison. It was because of this past history that Malik had first gone to his older sister for counsel, once he had learned who al-Tariq intended for his Chosen.

"He must be stopped," Malik had said, and Fatima had only shaken her head.

"Stopped how?" she inquired. She had been in the process of closing up her palace in the other-world, for she, too, had chosen a human to be her partner. In fact, Fatima would soon be the leader of the djinn community in that place called Los Angeles, since her human came from that area and so she would reside there as well, in order to make the situation not quite as strange for the man she had selected. "Malik, this is not the sort of thing where the elders will intercede. They have made their ruling and have determined how this new world of ours will run, but it has never been their practice to interfere in the individual lives of our people."

This was no more than the truth, but Malik thought there must be some way to prevent Omar al-Tariq from taking Leila Donovan as his own. She might be merely a human, but she certainly deserved better than that.

Apparently noting his inner turmoil, Fatima had laid a hand on her brother's arm and said, "If you wish to save this woman, then you must claim her as your own. It is the only way."

Malik responded, "And if I do that, then al-Tariq has the right to challenge me over the affront."

"True," Fatima replied. "But I know you, brother. Your strength is certainly equal to Omar al-Tariq's. I suppose it depends on how much you believe that he will harm this woman."

"You were involved with him. You should know."

The faint half-smile Fatima had been wearing abruptly faded. "Yes, I know," she said, her tone tight, almost too controlled. "Otherwise, I would not be encouraging you to challenge him over this. There are some who would say that it should not matter, that if she is saved, she should be grateful her life has been spared, no matter what the nature of her rescuer. But I doubt you believe that."

"No," Malik had said. "I do not believe it at all."

He thought it was in that moment he had determined to save Leila from Omar, no matter what. When he made his wishes known, of course al-Tariq took offense. But, because he was a bully and, like all bullies, a coward at heart, he had declared loudly that he had decided not to claim a Chosen at all, that an insipid human woman could never begin to compare to a woman of the djinn, and that he thought it would be far better sport to assist in chasing down those Immune who were not Chosen, and therefore put an end to the hated humans once and for all.

There the matter lay, and although Malik worried somewhat that Omar might interfere when it came time to make Leila his, he hadn't allowed that worry to interrupt his plans. Once the Heat had done its work, he had taken this house as his temporary home because it pleased him, thanks to its expansive views of the ocean and the water features which so gracefully enhanced its grounds. Unfortunate that he could not stay here forever, but the elders had been clear —all those who had taken a Chosen must live in their own communities, and Fatima had decreed that the community in this region would gather in the exclusive area known as Bel-Air. She was an earth elemental, and loved the hills and the rolling nature of the land there. Also, there would be no lack of opulent homes for the djinn and their partners to inhabit, an altogether pleasing situation for their little enclave. The elementals had no love for the signs of mankind's industry, and had vowed to remove as many factories and warehouses and other signs of modern manufacturing as possible from the landscape. That would take time, however. In the interim, it was better to retreat into their own worlds and pretend that those other areas did not exist.

Now, though…Malik looked up toward the house and permitted himself a sigh. The small grotto where he sat should have afforded him a view of one of the windows in Leila's room, but an unfortunately placed tree interrupted that view, so he could see nothing of her. He was able to sense her presence, though, knew that she had not tried to flee the property altogether. If she had attempted such a thing, she would not have gotten very far, and perhaps she had realized that any flight would be futile. Perhaps that was why she had retreated to the only sanctuary afforded her.

As much as he wanted to go up and speak to her, Malik knew she needed this time to gather her thoughts. It had to have been quite the blow, to realize that the djinn were the cause of all this pain and suffering. The disease had been designed to kill quickly and cleanly, but it still caused those afflicted with it to burn with a terrible fever, to fall into delirium. Those who had survived could only stand by and watch, for there was no cure, nothing that could be done to halt the progress of the disease.

Had Leila been forced to witness someone she cared for die from the sickness? Malik couldn't be sure; he had watched her for more than a year before the world changed, and so he knew that she lived a good distance from her immediate family and tended to only visit for special occasions, holidays and birthdays and such. Most likely, there wouldn't have been time for her to go home while the Heat was raging. But she had had a roommate. The problem was, he couldn't be sure. He had done his best to be near her so he might come and claim her when the time of reckoning finally arrived, but she had proved wily, had slipped away from the modest house where she lived without being seen. And so the chase had begun, one that had gone on for months, while his hope waned and he feared he would never catch up with her.

At last, though, he'd caught a telltale sign of her presence, had found her in that filthy alley, thin and wild-eyed and dirty. He hadn't cared. He'd only been relieved that none of the other djinn had found her, hurt her. Yes, the elders had said that those who raised a hand against a Chosen would meet their own punishment, but Malik feared that he and Leila had walked a fine line there, for while he had made his intentions known to the universe, he was not physically with her, not in any position to offer her any true protection.

Now, though…now she was safe.

How beautiful she had looked as she came out into the garden, the sea breeze blowing through her long, wavy hair, that same winds playing with her silken skirt and causing the gold threads along its hem to glint in the sunlight. Fatima had helped select the garments for Leila's new wardrobe, choosing human-style clothes made with fabrics that echoed the djinns' own attire, making sure that everything would be flattering and would fit properly.

"Far more entertaining than putting together

the clothes for my own Chosen," she'd said with a laugh when Malik attempted to thank her. "For the clothing worn by men in this region and this time was not very interesting at all. And if she is not grateful for these garments, then she must not possess any kind of eye for beauty in her clothing."

He couldn't comment on that particular remark, because during the times he'd observed her before the Heat swept over the world, he'd only paid attention to Leila herself—the big eyes of a startling dark blue, the graceful arch of her eyebrows, the succulent promise of her full mouth. What she'd been wearing hadn't been of much importance, although he'd noticed that she had been forced to wear the same plain uniform whenever she went to work, severely cut dark pants and an equally severe white shirt that still couldn't quite conceal the curves of her body.

No need for such a uniform anymore. Now she had clothing that would enhance her beauty rather than attempt to camouflage it.

If, of course, she would allow him to see her wearing any of those clothes. He had been sitting out here for the greater part of an hour, contemplating the sea and the sun and the wind, and still there was no sign that she wished to emerge from her bedroom.

Well, he could afford to be patient. After all, they now had eternity to play with.

―――――――

Leila sat on the bed and willed herself to breathe, slowly and carefully. As soon as her thoughts began to jumble again, going in circles like dogs chasing their own tails, she would focus on her breathing once more, do her best to remain calm. It was a mindfulness trick she'd read in a book several years before, and she'd adopted it as best she could, finding that it helped her to stay focused before an audition, to not let panic and the very real urgency to land a decent part get in the way of giving a good script reading. In the past, it had usually worked, but then, she'd never faced a situation like this before. Every time she thought she had a handle on her anxiety, it would come roaring back once more.

The djinn had done…*all* of this. Everyone dead, the whole world changed forever. All right, not everyone was dead, but so many were gone that it hardly mattered if there were still a few hundred or a few thousand survivors scattered around the globe. She wasn't really sure of the numbers involved, since her conversation with Malik hadn't gotten around to the nitty gritty details. The damning fact remained—the djinn had made sure that humanity would be completely wiped out, except for a pitiful few.

Why, she had no idea. All right, she would be the first to admit that mankind had done a pretty good job of screwing itself and the planet over at the same time, but she'd also always thought that eventually things would get turned around, that people would begin to make changes for the better.

Now they'd never get the chance to make those changes.

She thought of Tyrell then, of how strong he'd been in the face of so many losses. He'd been nominally in charge of Leila's group of survivors, probably because he'd managed to put his own panic behind him so he could focus on everyone's survival. They'd found a shortwave radio during one of their foraging expeditions at Caltech, had managed to make brief contact with more survivors. They were in Los Alamos, New Mexico, and the man on the radio said he was a scientist there. He was the one who told Tyrell and the rest of their group that their adversaries, the fierce, terrible beings who seemed intent on hunting down every human they found, actually were djinn—immortal, powerful, nearly unstoppable.

The scientist had a plan to stop them, though.

He'd come up with a device that somehow repelled the djinn, interfered with their energy. He'd even begun to transmit the instructions for how to create those devices, and Allan, who'd been a systems engineer at JPL, said he thought he could re-create one for the group here in Southern California. The scientist on the radio had explained how to use common components to make the device—touchscreens from iPads and iPhones, wiring from stereo equipment—and so everyone had hoped they would soon have the same sort of protection as the people in Los Alamos.

That hope was short-lived, though. The djinn had descended on Caltech soon after that, and the shortwave radio was lost during the survivors' desperate flight from their temporary sanctuary. And afterward they were all killed, one by one.

Except Leila. And now she knew exactly why —because Malik had chosen her to be his, and made sure none of the other djinn got close enough to harm her. Should she be grateful for that protection? She didn't know anymore what she was supposed to think or how she was supposed to feel.

She got up from the bed and went to the window. A tree blocked part of her view, but she thought she caught a flash of Malik's bright blue robes between the leaves. As far as she could tell, he was still sitting at the small round table where she'd left him.

Why hadn't he come after her? Surely a djinn couldn't be expected to understand the concept of needing some space?

Maybe he did. She knew nothing about the djinn except what she'd heard in her grandmother Neda's stories, and Malik didn't fit many of those descriptions, although there had been a few tales that described the djinn as possessing inhuman beauty. He wasn't a thing of air and darkness, dark smoke, a snake, or a dragon. He looked like an ordinary man.

Well, not *that* ordinary. Leila had spent a lot of time around actors, was used to seeing some pretty outstanding specimens of male beauty walking casually down the street, a latte in one hand and a cell phone in the other. But as gorgeous as those L.A. actors and models had been, she knew Malik would still have stood out among them. How could he not, with those perfect abs, that smooth warm-toned skin, those high cheekbones?

All right, he was kind of spectacular. But he was still a killer.

Or…was he? Her thoughts were jumbling again. He'd made it sound as though he'd had nothing to do with the Heat, or with the terrible hunting down of survivors that had commenced as soon as the disease finished burning its way through most of the population.

Then again, he could only be telling her what she wanted to hear. The djinn were supposed to be tricksters, making all sorts of promises that would never be fulfilled. But maybe their personalities bore little resemblance to what was described in those old folk tales, just as their appearance seemed to be markedly different.

If only her group had managed to maintain its communications with the Los Alamos survivors for a little longer. Leila hadn't been present for all those conversations, but she couldn't recall the scientist on the radio saying anything about the djinn being the cause of the Heat. He'd been more focused on letting the L.A. group know that they weren't alone, and that there might be a way to combat the djinn. Which was all well and good, but his encouraging words hadn't assisted them much in the long run. She hoped the scientist had been successful, though. It helped to know that somewhere there might be a group of survivors who weren't in bed with the djinn.

Literally.

The sensation of Malik's lips pressed against hers came back to Leila then, and she shook her head. What the hell had he been thinking, that one kiss was going to make her forget the last six weeks of running and hiding from his kind? That somehow she'd be swept away and conveniently ignore the myriad ways she'd seen her fellow survivors die at the hands of those vengeful elementals?

Not a chance in hell.

She turned away from the window, glad she'd only been able to catch that small glimpse of Malik and nothing else. It was a lot easier to harden her resolve against him when she wasn't actually in his presence. And what was with that strange fogginess that had come over her when he'd kissed her, that terrible moment of surrender before she seemed to wake up to herself? Had he cast a spell on her?

A spell. Leila wanted to laugh, but she knew she was in uncharted territory here. Dealing with the end of the world had been bad enough. Now she was supposed to figure out whether the djinn could cast spells?

Right then she wished more than anything she could have her grandmother there with her. Neda might be able to explain some of this. She'd been an educated woman, someone who'd worked as a sociologist for the government before the fall of the Shah forced her and her husband—and so many others like them—to flee for America and freedom. But for all her education, Neda hadn't forgotten the tales and stories from the small village where she'd been born. She might have been able to offer a few insights into dealing with djinn.

Unfortunately, Leila feared that Neda was gone, as well as everyone else in her family. Tyrell had spoken of watching his wife and daughter die, of going to check on his parents and finding them gone as well. If immunity to the Heat was at all hereditary, you'd have thought that at least one other person in his family should have survived. But they hadn't. They were all dead.

Tears started in her eyes, and Leila blinked them away. She'd gotten pretty good at that over the past hellish month and a half—tears didn't solve anything, and in fact just got in the way when you were running and hiding and trying to stay alive. There hadn't been much time to mourn, or even to stop and think about whether she had a reason to mourn. Fighting for survival had driven out just about every other concern.

Now it seemed as if she would have plenty of time to mourn, but she wouldn't allow herself to do so. It was just too big, to think that both her parents and her brother Dylan and her crazy Uncle Amir, the one with the expensive house in

Newport Beach but no visible means of support, were all gone. Her paternal grandparents and all the uncles and aunts and cousins in Boston that she'd only met once, at a family reunion when she was seventeen years old. Every last one of them…gone.

Damn it. The tears burned hot, unshed, in her eyes. Leila knew she needed something to distract herself, so she went to the closet and really looked around this time, noting all the gorgeous fabrics and expensive shoes. Where had all this come from? Was Malik like a genie of legend, someone who could just snap his fingers and make anything he wished appear?

Maybe he'd simply found all this stuff in shops and boutiques in Beverly Hills and magicked it over here. The jewels in the built-in drawers looked like something you'd get at Bulgari, heavy gold and cabochon gems, definitely with an Etruscan feel. She didn't see much in the way of glittering diamonds or platinum, and wondered at their lack, if all Malik had done was plunder a bunch of high-end jewelry stores. But maybe he'd thought the pieces he'd selected went better with the clothing he'd also provided.

She picked up a heavy ring set with a large ruby and tried it on. It fit the middle finger of her right hand well enough, but after staring at it for a moment, she took it off, holding it clasped in the palm of her hand. The thing hadn't looked right when contrasted with her broken nails and the half-healed scratches and scars on her fingers. It seemed as if she'd always been doing something to get banged up; more than once she'd been glad of her tetanus shots, and worried sick about what would happen once they ran out...not that she'd really expected to live that long.

A knock at the door made her startle and drop the ring. It fell into the open drawer, hitting a pendant set with emeralds and sapphires and making a loud *clink*. Leila held herself still, hoping if she remained quiet, he might go away.

Because of course that had to be Malik knocking at the door.

But then the knock came again. At least he was knocking, instead of simply barging in—or bringing down the door altogether, although she didn't know whether he would have gone to that extreme. He'd seemed quiet and well-spoken, almost diffident, as if he knew what an insane situation this was and didn't want to push her too hard.

Might as well go and see what he wanted.

Leila emerged from the closet and went to open the door. As she'd expected, Malik stood outside. What she hadn't expected was the tray of food he held, warm enough that steam curled up from it, bringing with it an aroma so delectable, her stomach gave an audible growl. Blood rushed to her face, but the djinn appeared not to notice.

"I thought you might be hungry," he said.

"Hungry" didn't begin to describe her current condition, especially with those savory smells filling her nostrils. Food like she hadn't eaten in months, cinnamon-spiced chicken and saffron rice and vegetables and a basket of pita bread. It was a feast that would've done her Persian grandmother proud. Where had he even gotten it from? Had he cooked it? The house had power, so maybe the food had been kept in a freezer all this time, even though it seemed too fresh for that.

"I could eat," Leila allowed. Even as she spoke, though, she worried what she was getting herself into. Maybe he'd drugged the food, done something to it to make her compliant.

As she took another breath and inhaled those wonderful aromas again, she thought that compliance might not be such a bad thing, if it meant a full stomach.

"Then take the tray and enjoy your meal," he said, offering her the platter of food.

She accepted it, feeling the silver of the tray cool against her fingertips, and also wondering why he was allowing her to eat alone. Yes, it was clear that he didn't want to push too hard, at least not right away, and yet she thought at some point he would have to do what he could to make her his Chosen in deed rather than in word alone.

Maybe so. For the moment, however, she thought it best not to ask too many questions. "Thank you," she said. "This smells delicious."

He inclined his head and moved away. For just the briefest moment, Leila thought of calling out to him to stay, to share some of this food, but she thought better of it. The last thing she wanted was for him to think she was okay with any of this. Yes, she'd eat, because she was hungry and this would be the first decent meal she'd had in weeks, but consuming the food he'd given her wasn't tacit agreement to go along with his plans.

At least, she had to hope he would see it that way. For now, though, she would eat, and gain some much-needed strength, and try to figure out what in the world she should do next.

FOUR

HE WISHED HE COULD GO VISIT HIS SISTER and ask her counsel about Leila, but Malik knew he shouldn't leave his Chosen alone in the house. True, so far she had made no move to escape, but what would happen once she realized that the djinn who had brought her here was gone?

Then again, there was no reason why he couldn't ask Fatima to come here to Malibu. They shared a bond, sister and brother, and so it was easy enough to call her to him.

She appeared in the living room a few minutes later, looking somewhat annoyed. "I was just about to sit down for drinks with Adam."

Adam being her Chosen, a man of twenty-five who'd once pursued an acting career, much like Leila. Or rather, not so much like Leila; while

Malik's own Chosen had supported herself by working in a restaurant while waiting for her "break," as she'd tended to call it, Adam appeared to have earned his livelihood by making himself a useful and charming companion to any number of wealthy women, some married, some not. Malik was not sure he approved of such opportunistic behavior, but he supposed it was none of his business. If nothing else, Adam's past liaisons had ensured his usefulness to older women...and Fatima was much, much older than her Chosen, even if she appeared to be around the same age, which would be in her middle twenties.

"I am sorry to have interrupted you," Malik said, and indeed he was. He should have stopped to think that the afternoon was wearing on to dusk, and to the time that the mortals in this town used to refer to as "happy hour." Not that djinn had any need to adhere to mortal schedules, but he'd gotten the impression that most of the community in Bel-Air had done that very thing, simply to make the transition easier for their partners. "I did not stop to think. I hoped that you might be able to offer some advice."

"About Leila, I assume," Fatima said, then chuckled as Malik raised an eyebrow. "Dear brother, the situation wasn't that difficult to deduce. It is the hour of dusk, and yet I see no sign of your Chosen, no glasses of wine, nothing to show that your progress with her is moving forward as you had hoped."

"She is proving somewhat…difficult," he allowed.

"Of course she is." A wave of one graceful hand, and a pair of glasses and a bottle of wine appeared on the inlaid coffee table in the living room. Fatima went there, and poured wine into each of the glasses before handing one to her brother. "What did you expect? It was not as it happened with most of the rest of us, simply going to our Chosen and telling them what their new lives would be—and casting a bit of glamour on them to smooth the transition if necessary. I am surprised you did not try that, Malik."

"I did," he said. "Only a little—not to coerce her, but to soften her fear. And while at first it seemed as if it was working, the enchantment did not last. She resisted."

It was Fatima's turn for her eyebrows to lift. "Interesting. There are not so very many mortals who can resist a djinn's glamour. It seems you have chosen a singular woman."

Malik had thought much the same thing— only in this particular case, he rather wished Leila was not quite so special. It would have been so much easier if she had been pliant, hadn't sought to argue with him. Then again, he did not want a limp doll as a partner. If Leila was prepared to fight him every step of the way, so be it. Her stubbornness now would only make her surrender later that much more rewarding.

If she surrendered at all. At the moment, it seemed more that she was prepared to dig in and shore up her defenses.

All he could do was shrug in response to his sister's comment. Fatima continued, "You must remember that she has spent weeks hiding and running. No doubt she has seen her companions killed…and you and I both know those deaths would not have been easy ones. The whole situation would have been much easier if you had only managed to take her right away."

"Which I did attempt," he said, the words abrupt. Fatima knew as well as he that it was through no fault of his that Leila had been so elusive.

"I know," she replied, "so there is no reason to take that tone with me. The only true counsel I can give you, brother, is to be patient. Soon enough she will see that you are nothing like the djinn who sent the Heat, or who hunted down her fellow survivors."

"I cannot be infinitely patient, Fatima," Malik pointed out. "The elders have given all of us only until the turn of the year to settle with our Chosen in the communities that have been selected for us."

To his surprise, Fatima's eyes twinkled with laughter. "As to that, brother—if you cannot make this woman fall in love with you in that span of time, then I will know there is something seriously wrong. Until then, do your best, but also be yourself. She will soon learn that she has been chosen by a jewel among the djinn."

"And if she does not?" he asked, somewhat irritated by the light tone his sister had adopted. He was not sure she quite appreciated the gravity of the situation.

At once Fatima's expression sobered. She pushed up the gold bangles on one arm with a faint metallic clatter, and tilted her head to one side, giving him a considering look. "Well, then, if she does not offer you her heart…you can always tell her the truth. Perhaps that would change her mind."

The truth? Leila moved back from the edge of the landing outside her bedroom and quietly tiptoed inside, then shut the door. The tray of food Malik had given her still sat on the small table by the window where she'd left it. Probably it was only lukewarm by now, but the second she'd heard voices coming up from somewhere downstairs, she'd abandoned her dinner, even though she'd only taken a few delicious bites, and gone to find out what she could overhear.

To eavesdrop, to be perfectly frank, but Leila felt no compunction about listening in on Malik's conversation. She'd only been able to catch a glimpse of his guest, a strikingly beautiful woman with black hair so long, she could probably sit on it. Even that small glimpse was enough to send an entirely ridiculous stab of jealousy through her—until she realized within a moment or two of listening to them talk that the woman was not some djinn lover Malik had summoned to take her place because he was already tired of her resisting him, but his own sister.

And it seemed he'd called the djinn woman here to ask for advice. In a way, it was sort of adorable that a being as strong and lordly and outwardly sure of himself as Malik would reach out to his sister for advice about his love life. There hadn't been anything in their conversation to set off too many alarms—well, except that bit about the "glamour," which Leila assumed must be some sort of spell—until they got to the end. When Malik's sister—Fatima, if she'd caught the name correctly—made that comment about "the truth," Malik had become downright subdued. His sister had taken the hint and not pushed him to pursue the topic, and then she left soon after, but clearly there was something important they'd been dancing around.

What that something was, Leila couldn't begin to guess. She certainly couldn't ask Malik. If he wasn't open to discussing a subject with his own sister, she very much doubted he'd be willing to talk to her about it.

You should still ask, she thought as she went to her neglected meal and made herself sit down and eat the rest of it. Really, it was almost a crime to let food this good get cold, especially after the short rations she'd been living on lately. *The worst he can say is no.*

Well, that wasn't necessarily true. He'd probably ask her how the hell she'd heard him bring up the subject in the first place, and then she would have no choice but to confess to her eavesdropping. Leila doubted her captor would be thrilled to learn she'd been listening to his conversation with his sister.

Captor. Could she even call Malik that? The door to her bedroom wasn't locked—that is, it had a lock, but she'd been the one to use it, not Malik. He hadn't even come after her when she'd fled from him on the patio. What would he have done if she'd kept running, had bolted right out the front door?

Probably then he would have pursued her. And any notions she might entertain of finding a car in the garage here and using it to get away might as well be put aside for now, because with the way he could apparently blink himself from place to place, he'd be able to catch up with her in an instant.

The excellent food suddenly didn't seem to be going down so easily. Leila reached for the glass of water on the tray and took a large swallow. For all she knew, the food she'd just eaten was drugged, but she didn't give that suspicion much credence. A being who could cast a spell to make a human compliant really didn't need to roofie anyone.

Then again, he'd said she'd fought of the glamour. He could be trying a different angle.

And if you keep second-guessing everything he says and does, you're going to drive yourself crazy, she told herself, scooping up the last of the saffron rice. The plate the meal had been served on was thin, translucent china, the kind of stuff you might see in a catalogue for around a couple grand a place setting, maybe more. She'd often wondered who could afford that kind of thing, but the people who'd once owned this showplace of a house were exactly the kind of consumers who wouldn't think twice about eating off plates that cost more than most people's mortgages. How much was this house worth, anyway? Or rather, how much had it been worth, back when real estate meant something? Twenty million? Thirty? Leila couldn't really wrap her head around that kind of sum and wasn't sure she wanted to.

Once she was done with the food, she wondered what she should do with the tray and the dirty dishes. She couldn't exactly rinse them off in the bathroom sink; there wasn't a garbage disposal built into the vanity. Probably the best thing to do was to stack them outside the door, just as she would have at a hotel where she was staying. Malik would come along and get them eventually, she supposed. The house was spotless, and she wondered for a moment whether the djinn had servants to keep the place clean, or whether his powers somehow took care of that particular detail as well.

She dabbed at her mouth with the hemstitched linen napkin that had been supplied on the tray along with the heavy silverware, then put the napkin on top of her scraped-clean plate and took the whole thing over to the door. Balancing the tray against her hip, she turned the knob—and then barely stifled a gasp of surprise when she saw Malik standing outside.

"How long have you been out there?" she asked, too startled to keep the accusatory note out of her tone.

"I just came upstairs," he replied calmly. "I thought I should check to see if you were finished with your meal."

"I am." Feeling a little foolish—or maybe the sheepish feeling she was currently experiencing was only guilt over her eavesdropping episode earlier—she handed the tray to Malik. "That was very good. Um…thank you."

"You are most welcome." He hesitated, as if he wasn't sure what he should say next. When he did speak, the words came out quickly, indicating that he wanted to get them out and over with before he had a chance to change his mind. "Would you like to come downstairs?"

Would she? Leila found herself hesitating as well, although for probably a completely different reason than Malik. After all, she'd fled to her room to get away from him. Going downstairs with him now would make it seem as if she didn't know what the hell she wanted.

Then again, that seemed like a fairly accurate assessment of her current situation.

"Sure," she replied, knowing he had to have

noticed the way she paused before answering. But what else was she supposed to do? This was all uncharted territory for her. She had no idea how she was supposed to behave around a djinn—especially a djinn who expected her to fall in love with him post-haste so they could move to Bel-Air and join the community of djinn and their Chosen that had been established there.

Malik smiled, and Leila found herself flushing for no reason. This was ridiculous. She'd been around her share of good-looking men—hell, she'd even dated some of them—and yet she couldn't seem to control the way she reacted to this djinn who had brought her to his Malibu hideaway. Even though he'd said that the glamour did not work on her, Leila couldn't help wondering whether his assessment of the situation was accurate. Some kind of magic spell seemed a more likely explanation for her behavior than simply overwhelming physical attraction.

"The night is still mild," he said. "I thought we could go out on the patio."

That particular setup seemed fraught with possibilities, not all of which she really wanted to acknowledge at the moment. But then, the living room presented its own issues, with that big luxurious couch. When you knew a man was intent on pursuing you, pretty much any scenario presented its share of problems.

"That would be nice," she said, hoping he wouldn't notice the way the words seemed to strangle in her throat.

Maybe he did, but he didn't react, only extended an arm toward the stairs. Leila exited the bedroom and couldn't help noticing from the corner of her eye the way Malik neatly made the tray he was holding disappear, presumably so he wouldn't be burdened with the thing as he went down the steps. A minor trick, but it made her wonder exactly what kind of powers he commanded, whether he could do just about anything he wanted.

That thought wasn't very reassuring. A shiver went over her, causing him to say, "Are you cold? I can get you a shawl."

"No, I'm fine," Leila replied at once. It was possible she'd regret turning down that shawl once she was outside, but she'd just have to tough it out. If she could sleep in the opening of a storm drain with only a jacket to keep out the night air, then she could handle a light evening sea breeze.

When she went outside, however, she was relieved to see that the temperature hadn't dropped all that much, even though the sun was long gone and only a faint smudge of dark orange lay along the horizon. Overhead, the sky was already midnight blue, the first stars pricks of light in the darkness.

Funny how many more stars she could see now, with all of L.A.'s light pollution a thing of the past.

The pool shimmered in that darkness like the world's biggest aquamarine. And it wasn't entirely dark; solar lights marked the edges of the path, and she could see several tall wrought-iron lamps casting their own glow on the conversation area beyond the pool.

It was there that Malik led her. On the table in front of the U-shaped sectional was more wine, this time rich and dark, along with a platter of fruit and cheese.

"I just ate," she protested.

"True," he said, still wearing a faint smile. "But I have not, and it seemed to me that you have gone so long without decent food, you need more now to compensate."

That might be true. To keep herself "camera ready," she'd spent so much of her time worrying about what she ate—even though she was naturally slender, with a metabolism her roommate had openly envied—that it was still hard to tell herself it was all right to eat more than the meager amounts she'd allowed herself in the past. Then she wanted to shake her head at herself. She was too thin right now, thanks to all those weeks of running and hiding and eating far less than what she needed. Anyway, it wasn't as if she had to worry about some overweight asshole of a casting director lecturing her about how she needed to lose ten pounds if she was really serious about landing a role.

Leila took a seat and Malik followed suit, although he was careful not to sit right next to her and instead maintained a polite distance. In silence she watched as he poured her some wine from the already open bottle, then placed a few pieces of cheese and some grapes on a small wooden plate.

"Thank you," she said as she took them from him. This felt too surreal, to be sitting in the warm dark of a Santa Ana wind and watching the bluish light from the pool reflect on the elegant planes of a djinn's face. Maybe she should have stayed in her room.

Too late for that now. Besides, there was always the chance that if she spoke with him, got more information, she might get closer to this "truth" Malik's sister Fatima had mentioned.

He poured wine for himself and made up another plate, this one with more food than the one he'd given her. Well, he had said that he hadn't eaten. In a way, it was fascinating to think that djinn had to eat, too, that they couldn't simply live off air, or possibly whatever element they called their own.

"Are you doing all this?" Leila asked, gesturing with the hand that held her wine glass toward the pool and the lights in the house beyond.

"Yes," he replied. "It takes very little of my power to make sure that the water is warm and the lights function in the way they were intended. I did not think you would want to sit in the dark, or take a cold shower."

"A cold shower is better than none at all, but yes, it was great to have hot water." Blood went to her cheeks again, and she was glad that the lighting where they sat wasn't too bright. Talking about showers seemed a bit…personal.

But Malik only nodded, silent for a moment as he sipped his wine. Leila thought she should have a taste as well, and took a modest swallow. Holy hell. She'd had her share of high-end wines, both on dates and also at the restaurant where she worked, since the owner liked the servers to sample the bottles available so they could speak knowledgeably on the subject, but she'd never had anything like this. Dark, with a hint of smoke, and subtle hints of earth twined around the richness of the grape. It was utterly entrancing.

But really, should she be surprised? If Malik had gone into this home's cellars to look for the wine, lord only knows what he might have found there. The people who lived in a house like this probably wouldn't have been stocking up on box wine or Two-Buck Chuck from Trader Joe's.

The djinn spoke then, his gaze apparently fixed on the still, gleaming waters of the pool, and not on her. "What made you come down?"

"I—" Good question. She gave a nervous little chuckle, then said, "I really don't know."

He smiled. "Thank you for your honesty."

Honesty. Guilt roiled in Leila at the memory of how she'd listened to Malik and Fatima talk in the living room below. Should she say something? Her mother had always told her, *A lie multiplies,* and warned her that not telling the truth took its own toll on the soul.

"Well, if I'm being honest…." Leila paused there as Malik turned slightly toward her and raised an eyebrow. In a rush, she continued, "I eavesdropped on you talking to your sister."

To her surprise, he only rewarded her with another one of those dazzling smiles. "I know."

"You *know?*"

"Of course. I sensed your presence up on the landing. I suppose you were curious when you heard another voice in the house."

"I—" That was pretty much exactly what had happened. Leila swallowed some more wine, knowing she did it a disservice by paying so little attention to it. "Why didn't you say something?"

"I saw no reason to. There was nothing I discussed with Fatima that could have come as much of a surprise to you." His voice was calm, measured, his profile perfectly chiseled and yet serene, backlit by the aqua-blue waters of the swimming pool. As Leila searched for the best way to respond, he went on, "You already know why I have brought you here. And certainly you could have guessed that I was hoping to get a more enthusiastic response from you."

Those words made her shift on the couch and give him a narrow-eyed look. "I suppose you djinn expect mortal women to fall all over you the minute you snap your fingers."

"Not precisely," he said, still unruffled. "But rather, I had hoped that a woman who had spent such a long time living in fear, who had been denied much of life's comforts for so many weeks, might have been a bit more grateful to be rescued from those conditions."

Leila cupped her hands around the wide bowl of her wine glass. "Well, maybe if you had said something instead of just trying to kiss me—"

"Judging by the way you responded to the

kiss, I was not sure explanations would have helped all that much." He shook his head and drank some more of his wine. "It was more that once you were here, once you realized you were safe, I had thought...."

Voice tight, she said, "You thought I'd fall into your arms out of sheer gratitude?"

"I see that I was being naïve."

Absently, she wondered where he had learned to speak English. His command of the language was perfect, although his diction was more formal than what she was used to. He'd been speaking English to his sister, too, Leila realized. Otherwise, she shouldn't have been able to understand a word they were saying, for surely the djinn must have their own language.

Even as these thoughts passed through her mind, she knew she was only attempting to distract herself from the matter at hand. It was obvious that Malik had expected her to come to him with no arguments, no reservations about casting in her lot with one of the very beings who'd engineered mankind's destruction. The height of arrogance, she thought, even as she wondered how all those other Chosen had reacted when approached by the beautiful elementals who had selected them. Maybe none of them had put up much of a fight, which would help to explain why the man who sat here with her now had expected her to behave in much the same way.

And even though she rejected his conviction that she should have succumbed to him immediately, she knew she had to be grateful to him on some level. It was only because of his protection that she'd survived this long. Because she was Chosen, apparently she was off limits to the other djinn, the ones who'd killed her companions and so many others. Had the djinn known in advance who would be immune, and so selected their future partners from some kind of list? It would explain why Malik had known what size clothing to obtain for her, although the thought of all those djinn coolly choosing their respective mates while the rest of humanity was about to die made her stomach want to curdle.

And how long would she remain Chosen if she continued to hold Malik at arm's length?

Since Leila wasn't sure she wanted to contemplate that question for very long, she decided it was time for some more wine. She drank, let the rich liquid flow over her tongue, and sat in the warm salt-scented darkness and wished she was the sort of person who could allow herself to succumb to him, one of those women who didn't think twice about climbing into bed with someone they found attractive. It would be a lot easier.

Abruptly, she asked, "What did Fatima mean when she said you should tell me the truth? The truth about what?"

Malik seemed to go very still. He had already been sitting there quietly enough, one strong hand resting on the base of his wine glass where it sat on the tabletop, but now it felt as though he was barely breathing, that he was doing his best not to react to her questions. When he spoke, his tone was still even enough, but there was an underlying edge to it, a tension Leila hadn't thought she'd heard before.

"There is another djinn," he said. "His name is Omar al-Tariq, and he wished to claim you as well. I could not let that happen."

"Why not?" From where she was sitting, one djinn seemed as good as another….

Then again….

Leila thought of those cruel, beautiful shapes diving from the sky, or shivering into existence in the middle of the street, intent on vengeance. For what, she still didn't know. She'd only known that to see a djinn was to die not long afterward.

Considering the kindness Malik had shown her so far, she thought she might have to revise her opinion about all djinn being equal.

"He is a cruel person," Malik said, still in that even tone. "He takes his joy in tormenting others, especially women. Not physically, but the kind of cruelty of the mind that leaves its own terrible scars."

A shiver went over Leila. She'd been fortunate enough to avoid those kinds of gas-lighting bastards when she was dating, but she'd had a few friends who weren't so lucky. Malik was all too correct about the mental scars such relationships left in their wake.

When she didn't immediately reply, he continued, "I determined that al-Tariq should not have you. In such situations, it is the normal practice for the parties involved to have a duel."

"'A duel'?" Leila echoed, a small chuckle escaping her lips despite herself. "You fought a duel over me?"

"No, I did not. I would have," he added, as though to inform her that he was no coward. "But when al-Tariq saw that I was serious about pursuing you, he relinquished his claim, saying that it had never been his true intention to take a human woman as his partner."

"Sounds like a real prize," she remarked.

"No, he definitely is not that. He is one of those who thinks himself strong…but only when he knows he has the advantage. He could not be sure of prevailing against me, and that was why he withdrew."

"So…." Leila let the word trail off, mostly because she was still trying to put it all together, doing her best to figure out exactly what Malik was telling her. "Does this mean you really hadn't intended to take a Chosen until you decided to be my guardian angel?"

He lifted his glass, swallowed some of the dark wine within. "Perhaps an over-simplification, but yes, at first I hadn't thought I would."

"You didn't think a human life was worth saving?" She was doing her best to keep her voice as calm and controlled as his, but even she could hear the anger that underlaid her words, like the first flame racing along the bottom of a log before it caught.

"That is not what I said."

"Then please—explain it to me. I'm just a simple human, after all."

This time he shifted on the couch so he faced her directly. His jaw was set, and although it was fairly dark out here, despite the lights that had been set up to illuminate the area, she thought she could see true anger in his eyes. "You are much more than that, Leila Donovan, and I think you know it." Before she could open her mouth to reply, he went on, "I did not agree with the decision to let the Heat loose upon your world. Unfortunately, there were far more who wanted their revenge than those of us who counseled moderation."

"Revenge for what?" Leila asked. Once again she had the feeling that there were undercurrents here she knew nothing about. "What did we ever do to you djinn?"

"To be absolutely precise, you mortals did nothing. It was God who took this world from us and gave it to humankind, who made us exiles in the otherworld. But because we could not take our revenge against Him directly, the djinn decided that it was humans who would pay the price."

God. He was talking about *God*. Leila's head swam, and she was fairly certain it wasn't from the wine, not after the healthy meal she'd just eaten. She'd heard bits and pieces of the legends about the origins of the djinn, that they were so vengeful because they had been the original inhabitants of this world before it was taken from them, but she'd only thought those details were part of a story, a piece of a fairytale like Aladdin and his lamp or Ali Baba and his treasure cave.

But now she sat opposite a real-life djinn, a being who lived and breathed just as she did, and who had just casually spoken of God the way someone might talk about an inconsiderate boss who kept asking for overtime with no pay and perpetually "forgot" about holiday bonuses. So was it all real, all the legends, all the stories? Or did those tales only contain kernels of truth, while the rest was all embellishment?

Speaking slowly, she said, "If God gave us this world, why did He allow you to use the Heat on humans at all? You'd think He would have stopped you."

Malik let out a small sigh, one Leila was fairly certain he hadn't intended her to hear. "In my heart of hearts, I had thought that He would stop us. That was why I did not at first select someone to be my Chosen—I truly believed it would not be necessary. But when I heard that Omar al-Tariq had chosen you, I knew he must be stopped, even if the djinns' plans turned out to be for naught. Then the Heat was loosed, and…." He stopped there, and took another swallow of wine.

"And it killed everyone, just as the other djinn had planned," Leila said, her voice hard. She'd put that steel in her tone, because otherwise she feared she might lose control, might begin to cry. The only way she had survived so far was to not think of how big and terrible all this was, and yet each conversation she'd had with Malik so far had only driven home how much the world had changed, how much she'd had to change to deal with it.

"Yes," Malik replied heavily. He reached for the bottle that sat on the table and poured himself some more wine, and then, in silence, filled Leila's glass as well. "God did not stop us. Those of the One Thousand—the djinn who wished to save some of humanity—went forth to claim their Chosen and take them to their new homes. I intended to do the same with you, but you proved to be too quick to run away. The rest, you know."

Almost mechanically, Leila lifted her glass of wine to her lips and drank. Magnificent as this wine had tasted a few moments earlier, now it was bitter on her tongue, reminding her of all the losses she had suffered…the world had suffered.

Nothing would ever be the same.

They were both quiet again, but this time the silence wasn't quite as awkward. He'd spoken, and he'd told her the truth. Oh, Leila supposed Malik could be lying about his motives, or even about this Omar al-Tariq person, but she didn't think so. She'd spent way too much time around people who could lie as naturally as they breathed and had learned to spot the signs…and she'd heard the ring of truth in the djinn's words.

"Thank you," she said softly.

He didn't ask why she was thanking him. He

only replied, "It is nothing. You deserve the truth. I thank you as well, for telling me that you had listened to Fatima's and my conversation. I wondered whether you would."

"You didn't trust me?"

"It's not that," he said at once. "You have been running for a very long time, after all. I can see why confidences would be difficult for you."

Sitting there and listening to his deep, warm voice, watching his fine profile backlit in the darkness, Leila felt something tight and terrible in her chest begin to loosen. She didn't quite know what was happening; she only knew she'd never felt this way before.

It frightened her.

She pushed the wine glass away and stood. "I'm—I'm pretty tired. Is it all right if I go to sleep?"

His expression was unreadable. "Of course it is. You don't need my permission for such things —this is your home as much as it is mine."

It didn't feel like home. It felt as if she was staying at the Ritz Carlton. But she didn't bother to tell Malik that. Instead, she inclined her head at him, then murmured a quick good night and fled.

Apparently, she was going to keep running.

FIVE

HAD HE TOLD LEILA TOO MUCH? MALIK couldn't be quite sure; he had certainly had his share of relationships over the long, long centuries of his life, but he had never interacted with a human woman before. By necessity, the balance of power in such a liaison was quite different. A djinn woman's powers were often the equal of—or sometimes greater than—those of the man she partnered with, while with a human woman, the situation was not remotely the same. All Chosen drew a little power from the elementals who had selected them, or otherwise they would not be blessed with long life to match that of their partners, and neither would they have the power to heal with astonishing rapidity, and to withstand all manner of illness and disease. Even so, those more-than-human qualities did not make them the equal of a djinn.

When he had resolved to take Leila as his Chosen, Malik had also resolved to treat her as a peer, even though she was only a mortal. He did not want to spend eternity lording it over a human woman, which was probably what Omar al-Tariq had planned for her before Malik thwarted his little scheme. That was why he had told Leila the truth and nothing else. He did not wish to play games with her. From what he could tell, she respected him for this treatment. It seemed that she had softened a little, unless his eyes and his ears were deceiving him. Unfortunately, any perceived softening had not prevented her from running away, there at the end.

He lay in his bed and stared at the ceiling, wishing sleep might come to calm his racing thoughts. Would Leila be amused to learn that djinn slept as well? They were similar to humans in this basic need, although djinn did not require nearly as many hours of slumber.

Perhaps if he was lucky, he would have Leila sleeping next to him in the near future. In her room, though—he had given her the largest bedroom, hoping she would appreciate the gesture, and he would very much like to take up residence there with her. This room was quite elegant, if not so large, but it lacked the expansive ocean views of her current quarters. He could still hear the sea, though, could sense the ever-present rumble of the waves crashing on a shore that was many feet below the promontory where this house had been constructed.

Leila slept. No wonder—he imagined that she had not had many hours of uninterrupted sleep since the Heat had changed the world. She had shut her door, of course, but when he walked past earlier this evening, his sharp djinn ears had been able to catch the sound of her regular breathing. He thought of her now, thought of her eyes closed in sleep, lashes dark against her cheeks, the wealth of her long, near-black hair spread across a pillow.

She was so very beautiful, as beautiful as a djinn. It was possible, he supposed, that she might carry some elemental blood within her. He knew that her mother's family had come from Persia, a place where the djinn had once mingled with mortals, although such liaisons were frowned upon among his people, and the offspring of such unions shunned. But perhaps a djinn had once visited one of Leila's distant ancestors, and the woman had passed off the child as the result of her marriage bed. Those things happened, even if they were never spoken of.

Djinn blood would explain why she had been

able to fight off the glamour he had tried to cast on her. It was a power that only worked on mortals, as he'd learned to his chagrin once when he was young and very foolish. Luckily, the djinn woman who had been the object of the glamour had been older and far more experienced than he, and so she had laughed and told him that he could only rely on his charm when it came to the likes of her kind. Luckily, she had been forgiving…and all too happy to teach him the arts of love.

He wished he could share that knowledge with Leila now, but he knew he would have to tread with care. As to the question of whether his Chosen had djinn blood…well, he was not certain of the reception such an inquiry would provoke, and so he thought it better to hold his tongue for now. The djinn did not have a way of testing for such things, and at any rate, even if some long-ago ancestor had been half-elemental, the blood would be so diluted by now as to hardly matter at all.

No, it would be better to keep silent on the subject. Malik had to hope their continued proximity to one another would continue the softening he had seen in her expression earlier that evening. Perhaps, in the not too distant future, she would realize he truly intended only the best for her. He did not love her yet, of course; he hardly knew her. But he thought he could love her quite easily.

With any luck, she would feel the same way about him. If she did not...no, he wouldn't allow himself to consider that possibility. She must come to love him, or she could not remain his Chosen.

And then she would surely die.

Sunlight woke her, a diffuse brightness outside her eyelids. Leila blinked and sat up, staring at her luxurious surroundings for a confused half-second before she realized where she was. No, this was certainly not an abandoned warehouse, or a storm drain, or even one of the few bedrooms in empty houses where she'd stolen some sleep, knowing she had to risk it for a few hours because otherwise she would have dropped from exhaustion where she stood.

This was the house in Malibu, a place so far beyond anything she'd ever experienced in real life, it might as well be a movie set. She'd been so tired last night when she climbed the steps to her room that she'd forgotten to close the drapes, but thankfully, because the space had a west/north-west orientation, all she had to deal with was reflected daylight and not the actual sun blazing in.

She pushed back the silken duvet and went to the window so she could look out at the sea. It was a serene dark blue, barely ruffled by the wind. It seemed that the rough Santa Ana winds had died out, to be replaced by a normal sea breeze.

Movement closer to the house caught her eye, and she looked down at the pool. A dark shape was cutting through the blue-green water, sleek and fast.

Malik.

He moved with the speed and grace of an Olympian swimmer, barely leaving any ripples in his wake. All the way to one end, then back to the other, doing laps as though he truly was training for the Olympics. In that moment, Leila thought water must be his element, even though he hadn't told her which one he controlled. She somehow doubted a fire elemental would be so happy in the water.

As she watched, he came to the shallow end of the pool and climbed the steps. He wore dark, tight-fitting trunks that clung to his thighs and ass, and did very little to hide the perfection of his form.

Leila swallowed and backed away from the

window, her cheeks flushing with sudden heat. Amazing as the sight had been, she wasn't sure whether she really wanted to see that much of Malik. True, the open robes he wore didn't do much to hide his broad chest or the perfection of his abs, but at least his arms and legs had been covered. Now she knew that the rest of him was just as flawless as the glimpses she'd already caught, and she wasn't quite sure what to do with that knowledge.

You can think someone's attractive without wanting to jump into bed with them, she told herself as she went into the bathroom. It seemed foolish to shower and wash her hair again when she'd done that very thing only twelve hours or so earlier, but she didn't know what else she was supposed to do, so she showered once more, although this time much more quickly.

The thing was, the flush that had gone over her at the sight of Malik's nearly naked form hadn't completely been one of embarrassment. Leila could lie to herself all she wanted, but she knew desire when she felt it. Yes, it had been a while. Still, there were some things you just didn't forget.

It's only natural, she thought as she rinsed the conditioner out of her hair. *You're alone with one of the most amazing male specimens you've ever seen. How the hell did you think you were going to react?*

Well, preferably not like a silly girl in junior high crushing on some guy in algebra class.

Leila got out of the shower and dried herself off, debated brushing her teeth, then decided against it. She hadn't eaten anything yet, so she'd just have to do it all over again...assuming they ate anything at all. Maybe djinn weren't into breakfast. Aside from that, toothpaste was guaranteed to make coffee taste weird. She assumed Malik would have coffee here. He certainly seemed to have everything else.

Another day, another gorgeous silky skirt and simple top. Jeans would have been nice, but apparently Malik didn't want his Chosen wearing pants. Just old-fashioned, or did he want her in skirts and impractical shoes because it would be harder for her to run away when dressed like that?

Watch me, she thought as she descended the stairs. *Even before the Heat, I could climb a chain-link fence in four-inch heels.*

She couldn't help smiling at the memory, at how one of her college boyfriends had thought it would be a good idea to go trespassing at the Goodyear blimp airfield in the South Bay. They'd gone there after attending a friend's birthday party, and were both pretty tipsy...but not so out of it that she hadn't gone up and over that fence like a pole vaulter in training after a security guard started chasing them.

The scent of coffee came to her near the bottom step—a good thing, since she needed something to help guide her to the kitchen, which felt like it was miles away from the staircase. How big was this place, anyway? Six thousand square feet? Eight thousand? The people who'd lived here probably needed walkie-talkies to keep in touch.

She came into the kitchen, a huge space dominated by enormous Thermador stainless steel appliances and what appeared to be miles of granite countertops in warm, sandy shades that echoed the natural materials used in the rest of the house. Standing at one end of the counter, pouring coffee into a pair of bisque-glazed mugs, was Malik. To Leila's relief, he was out of the swim trunks and back into one of his robes, this one a deep blue faintly tinged with green, a color that echoed the ever-changing waters outside the window.

"Good morning," he said politely. "Did you sleep well?"

"Very well," she replied, relieved that he was acting like she was simply an honored house guest, and not the woman he wanted to make his partner for eternity. That was way too big a concept to think about before she'd had her morning coffee.

"How do you like it?" he inquired, lifting one of the mugs toward her. "There is cream in the refrigerator and sugar in the pantry."

"Black is fine," Leila said. Her fingers briefly brushed against his as she took the mug from him, and again she could feel that unwelcome flush in her cheeks. Back in her college days, she'd drunk her coffee heavily doctored, milky and sweet, but she'd trained herself to drink it black after she discovered how many calories that particular indulgence cost her.

"Very good."

Neutral words, meaning nothing. Did he know that she'd been standing up at the window, watching him as he swam in the pool? After all, he'd been able to tell that she had eavesdropped on his conversation with his sister. True, they'd been much closer when they were having that discussion than he had been while in the pool, but still…she just didn't have any idea what a djinn could and couldn't do. That uncertainty unsettled her; she didn't like not knowing what to expect from him.

"It looks like it's going to be a pretty day," she remarked. More words that didn't mean much. But what the hell was she supposed to say to him?

It wasn't like they could talk about the recent crop of movies that had come out, or the latest shenanigans in Washington, D.C.

Actually, when she put it that way, Leila thought the end of the world might not be so bad after all.

"For now," Malik allowed. "And for a few more days. But I believe a change in the weather is coming."

"You're a meteorologist, too?" she asked, faintly amused, then took a sip of coffee. It was almost too hot to drink, but she needed the caffeine. Despite its temperature, it was very good. French roast, strong but smooth. Malik definitely could brew a decent cup of coffee.

"I have not studied the science of weather, if that is what you mean," he replied. "My element is water, not air, but I can still sense when conditions are going to shift."

So her suspicions had been correct. No wonder he seemed so at home in the pool—and no wonder he'd chosen a house surrounded by water, one with water built right in, when you considered the indoor water feature in the atrium and the waterfall that cascaded down into the koi pond just outside the living room.

Leila glanced outside. The palm trees planted near the pool shimmered in the sunlight as their fronds caught the morning breeze. It certainly didn't look as though rain was anywhere close by, but she knew those things could turn on a dime, especially lately. No one in her little group of survivors had been a meteorologist or a climatologist or anything close to that, but they'd all noticed the way the weather had whipsawed this autumn, swinging from hot, dry Santa Ana winds to sudden rainstorms, far more than they usually should have been getting at this time of year. Then again, Southern California was in a drought half the time, so it was difficult to say what was normal.

"Crazy weather," she remarked before she sipped again at her coffee.

Malik's brows drew together, and he also looked outside for a brief moment before returning his attention to her. "I'm not sure 'crazy' is precisely the right word. Your climate is attempting to readjust, to return to normal now that it does not have any new pollution to contend with. Things may be a bit unsettled for a while. The effect is probably more noticeable here, where there were so many people and so many cars and factories, so much industry, than it would be in other, less populated areas of the country."

It wasn't the sort of thing she'd really had time to consider. Sure, climate change had been in the back of her head as something she needed to worry about, but she'd been too busy to do much about it besides do her best to recycle and make sure she was careful about turning off unnecessary lights, that sort of thing. She definitely hadn't stopped to think about what the effect might be of suddenly removing all the carbon overload. No more millions of cars on the roads. No more factories belching smoke. No more…well, no more of almost everything.

"How many djinn are there?" she asked abruptly, not sure whether Malik would even reply.

However, he barely blinked as he said, "Some twenty thousand of us. Not so very many to be spread all over the earth. There will be little concentrations here and there, because of the settlements where the Chosen and their djinn live, but even the populations of those settlements will only number in the hundreds."

Twenty thousand, and about a thousand more Chosen, if Malik's comment about there being one thousand of the "good" djinn was correct. No, that wasn't much compared to the billions who had once called Earth their home.

Then she asked, halfway dreading the answer, "How many were immune?"

His hesitation was obvious, but he didn't try

to dodge the question. "I am not sure. I was told that the Heat killed more than ninety-nine percent of the population, but even that mortality rate would still leave millions alive. However…."

He stopped there, and Leila thought she knew the reason why. There might have been millions left after the Heat had done its dirty work, but now, almost two months later, she wondered how many of those immune people were still alive. The "bad" djinn had done their due diligence, picking off survivors wherever they found them. Even if there were ten thousand or more of them on the hit squad, it would still take time. There might be hundreds of thousands of people left, just waiting for the hammer to fall.

Her hope must have shown itself on her face, because Malik said quietly, "There is nothing we can do to save them. Indeed, those of us among the One Thousand are forbidden to make the attempt. It was part of the bargain we made. We could only protect our Chosen, and no one else."

"Seems a little harsh," Leila said, her tone intentionally brittle. She still couldn't see how anyone—even a djinn—could just sit back and allow millions of people to be murdered outright. This wasn't even about the Heat, but the calculated genocide of those remaining.

"It *is* harsh," Malik returned, surprising her.

"We djinn are a harsh people, in many ways. We were forced to live for millennia in the otherworld, and it is not a place for the soft of body and spirit."

She tilted her head to one side, considering him. Once again, he wore that calm expression, and she wondered how much of it came from inner serenity, and how much from rigid self-control. "The otherworld. You mentioned it yesterday. What is it, exactly?"

A sip of coffee, as though he needed it to fortify himself for the explanation to follow. "It is a place beyond this world—on another plane, for lack of a better way to describe it. There is no night and day, only a sky tortured into a thousand colors. Nothing grows there, save what we can nurture in the courtyards and gardens of our palaces. The wind blows ceaselessly." He paused before adding, "No human can survive there, for the air is not sufficient to support your lungs."

The picture he painted was a horrifying one. No wonder the djinn had been so angry with God, had been willing to do whatever it took to make Earth theirs again. The terrors of the otherworld weren't enough justification for the death and destruction they'd unleashed, and yet Leila began to see how the djinn might have thought so.

A silence fell, one in which they both sipped their coffee, not quite looking at each other. When it got too awful, Leila said, "How long do you think it will take for the weather to settle down?"

His shoulders lifted, and the blue-green of his robe shimmered as it shifted slightly. "I honestly can't say. Some years, I would think. At least here in this region there is little chance of tornadoes or hurricanes."

Thank God for small favors. She smiled slightly, then said, "But we have earthquakes."

"Oh, they are nothing to worry about," he assured her. "The earth elementals can sense them coming, and send the energy elsewhere before they can do much damage."

Leila began to realize there were ramifications to djinn powers that she hadn't really considered. Too bad the djinn weren't altruists; they could have stopped the Northridge quake before it contributed to so much loss of life, or the destructive quakes down in Mexico. But apparently they were only concerned about mitigating the damage now that they were residents of this planet.

"If that's the case," she asked, "can't air elementals stop tornadoes?"

"I suppose they can," Malik replied. "I would

rather not put it to the test, however. Unsettling things, tornadoes."

His comment almost made her smile. Not because she was a fan of tornadoes, either, but because it amused her to see that Malik had a bit of a phobia. Maybe that was too strong a word. Clearly, though, he didn't like them, maybe because he couldn't control them the way he probably could a tsunami.

"Is your sister a water elemental, too?" she asked.

"No, she controls the earth."

"Siblings don't have to have the same powers?"

"No." He sipped some more coffee, then added, "As far as we've been able to tell, there is no clear genetic pattern when it comes to whether a djinn will control a particular element. It is not the sort of thing that runs in families. It appears more that nature guides us in this, for there is always an even distribution among the four elements, no matter how many children are born to a particular family."

She hadn't even thought about children. But if Malik had a sister, then it stood to reason they must have parents somewhere. She hadn't really stopped to consider the concept of djinn reproducing, because before she met Malik, the elementals had been one large consolidated force of evil, as far as she was concerned. You didn't worry about your arch-enemies having parents, or siblings, or any kind of families.

Did the djinns' partnerships with their Chosen mean that they, too, could reproduce together? Leila wasn't sure she wanted to ask that particular question—it would sound as though she had a personal interest in the answer. Children had been one of the last things on her mind before the Heat struck, and she hadn't thought about them much after the disease had wiped out most of mankind, except on the rare occasions when she'd had a little time to stop and realize she hadn't seen any survivors under the age of about sixteen or seventeen. Whether that meant the disease had struck the young particularly hard, or only that they weren't as equipped to escape their djinn pursuers as adults, who generally had more resources, she couldn't begin to guess. About all she could do was experience a weary relief that no children seemed to have survived to live through the horror of the world as it was now.

Had Malik guessed at her uneasiness regarding their current topic of conversation? Leila couldn't tell for sure. She sipped her coffee, while the djinn drained the rest of the French roast in his mug and refilled it from the carafe that sat on the coffeemaker's warming plate.

Coffeemaker. That was an understatement. The thing was an enormous stainless steel industrial unit that looked like it could make espresso and lattes for an entire film crew without breaking a sweat. Using it to make a couple of mundane cups of coffee was like using a Ferrari to go grocery shopping.

"Would you like some breakfast?" he asked after he finished filling his mug.

Breakfast for her used to be a cup of yogurt and some fresh fruit. Lately, it had been energy bars—if she was lucky. It had been so long since she'd had a real breakfast, about all she could do was blink at the djinn and repeat, "Breakfast?"

A flash of a smile, dazzling as the bright sun that poured down on the patio outside. "I assumed that was the meal you mortals consumed in the morning. Eggs, toast…bacon?"

Oh, God, bacon. When was the last time she'd eaten any bacon? Maybe at the brunch she and Dylan had attended on the weekend of their father's birthday nearly a year ago, although now that she thought about it, she'd skipped the bacon and waffles, had only eaten eggs and fruit and one piece of sourdough toast, since she had an audition coming up and didn't want to look puffy.

Well, no worries about auditions anymore, that was for sure. And clearly Malik wasn't one of those controlling types who scrutinized every mouthful his girlfriend ate to make sure she didn't plump up on him.

"Bacon sounds great," she said, then lifted a dubious eyebrow. "You know how to make bacon?"

Another smile. "These things are easy enough for us djinn."

Suddenly, the smell of fresh-cooked bacon hit her nose. Leila looked over at the counter-height table and chairs that were set off to one side in a nook, and saw that the table was suddenly set, and in the middle of the table was a platter of bacon, a bowl of scrambled eggs, and a plate of toast cut into perfect triangles.

"What the—?" she blurted, then stopped, sending an inquiring glance up at Malik. "You can do all this?"

"Oh, yes," he replied. "Some of my people like to cook much as mortals do, making everything from scratch, but it's not necessary."

The scent of bacon was too enticing. Leila took her mug of coffee with her and went over to the table, then reached out with her free hand and picked up one of the perfectly browned and crispy morsels. One bite was enough to send endorphins flooding all through her. Holy hell, that was good.

"You like it?" Malik asked, then came over so he could pull out one of the chairs and sit down.

"Best bacon I've ever had," she said, and that was only the truth. She could have tried to explain her reaction to the food by telling herself it was only that she hadn't had bacon in a long, long time, but that would have been a lie. It really was the best she'd ever had.

So were the eggs, and the toast, neither of which appeared inclined to get cold the way they usually did when they'd been sitting out for a little while. Leila justified the alarming pile of food she put on her plate by telling herself that she'd been on basically starvation rations for the last few weeks, and so overindulging now certainly wasn't going to make much of a difference.

Malik wore a small smile as he watched her eat, but he didn't comment, possibly because he, too, did some serious damage to the bowl of eggs and the plate of bacon. Did djinn have to worry about their weight? Probably not; they seemed to be pretty perfect physical specimens, as far as she'd been able to tell.

Once she'd slowed down a little, she asked, "You can conjure any food you want, just like that?"

"Yes, as long as the components for that food exist somewhere. We djinn cannot make something out of nothing, but the world is rich, and we can use what is already here."

That made sense. In a way, it helped to know he wasn't just snapping his fingers and pulling this stuff out of thin air. "The wine, too?"

His smile broadened. "Not that. What was left here in the house is more than sufficient to our needs."

She couldn't argue with that, not after the exquisite Bordeaux they'd shared the night before. "But you could if you wanted to. You could just snap your fingers and have a '61 Chateau Lafitte Rothschild appear here on the table, right?"

A snap of his fingers, and a dusty bottle sat on the table before her, an incongruous contrast to the plates of breakfast food that occupied the same space. She peered at the label. Yes, that was definitely the wine she'd requested.

"It did not have to come so very far," Malik said in reply to her astonished silence. "One of the neighbors down the street had it in his cellar. But I could have summoned it from the other side of the world if necessary."

Right then, Leila was glad she was already sitting down. Oh, she'd known Malik possessed otherworldly powers, or he wouldn't have been able to blink her here from that alley in Highland Park, but between the wine and the breakfast, she wondered how much more he could do. She was afraid to ask.

Instead, she murmured, "Impressive," and took another bite of her toast, partly to cover up her confusion.

"It is part of what we are," he said. "Nothing more, nothing less. Certain powers have been granted us, but we certainly are not gods, or anything close to it."

Could the djinn die? They were living, breathing creatures, and so one would think that was always a possibility, but Leila couldn't know for sure—and again, that was a question she really didn't want to ask.

Voice softer, he added, "There is nothing I would not get for you, if you requested it of me."

Blood rushed to her cheeks, but she made herself say, her voice level, "I'm not sure there's anything I need, thanks to that closet full of clothes you gave me."

"Material comforts," he replied, giving a negligent wave of one hand. "What is something you *really* want?"

What did she really want? For things to go back to the way they were, she supposed, although she knew that was impossible. She couldn't ask for Malik to let her go, because she knew as well as he did that she would be vulnerable to pursuit from the bad djinn as soon as she was no longer under his protection.

But there was one thing, one request she could make. Something that had been preying on her mind ever since the world had died silently, shuddering out its last breath as its inhabitants burned out their lives in a fever that was nuclear hot. She'd never been able to check for herself, because the distance was far too great to even think about covering on her own, but now she had Malik to help her.

Meeting his dark eyes directly, she said, "I want you to take me home."

SIX

MALIK HADN'T KNOWN WHAT LEILA WOULD request of him, but her response surprised him nonetheless. For a second or two, he could only stare at her, not quite sure what she was asking. "You want to go home to Highland Park? You know that's not possible."

"No, not there," she said with a wave of her hand. "I'm not talking about going back to stay. I know it isn't safe. I meant that I wanted you to take me home to Irvine, to the house where I grew up. I need to see it for myself. I—" She stopped there and drew in a small, hitching breath, as though she was attempting to hold back a sob. Indeed, her dark blue eyes did look suspiciously bright. "I need to know that they're really gone. Can you do that for me, Malik?"

Of course he could. He deemed the journey safe enough, for there were no other settlements of djinn in that area. Down the coast in Laguna Beach, yes, and then another a hundred miles away and more in San Diego, but none in Irvine, the sprawling suburban town where Leila had grown to adulthood.

"Yes," he said. "It will be no problem. But what precisely are you hoping to find?"

Her fingers played with the handle of the fork where it rested next to her plate. "Closure," she said simply.

How he wished he could take her in his arms and offer her comfort, for he could tell that she was still fighting to maintain control. Clearly, the thought of what she might find worried her, and yet she needed to confront it.

He could understand that. In fact, he was glad of her need to confront her past, because once she had done so, he hoped she would be able to face her future—her future with him. They could move on together.

"Very well," he said. "You wish to go now?"

"If that's all right." She pushed her empty plate away, then put her napkin on the table. "I couldn't eat another bite anyway."

Malik was feeling quite full as well. Normally he did not eat so much in the morning, preferring to have larger meals at other times of the day, but he had consumed a healthy helping of eggs and bacon so as to keep Leila company. Despite her subdued expression, he thought the big breakfast had done well for her, as her cheeks had a warm, healthy color to them, and already some of the hollow-eyed thinness he'd noted when he confronted her in the alley was beginning to disappear. He would have to make sure she ate well so she might return to her healthy, happy self.

He waved his hand over the table, and all the dirty dishes instantly disappeared. Leila's mouth opened slightly in astonishment. "Where did they go?"

"They have all been cleaned and returned to their proper places on the cupboard shelves," he replied as he stood. Leila rose as well, shaking her head.

"That's convenient. I would have killed to be able to do that sort of thing back when I was a kid and got stuck with kitchen duty."

It was such a small thing, Malik was almost embarrassed to have Leila take such note of it. He stepped away from the table and extended a hand to her. "I will have to hold you, so you might travel with me as I journey in the djinn way."

Her expression sobered. From the careful, measured way she came over to him, he could tell she wasn't overly thrilled about having to get this close. And yet, he sensed no fear in her, no revulsion for what he was. It was more that she wasn't entirely sure of her own responses to him, and therefore preferred to keep her distance until she was able to sort out her feelings.

That would have to wait until later, however, because the only way Malik could have her travel in the blink of an eye was for him to hold her firmly. She stepped closer, let him wrap his arms around her waist. This was probably the closest he would get to that kiss he had wanted to steal from her, although he told himself not to enjoy their proximity too much. The last thing he wanted was to startle her, make her attempt to draw away from him at an inopportune moment.

Still, he allowed himself to relish the feel of her slender waist, breathe in the sweet scent of her hair. The djinn could not travel to places they had not visited before, or at least seen, but that was no impediment here. He had come to see Leila's childhood home when he was watching over her, trying to decide whether or not to make her his Chosen. Therefore, it was easy enough to summon the image to his mind of the large two-story house with the well-grown trees around it, slender pines and tall white-barked eucalyptus, and what once had been a well-tended lawn but was now probably yellow and dead. Nothing anywhere close to as lavish as the house where the two of them now resided, but still the sort of place where comfortable, prosperous people lived.

Within the next instant, they stood on the sidewalk in front of the house. As soon as her feet touched the pavement, Leila let go of Malik. He had been expecting her to do that very thing, and yet he still experienced a stab of disappointment when she withdrew her arms from around his waist and took a few steps away from him. Her jaw tightened as she looked at the dry, weed-infested lawn.

"My father would never have let it get like this," she murmured.

Sensing that she didn't expect him to reply, Malik held himself to one side and watched as she turned away from the house so she could survey the rest of the cul-de-sac where it was located. All of the front yards showed similar signs of neglect, but, unlike some of the other mortal neighborhoods he had visited after the Heat had done its work, there were no abandoned vehicles in the middle of the road, no signs of a hasty attempt to flee the sickness.

"I suppose we'd better go inside," Leila said next.

He made no protest. If she wanted to see this,

so be it. At least she would not be doing so all alone, would have him there with her.

Then again, perhaps she did not find his presence as comforting as he hoped she did. Malik did not much wish to consider that possibility, for he wanted her to be comfortable with him, to see him as a source of solace.

He followed her up the front walk. She touched her fingers to the aged-bronze door latch. "It's locked."

An easy enough thing for him to manage. He reached out and pressed down on the latch, and the door swung inward a few inches.

She cast a surprised glance up at him, then gave a resigned little shrug. "I suppose I should have expected that."

Without waiting for him to reply, she pushed the door open all the way and went inside. Malik followed a few paces behind her, taking in his surroundings. The entryway and the living room just beyond it boasted very high ceilings, probably at least twenty feet tall. The floor was pale tile in the entry, but turned to hardwood in the living room and the dining room just beyond that.

Everything was covered in a fine layer of dust, but he could tell the furniture had once been good, understated and spare but of high-quality materials. The walls had an eclectic collection of art, including a very fine page from an illuminated manuscript picked out in gold leaf.

Leila must have noticed his attention because she said, "My grandparents gave them that as a wedding present. It was one of the few things they were able to smuggle out of Iran."

Malik nodded. "It must have been difficult to start over in a new place."

"It was. My grandfather was a doctor in Iran, but he had to do general office work for five years before he could get his license reinstated so he could practice here." Leila paused, her attention focused on the painting—probably so she wouldn't have to look directly at him. "But he was never bitter. He was proud of what he was able to do here, always said that America was the grandest country in the world."

Now it was impossible to ignore the glitter of tears in her eyes. Once again Malik wished he could hold her close, allow her to weep for all she had lost. "Did your grandparents live here in Irvine as well?"

"Yes. Their house is over in University Park, though. It's smaller than this one, but my grandparents were proud of it as well." Leila swallowed, then reached up to touch the pad of her ring finger against the outer corner of one eye, trying to catch a tear before it fell down her cheek. "They bought it for cash with the money they brought out of Iran with them. Of course, back in the seventies you could still buy a house here for less than a hundred grand. Anyway," she went on, "I guess we'd better go upstairs."

Malik didn't argue. He hadn't seen any signs of the pale gray dust that signaled a human had died of the Heat in a particular spot, which meant Leila's parents had most likely perished in their bed, if they had been home at all. The symptoms of the disease came on quickly, but they usually allowed enough time for its victims to reach their homes before the truly virulent phase took hold.

She went up first, with him following a step or two behind her. Up on the second floor were four bedrooms, although one of them appeared to have been used as a study or office, judging by the bookshelves that lined the walls and the large desk with the now-dark computer sitting on it.

Leila ignored that room, however, and the one next to it, instead going to the end of the hall. The door to that room stood open as well.

At first, it didn't appear as if anything had been disturbed. The bedclothes were turned back, true, but everything else was neat and in order, from the line of perfume bottles on the dresser to the gold earrings and necklace that lay in a dish on one of the nightstands.

It was only when he drew close that Malik could see the small piles of gray dust on the pillows, the larger ones on the sheets below those pillows. From what he could tell, Leila's parents had died here together. That was something, he supposed, although he knew the Heat caused such a dreadful fever that the delirium it brought on probably would have prevented either of them from realizing they weren't alone after all.

Leila stood there for a long moment, hands clenched at her sides as she stared down at the bed. Malik said nothing; he guessed that she must know precisely what those small piles of gray ash meant.

When she spoke, her voice was hard, tight, barely sounding like herself at all. "I should have known. That is, I think I did know. I didn't want to believe it, but I knew."

"I am sorry," Malik said, although he didn't know for certain whether she would want to hear those words from him, a djinn.

A lift of her shoulders. "You didn't kill them. I mean, you probably knew the people who killed them, but that isn't the same thing, is it?" She turned toward him, anger and sorrow making her lovely features appear more like a mask than her true countenance. "Malik, tell me it isn't, or I don't know how I'll be able to stand looking at you."

Anger moved in him as well, but not at her. No, it was directed solely at the twisted minds who had thought this was the only solution that would allow them to call Earth their home once again. "It is not the same thing," he said quietly. "I knew none of them personally, and none of them came from my clan. That may be cold comfort to you, but it is the only comfort I can offer."

"It's…something." She stood there, looking at him, but it seemed more that she was looking *through* him, perhaps attempting to seek out those who had caused such destruction. Or perhaps she was merely imagining this same scene replicated in her grandparents' home.

He went to her then, took her in his arms. At first she stiffened, and he worried that she would attempt to push him away, wriggle out of his embrace, but then her head was pillowed on his bare chest, her hair soft against his skin. He bent and touched his lips to the top of her head. "Leila, let me take you from this place. Let me take you home."

She didn't argue at his use of the word "home." Perhaps she was in shock, or perhaps her sorrow wouldn't allow her the strength to fight him. At any rate, she gave a quiet nod, and so he tightened his arms around her, then blinked them back to the house in Malibu, out to a part of the parklike grounds where she could stand on green grass and be surrounded by trees, and let some of the abundant life there help to drive the visions of death from her mind.

To his surprise, she didn't attempt to pull away from him right away. Perhaps she needed the comfort of someone—anyone—at this time, even if that comfort was offered by a djinn. She stood there for a long moment, quiet in the circle of his arms, then raised her head and looked around at the trees, at the carefully clipped hedges. He had made sure the grounds here would suffer no degradation simply because there was no longer a staff of humans to maintain them, and so everything looked much the same as it had when the Heat first began.

"Where are we?" Leila asked.

"As I said, home," Malik replied. "You have not seen this part of the grounds yet—that is all."

She was silent again, looking around them. The sea breeze caught at her loose hair, blowing wavy tendrils over her shoulders. Tears still glittered in her eyes, but he thought she would not allow them to fall. "It's beautiful," she said at last.

So are you, he thought, although he kept those words to himself. He did not think she would appreciate compliments now, with her sorrow fresh in her mind. "I do like to walk here among the trees. It helps to clear the mind, I think."

"Thank you for bringing me here." She drew in a deep breath, then shut her eyes for a moment. "I'm not—I don't know what I should do next."

He touched her hand, wrapped his fingers in hers. "You don't have to do anything. But I would suggest walking with me over to the pool. There you can sit in the sun for a while, and take as much time to rest as you need."

Her fingers tightened against his. When she looked up at him, her eyes were the same deep, dark blue as the wild Pacific, now hidden by the trees of the grove where they stood. "Will you sit with me, Malik?"

A rush of hope went through him at her question. He had feared she would want to be alone, would not wish to have a djinn anywhere near her as she fought to face the very real confirmation of her worst fears. Surely she must have known her parents weren't still alive, but it was one thing to hold such a belief in one's mind, and quite another to be confronted with concrete evidence.

"Yes," he said, heart swelling with relief at her request, "I will sit with you."

Even through her closed eyelids, Leila could see the reddish glare of the sun, bright and warm. It beat down on her, soothing, returning some heat to her chilled limbs. There was no reason for her to be cold, not on a bright sunny day that could have been an advertisement designed to entice snowbirds from Illinois and Michigan to Southern California for the winter, but after standing in the house where she'd grown up, seeing what had become of her parents, she'd been overtaken by a chill that would take the hottest sun to dispel.

The chaise longue next to her creaked as Malik shifted his weight. He'd brought her here to lie down by the pool, to bake in the sunshine. On the table that separated the two chaises was a pitcher of iced tea he'd conjured from somewhere, but Leila had only taken a few sips before she lay back and closed her eyes. If God was merciful, He'd let her sleep, let her forget what she'd just seen. Then again, if God was merciful, He wouldn't have allowed any of this to happen in the first place, would He?

She let out a sigh and hoped the sound of the breeze ruffling the fronds of the palm trees around them would be enough to drown out the sound. Maybe it wasn't such a good idea to be lying here with her eyes shut. For all she knew, Malik had changed his position on his lounge so he could lie in a better position to watch her.

That seemed to settle it. She pushed herself up to a sitting position, ostensibly to reach for her glass of iced tea and take a sip, but more so she could check to see what the djinn was doing. To her relief, he lay flat on his back, the silken folds of his robe falling away to either side and exposing the hard, flat contours of his stomach and the strongly muscled expanse of his chest.

Leila forced herself to look away, to hold the glass of iced tea and pretend to be staring out to sea. She thought she spied the smallest smudge on the horizon. One of the Channel Islands? She'd never spent any real time in Malibu, except for one excursion when she and a group of friends had driven along Pacific Coast Highway and then stopped at Gladstone's for crab legs and grilled swordfish. That brief trip hadn't been enough to give her any kind of familiarity with the area, so she couldn't say for sure whether there were any islands visible from Malibu's coast or not.

Malik's chaise longue creaked again, this time so he could push himself up to a sitting position, just as she had. Just the briefest of glances in her direction, as if to ascertain her mood, and then he seemed to follow her gaze out to sea.

"The weather will remain fine for some time, although a storm will be here in a few days," he said before reaching to pick up his own glass of tea.

"It's hard to believe," she replied as she looked up at the bright blue sky, at the gulls circling over the seashore hundreds of feet below them.

"Ah, but it's out there, a thousand miles away. We will have sunshine for now, however." He paused, then said, still with his gaze fixed on the horizon, "I am here, if you want to talk."

She really didn't. About all she could do was shrug as she drank once more from her iced tea. Just as well that there wasn't anything alcoholic added to it, but at the same time, she thought she could use a drink. If she asked, would Malik conjure a pitcher of margaritas, or maybe a couple of daiquiris, complete with little paper umbrellas?

Better not to. Leila didn't know what time it was, but she guessed it was barely noon. If she started drinking now, she'd be a mess before the day was half over.

"What is there to talk about?" she said in response to Malik's offer. "I knew it was a chance in a million that they could have survived. The same for my brother, I suppose."

"You haven't spoken of him very much."

No, she hadn't, because she really didn't know

what she could say. They emailed occasionally, but he had his life and she had hers. She knew he hadn't spoken to their parents for more than six months. There had been a blowout at Christmas, one so bad that he'd gotten up from the table and walked out before their father had even finished carving the turkey.

"Dylan was...." Leila let the words trail off because she was searching for a way to explain her brother to Malik without sounding as though she was making excuses for him. Also, her own feelings were more conflicted than she really wanted to admit. She'd expended so much energy during her childhood and high school years trying to watch out for Dylan that she'd felt guilty for going away to school, even if it was just to UCLA, and guiltier still for settling in Los Angeles after she graduated rather than returning to Orange County. "Dylan was really brilliant. All those tests —genius IQ. And he could paint like you wouldn't believe. He was accepted to Art Center in Pasadena, Otis Parsons, a couple of other places I can't remember." She paused there, wondering if the djinn even knew what those schools had been...not that it mattered now. "He was also gay, and bipolar. You know what that is?"

"He preferred the company of other men, and was manic-depressive?"

Somehow it sounded so much harsher when phrased that way. And while Leila supposed she could have attempted to explain the DSM-V definition of bipolar disorder and why manic-depressive really wasn't a good description of the condition, right then she felt like she didn't have the energy. "Yes," she said. "My parents were good people, but they could never handle Dylan very well. They fought all the time, mostly because he struggled with taking his medications when he was supposed to or showing up to appointments with his therapist. I know they were still supporting him, though. Financially, I mean. He'd finally ended up going to Art Center and was living in Altadena when—well, when all this happened. I kept thinking I might run into him, since Altadena was right next to Pasadena, and we were hiding in Caltech for a while, but...."

"I am sorry," Malik said. "No, I am sure he would not have survived the Heat. Those who designed the disease made sure there was no genetic factor involved, for they did not want families to survive together and thus be stronger. I think what they did not take into account was how you mortals make your own families when the people of your blood have been taken away."

How true that was. Leila thought of Tyrell, tall, strong Tyrell, who never seemed to let anything ruffle him, no matter how bad the situation got. Macy and Jack, both of whom had been students at Caltech, and Allan, who'd worked at JPL. Pretty Taylor, and Jared, who could start a fire from nothing and had once been an Eagle Scout. And fiercely independent Bailey, who—perhaps inspired by her name—had bailed out early, saying she hated skulking in the dark and would find a way to survive on her own. She'd left the group, and Leila had no idea what had happened to her. Surely she must be dead by now, though. All of them had created a family out of necessity, out of their desire to survive.

All gone now. All of them.

She didn't even realize she was crying until she felt the tears sliding down her cheeks. Why they had come now, and not when she was standing next to the bed where her parents had died, Leila didn't know. But then she felt strong hands taking hers, lifting her from the chaise, and in the next moment she was folded into Malik's arms.

He'd held her before, but this time she burrowed her head into his chest, taking some much-needed comfort from the strength of the muscles she felt beneath her cheek. In all the time she'd been with Tyrell's group, she'd never gotten close to anyone—hadn't allowed herself to, because she knew how precarious their situation was. She'd already lost too much. If she'd let herself care about any of them as anything more than companions in survival, the pain of losing them would have been even more unbearable.

Did this mean she had begun to care for Malik? No, that was a ridiculous notion. She barely knew him. She was only letting him hold her now because she desperately needed to feel as though she wasn't alone. Besides, she didn't have to worry about losing Malik—more the opposite. He had chosen her. If either of them was going to walk away from the other person, it would not be him.

She felt him kiss the top of her head, very gently, almost as though he didn't want her to know what he had done. Rather than stiffening in surprise, she pushed closer to him. This was good. She'd forgotten how good it felt to be held by someone...even if that someone happened to be a djinn.

Although she wondered whether he was going to bend down and kiss her on the mouth, apparently he didn't seem inclined to push things. His hand passed over her hair, warm and heavy and strangely reassuring, and then he let go of her, taking a step back. Dark eyes searched her face, as though looking for a sign as to whether he'd overstepped, cautious and gentle as the embrace had been.

"Thank you, Malik," she said, and meant it. She knew it was probably crazy to feel comforted by his presence, but she was. With him near, she wasn't alone. Everyone else might be gone, but he had been protecting her this whole time, even if she'd been too blinded by her own fear to realize it. Still, she knew she needed some time alone, some time to come to terms with all that he'd told her…and also, to attempt to decide what she should do about these strange feelings he seemed to arouse in her.

"Is it all right if I go walk on the beach for a bit?" she asked. "I promise I won't go far."

Expression somber, he nodded. "Of course. You are safe here. Walk as far as you like. If you follow the path through the garden, it will take you to a set of stairs that leads down to the beach."

Trying to ignore the flicker of disappointment in his eyes, she said, "I won't be long."

Then she turned and walked away from him, and hoped she hadn't just done exactly the wrong thing by rejecting his company.

SEVEN

MALIK WATCHED HER WALK AWAY AND MADE no move to stop her. Somehow he knew that if he did not give her this time now, she would never come to a place where she would accept him. It was difficult, for every vein in his body seemed to pulse with need for her, but he made himself go inside the house. If she caught a glimpse of him watching her when she thought she was supposed to be alone, she would never forgive him. After all, hadn't he just told her that she was safe here? What reason would he have for observing her, unless it was to protect her from some kind of danger?

He wished there was something more he could do to show her that he meant her no harm. Yes, she must realize that he had brought her to a place of shelter, that he had kept the other djinn from pursuing her and making her yet another victim, but he didn't know whether that was enough. Unfortunately, he feared that all he could do was allow her enough time to grieve, and hope she would at last come to a place of, if not acceptance, then understanding.

In the meantime, he walked through the empty rooms of the house he had borrowed, whisking away some dust here, summoning flowers to fill a vase there. Whatever he could think of to make this place a sanctuary for the woman he had chosen, small touches she might not even notice consciously, but might help to soothe her soul. Once it was calm enough, perhaps she would find herself reaching out to him just as he longed to reach out to her.

For now that he had held her, he could think only of how much he wanted to embrace her again, to feel her slender body in his arms, to sense the fierce energy of her spirit. It was that spirit which had kept her running, even though she must have wondered, in the depths of those long, dark nights spent in hiding, whether such an existence was truly worth the effort.

He had to hope she would come to realize that her life was worth a great deal...and that he wanted to make sure it was as rich and rewarding as she deserved.

———

The wind caught at her hair, wild and heavy with salt. It felt good to breathe in the sea air, to give herself the luxury of a solitude that didn't consist of stolen minutes spent in hiding.

Even so, all the salt air in the world couldn't quite get rid of the ache she felt now, the one that seemed to have lodged itself firmly under her breastbone. She'd known her family must have been gone, but....

At least her parents had died together. That was something—what they'd always wanted, really. They used to make jokes about not outliving each other so neither of them would have to go on alone after the other one was gone. Somehow she'd known that if one of them passed away before the other, the parent remaining wouldn't last for very long.

It bothered her far more to wonder what had happened to Dylan. Of course he wouldn't have been anywhere near Irvine when the Heat struck —he would have been at his apartment in Altadena, or possibly in a class at Art Center. She hadn't been completely aware of his schedule there toward the end, although she knew he'd cut back on his classes because his medication made him feel foggy and not always able to concentrate, to create. That was why he skipped taking his meds sometimes, and although Leila would argue with him about ignoring the medication that made him even remotely functional, she couldn't really blame him. If their situations had been reversed, would she have acted any differently?

But she knew Dylan's death would haunt her, like the ending of a book she'd never finished. She supposed she could have Malik take her to Dylan's apartment, but if she didn't find any evidence of her brother being there, she still wouldn't have any true closure. Maybe in a way this was better. She could imagine him surviving, even though Malik had said the odds of that happening were very low. Survival was a one-in-a-million thing, and since she'd escaped the Heat unscathed, the chance of anyone else in her family sharing that immunity was pretty much nil.

She paused at the water's edge, watching the waves come up just to barely touch her toes before receding. The air temperature was mild enough that she could almost imagine the world was still caught in the tail end of summer, but she knew better. That water held its own chill, a reminder that winter was soon to come.

And what would that winter be like? From the way Malik and his sister Fatima had talked, it sounded as though he had until the first of the year to live here at the house with his Chosen, a little more than a month to convince Leila that she needed to settle into this new life with him. Was that time enough? She honestly didn't know. Her body's response to him was obvious, but a lifetime of forever needed a little more than simple lust.

All right, then. He was gentle and kind, and yet somehow proud and passionate as well. An interesting combination. Just the idea of Malik was entrancing in its way, an immortal godlike being who wanted to make her his own. Almost like something out of a fairytale, although even the grimmest Grimm story didn't involve the premeditated deaths of billions of people.

Not Malik's doing, of course. But still....

She walked back over to the base of the stairs, then paused so she could slip her sandals back on. It had been too difficult to walk in the sand while wearing them, but she needed the shoes now to protect her feet from the rough cement as she made the steep climb back up to the house.

And after that? She honestly had no idea.

Leila came back inside, windblown and more beautiful than ever to Malik's eyes. She asked for a glass of water, and he fetched one for her from the kitchen, although he could have summoned it from thin air if he'd wanted. Somehow, though, he thought it better to show how he wanted to make an extra effort for her.

If she noticed, she gave no sign. She thanked him absently, then went upstairs to her room. And when he knocked hours later, close to the time when many mortals chose to take their evening meal, she told him she would like a tray, if it wasn't too much trouble.

Of course it was no trouble at all, except that he did not see how they could grow any closer if she did all she could to hide herself from him. But he reminded himself that she had suffered great losses, and he must be patient, and so he conjured a tray of grilled fish and vegetables and rice, and left it on the floor outside her door.

This went on for several days. Malik wished she would talk to him, but she seemed determined to work through her struggles on her own, and he already knew that trying to impinge on her soli-tude would only make her withdraw that much more. He did his best to remain patient, although he was all too aware of time passing, of how this window in which she would be allowed to accustom herself to her new situation was closing ever further. But even with that growing sense of urgency, he understood he could do nothing but wait.

From time to time, she would emerge and go walk in the garden, or down by the ocean. The library in the house contained a great many books, and she would fetch herself one from time to time, so he knew that must be how she also spent some of her mornings and afternoons. Her attitude was not cold—no, she would smile at him and thank him for the meals he provided, but she did little more than that. It was as if she thought she needed to allow a certain number of days to pass before she felt comfortable spending any time in his presence.

At last, though, she came to him on a bright morning, one where the warm winds from the east had blown across the city yet again, and suggested that he accompany her when she walked on the beach. What change of heart had brought her to this moment, Malik couldn't say, but of course he accepted her invitation with alacrity, following her as she led him from the house and across the gardens, and finally down the long white sand beach, with the gulls calling overhead.

Ah, yes, this was what he had dreamed of when he imagined his future life with Leila. He knew they couldn't stay here in Malibu, not forever, but he would cherish this time at the shore while he could.

She'd taken off the silvery sandals she wore and hitched up her long embroidered skirt so she could walk along the waterline without getting the hem wet. Her feet and ankles were slender and lovely, just like the rest of her. And he loved the way the ocean breeze caught her long, dark hair and blew it around her like a cloud of silk.

Most of all, he loved remembering the way she had felt in his arms when he'd held her after their journey to Irvine, the sweet scent of her hair as he'd bent to kiss the crown of her head. In the days since, he hadn't dared to attempt anything like that again, since she'd seemed so distant, and he couldn't know how more overt advances might be received. That day, she'd gone into his arms more out of a need for comfort than anything else —not that he blamed her for seeking reassurance. When confronted by the reality of her parents' deaths, she'd needed someone to offer some kind of solace. If that solace was offered by a djinn, well, better that than nothing.

The clouds on the horizon were closer now, but not so close that they risked blotting out the bright sun overhead, now moving toward the west as it continued on its daily journey. Some rain would be a good thing, soaking land that was now parched after several days of the hot, dry winds the former inhabitants of this region had called the Santa Anas. And it would be good to be safely inside with Leila, listening to the rain fall on the roof. Perhaps a fire in the living room's enormous hearth, a good bottle of wine…who knew what might happen next, now that she seemed to have begun to soften toward him?

"Look," she said, coming up to him with something clutched in one hand. She opened her fingers, revealing a large cowrie shell with a tortoiseshell pattern of spots on its surface. "I've never found one so large before."

"It's beautiful," he said. "Perhaps you were always thwarted in the past because other beach-combers found the choice shells before you did."

The smile she'd been wearing faded as she gazed past him, toward the empty beach that stretched northward to the next promontory. "Yes, I suppose there's not much competition anymore."

Damn, he knew he should have watched what he said. All around them were constant visual reminders of their isolation; he didn't need to open his mouth and reinforce that fact. "I've always enjoyed looking for shells along the beach," he said lamely, not sure how to save the conversation.

To his relief, the sad, distant expression left her dark blue eyes, and instead her full mouth quirked back into a half-smile. "How many beaches have you walked, Malik?"

"A good number," he said. "Although we djinn were exiled to the otherworld, we were permitted short stays here on Earth, as long as we did not abuse the privilege and attempt to make permanent homes here. I have been here in Malibu, and along Australia's Gold Coast, and the French Riviera. Cape Cod, and Cape Town. There were very many beautiful places to see."

Her eyebrows lifted. "A real world-traveler, then. I'm jealous—the farthest afield I ever made it was Hawaii one year in high school, and then to Cancun for spring break when I was in college." Her lovely features thoughtful, she looked out to sea, as though visualizing the distant lands that lay far behind the horizon. "I don't suppose I'll get to see anywhere else now."

A pang went through him at the note of regret in her voice. Did he dare reach out and take her hand? Almost hesitant, he stepped closer to her and wrapped his fingers around hers. She didn't flinch or try to move away, and he let out a relieved breath. "No, I fear not. The communities of djinn and Chosen were set up to keep them apart from the rest of the djinn, and that means traveling beyond them, except perhaps to other djinn settlements or areas nearby those settlements, is not allowed."

She was silent for a moment, appearing to absorb what he'd said. Fingers still clasped in his, she asked, "What of all those other djinn? What are they going to do with themselves, now that the world is theirs?"

Malik had expected her to ask this question at some point. Still, he knew he would not much enjoy giving her the answer. "Once they know the Earth is truly…cleansed…then each of them will go to settle on his or her lands. The elders have determined who will live where. I do not know much about that, because once I had decided to make you my Chosen, I did not pay much attention to where the others would make their homes."

"They'll live by themselves? Don't djinn get married and have families?"

"Not in the way you mortals did," he replied. "Of course we reproduce, or else I would not be standing here and speaking with you, but our families are small. It is most usual for a couple to have only one child and no others."

"But that couple aren't husband and wife?"

"No. Because of our long lives, we understand that it is not feasible or even desirable to be with one person for all of eternity. Djinn form bonds lasting for decades or even centuries sometimes, but they never last forever."

Leila was silent for a moment, clearly pondering his words. A small pucker of a frown pulled at her eyebrows as she asked, "If that's how you djinn feel about such things, then why are you supposedly with your Chosen for all time? That doesn't seem to make much sense."

Good question. Malik did not have a concrete answer for her, but he had several suspicions. "The elders never told us precisely why they stipulated that a djinn-Chosen bond must last forever. However, I think I can guess. For one thing, having saved our Chosen from death at the hands of the other djinn, it would not be precisely fair to leave them to fend for themselves if the elemental in the relationship decided that he or she did not wish to participate in it any longer." He stopped there, thinking he had already said enough.

But it seemed that Leila had guessed he had more to say on the subject. "That's the only reason?"

"The reason most djinn believe," he replied. "But I think they also did so in order to appease the djinn who wished to destroy mankind. I believe it was the elders' way of telling them that they would allow us to save some humans, but at the price of giving up our freedom for eternity. No doubt the other djinn would think that a very good joke."

"Did you think that?" Leila asked, her tone almost hesitant, as if she did not wish to hear the answer.

"No," he said at once. "When I determined that I would make you my Chosen, Leila, I understood everything such a decision entailed. And I also knew that I would never regret it."

For a moment she only stood there, her hand clasped in his, her eyes searching his face, seeking the truth there. He remained still, allowing her to make her inspection, but a faint tremor went through him. She stood so very, very close, and he had been trying so very hard to allow her the time to accept him, to accept what her new world would be.

And then she was up on her bare toes, her mouth pressing against his. A second of shock, and then he pulled her toward him, his lips touching hers, tasting the faint tang of the lemon from the iced tea she had drunk earlier that morning, and an even fainter flavor of salt from the sea spray that had misted her face as she walked along the shoreline. But then she was all sweetness and wildness as her arms went around him and tightened, holding on to him as though he was the only solid thing in her world.

Perhaps he was.

The kiss lasted for years, decades. Malik did not know for sure, just as he wasn't sure whether the pounding he heard in his ears was only the beating of the blood in his veins, or the roar of the surf on the beach. At last, though, Leila lifted her mouth from his and looked up at him with an almost sheepish expression.

"I'm not sure why I did that," she said at last.

"I am glad you did." That was severely understating his reaction, but although she had initiated the kiss this time, he still did not want to frighten her off with his ardor.

A faint lift at the corner of her mouth. "I think I am, too. I just—" The words broke off there as she slipped from his embrace and stood a pace or so away from him.

He let her go, because he knew she needed some time to gather herself. "You just what?"

"Did I only go to you right now because I still needed comfort from someone…anyone?"

A few minutes ago, he might have asked the same question, but he'd tasted the truth in that kiss. He had observed Leila for some time before the Heat transformed the world, and he knew she was not the kind of woman to give of herself lightly. No matter how afraid and alone she felt, no matter how much she still grieved for the losses she had suffered, she would not have gone into his arms if that had not been exactly what she wanted to do.

Shaking his head, he said, "I think you already know the answer to that, Leila."

She was silent for a moment, then bent to pick up the cowrie shell she had found earlier. It must have fallen from her hand when she kissed him, although he had not heard it drop to the sand. Not so surprising; that kiss had so consumed him, he rather thought he wouldn't have heard even a bolt of thunder crashing overhead.

A small smile touching her beautiful mouth, she looked up at him, the shell nestled in her palm. "Shall we find a place for this?"

The cowrie shell was given a place of honor on the mantel in the living room. Looking at it, Leila thought she could be happy here.

Don't get too attached, she told herself as Malik produced—from apparently nowhere—a couple of salads garnished with roast chicken chunks and slices of strawberry and dressed with vinaigrette. *This isn't home. It's just a…way station.*

The world's most luxurious way station, to be sure, but she had to remind herself that she and Malik couldn't stay here. Eventually, they would have to relocate to Bel-Air. Not so eventually, to be accurate; in the conversation she'd eavesdropped on, Malik's sister Fatima had said that Leila and Malik would need to be gone from Malibu by the turn of the year, less than six weeks from now.

And how crazy was it that she wanted to stay here, when only a few days before she'd wondered how in the world she could get away. Had so much about her changed in so short a time?

Apparently, it had.

Malik brought the plates of salad over to the same table where they'd had breakfast the first morning she'd spent here. The house possessed an enormous formal dining room, but that seemed like far too lofty a space for a simple meal such as this. How he'd known that she would want something light, she didn't know, but she had to appreciate his thoughtfulness.

Which is probably the last quality I'd expect from a djinn, she thought. Not that anyone could fault her for that particular assessment, given the murderous specimens she'd encountered before meeting the man who'd made her his Chosen.

Neither would she have guessed that a djinn could be such a good kisser. A little shiver went over her as she recalled the touch of his lips against hers. A good kind of shiver, the warm, tingly kind that told her she would probably be happy with a lot more than merely a kiss.

And here you were telling yourself when you first came here that you couldn't possibly allow yourself to be with him, she scolded herself. True, that was before she'd seen his kindness, his quiet strength. If she wanted to be completely honest with herself, Malik was pretty much exactly the kind of man she'd been looking for before the world went haywire. She'd had enough of flashy actors and musicians and screenwriters who said the most soulful things but who could be counted on to bail out exactly when she needed them the most—say, after a particularly painful audition or another bout of trying to patiently explain to her brother over the phone why it was so important that he not stop taking his meds.

The only good, true relationship she'd had—well, she'd sabotaged that one herself. Luke was a few years older than she, out of law school and getting started in his first real job with the California Conservation League, practicing environmental law. He'd wanted to get married. But at twenty-three and with only a year of freedom after college under her belt, she'd balked at the thought of settling down so soon. She wasn't ready for the house and the picket fence and the 2.5 children. In hindsight, she'd realized Luke hadn't wanted those things, either, at least not yet. He had enough debt from law school that buying a house was out of the question in the short term, and as for kids, well, they were expensive, too. But he'd wanted her, wanted to share his life with her, and she'd freaked out and run for the hills, and everything had kind of gone to hell after that, thanks to the parade of actors and musicians who looked good and were fun to hang out with but were never there when she needed them.

Malik, she thought, would always be there for her. He'd already proven that much in a very short span of time, proven that he was willing to wait as long as necessary. After that kiss, though, she wasn't sure she wanted to wait anymore.

She smiled at him as he settled into his chair. "This looks good."

"I believe it will be." He picked up his fork but paused, head tilted at her in question. "Do you cook?"

"Oh, God, no," she replied. "It's a good thing that you can just conjure food out of thin air the way you do. If I tried to feed us, we'd probably get poisoned."

"It is very difficult to poison a djinn," Malik said, his tone so neutral, it took Leila a moment to realize he was teasing her.

"Well, humans aren't quite so sturdy." As soon as the words left her lips, she wished she hadn't said anything. Her companion's expression went blank, and he couldn't quite meet her eyes. She guessed he must be thinking of the piles of dust they'd found at her parents' house, of all the mortals who had perished thanks to djinn intervention.

They both ate in an awkward silence for a few moments. Then Malik set down his fork so he could reach for his glass of water and take a drink. Once he was done, he said, "I would like to make a true dinner for you tonight. Would that be all right?"

Considering the quality of the food he'd fed her so far, she thought that would be much more than all right. And it couldn't hurt to have a few more days of sloth and eating whatever she wanted; she figured right now she was probably thin enough to satisfy the most critical of casting directors. If Malik kept this up, then yes, she'd need to start thinking about exercising. Running on the beach was great for your calf muscles....

But soon enough you won't be here to run on the beach, she reminded herself. *You'll be in Bel-Air, miles away from the coast.*

Leila wasn't sure she wanted to reflect on the sort of thought process that made relocation to one of the country's ritziest suburbs sound like some sort of prison sentence…especially when only a week ago the thought of being able to sleep indoors had seemed like the height of luxury.

"A dinner sounds lovely," she said. "Maybe that storm you were talking about will have come in by then, and we'll be able to listen to the rain as we eat."

"I would like that." He offered her a hesitant smile, one that made her think he was still coming to terms with the change in their relationship. Surely he must have thought that at some point she would stop holding him at arm's length, but he probably couldn't have guessed it would happen so soon.

Well, that made two of them.

Still, she had no desire to take back that kiss. It had felt right. Possibly it had been spurred on by the old notion about wanting to reach out for intimacy when confronted by death and loss, but Leila knew it was more than that. She'd wanted Malik, wanted to feel the touch of his lips against hers. The kiss was everything she'd hoped for, and far more. She couldn't remember the last time when even recalling such an embrace was enough to get her running hot and cold all over again, making her glad that she was seated demurely at the table so he couldn't see how her legs had gone shaky and weak with desire.

This certainly wasn't normal behavior for her, but she found she didn't mind too much. In a way, she appreciated being able to indulge her attraction to him. She wouldn't have to worry about him standing her up or leaving her for another woman. No, because she was his Chosen, his faithfulness was pretty much a given. There was something to be said for that kind of constancy.

"Is there anything in particular you would like to have for dinner?" he asked then, pulling her out of her reverie.

"You can surprise me," she said. "I'm not picky. Only no sushi, please. I'm probably the only wannabe actress in L.A. who couldn't stand the stuff, but I just could never get into it, no matter how hard I tried."

"I understand. It's nothing I would have selected, either. I will surprise you, but not with raw fish."

She grinned at him, and he returned her smile. Yes, the pain was still buried down there, an ache of loss that might never truly go away, but Leila hoped that the kiss she'd shared with Malik was the first step to moving forward, to accepting this new world and the new life she would have in it. She reminded herself that her parents had died in their own bed, next to each other. They hadn't been alone in the end.

That was something. It had to be.

EIGHT

THE DAY GREW DARKER AS THE CLOUDS
rolled in, the bright sun that shone down on their
kiss now hidden behind a blanket of somber gray.
Malik found he didn't mind so much, because he
could also feel the approaching moisture, the rain
that would bring some relief to Southern California's parched hillsides.

He'd told Leila that he wished to take care of
all the preparations, and informed her that she'd
have to find something to amuse herself for a few
hours. Doing so didn't appear to be much of a
hardship for her, because she'd gone exploring and
discovered that the house possessed its own movie
theater, a little jewel box of a viewing room that
could seat up to twenty people. Of course the two

of them had no need to accommodate that many, but it was still enough to keep Leila occupied, especially when she announced that the former owner of the house must have been a producer of some sort, since she'd located a stack of "screeners" while poking around in the media room.

What a "screener" was, Malik couldn't be sure, but he was glad to see her so happy. He was also pleased with all the pieces he collected as he was preparing the dining room for their special dinner —elegant china from England, a beautiful ivory silk damask tablecloth to cover the long walnut table, heavy silverware in an intricate pattern to complement the embossed gold leaf on the dishes. Fine crystal goblets for the wine, and a grouping of large silver candlesticks to march their way down the table. It, too, could have seated several dozen people, but he chose to ignore that large unused expanse and concentrated on the place settings he put at one end.

He had just conjured into being a large centerpiece of lilies and roses, all in shades of cream and ivory, when the first drops of rain began to fall outside. They pattered gently on the flagstone walkway, made little plinking noises as they hit the koi pond just outside the window, and he smiled. Good. He had wanted this dinner to feel intimate and cozy, and he thought there was nothing cozier than being warm and safe inside while the rain fell outdoors.

There had been no rain in the otherworld, no precipitation of any kind. Malik could feel the air grow richer because of the moisture it now contained, and he pulled in a deep breath. Yes, that was better. This Southern California was quite a dry place, not usually the sort of setting a water elemental would seek out. He had his eye on several places in Bel-Air that had water features and ponds in addition to a swimming pool and spa, and he hoped that Leila would care enough for one of those houses to accept it as her new home.

First things first, though. He had an idea how this evening would end, if the fire in Leila's kiss had been any indication, but he did not want to presume too much. It would be better to seal their connection to one another before he began any talk of relocation. There was still plenty of time, and Fatima had been informed of the delicacy of the situation. She would allow him to let matters with Leila proceed naturally…as long as they did not drag out for too long.

Now that the dining room was arranged to his satisfaction, he went into the kitchen and stood in the middle of the large space, arms crossed, brow furrowed in thought. He wanted to make sure that the dinner he created for Leila would be something memorable, and yet he also did not wish to serve anything too heavy, not when he hoped the evening might end with her in his arms.

No red meat, then. A pity, because he tended to prefer that sort of dish, but they could indulge themselves with a main course of that type later on. Chicken was far too prosaic, but some kind of game bird might work—duck or quail, perhaps. Yes, he thought quail would do quite well, with a stuffing he'd had once long ago, wild rice and golden raisins and subtle seasonings. Vegetables basted with balsamic vinaigrette and grilled, and a good crusty bread to go on the side. For dessert, crème brulée with fruit…or would she prefer something chocolate? No, again, that could wait for a heavier meal.

Satisfied with the menu, he blinked himself down to the wine cellar and began perusing the ranks of gleaming bottles that lined its walls. The air was much cooler here, held to a perfect constant temperature so that the precious wine would come to no harm. With a game bird, rosé seemed the best pairing. Luckily, it seemed the home's former owner had an affinity for that style of wine, as there were several cases' worth of the pale pink alcohol. He selected a pinot-based rosé from the Rhone, and blinked himself back up to the kitchen so he might stow it in the wine refrigerator there until the time came to drink it.

He glanced at the clock on the stove. Time mattered little to djinn, but he knew that mortals tended to appreciate set schedules, especially when it came to their mealtimes. But he was relieved to see that the time was now nearly seven o'clock, a good hour for the evening repast.

A quick glance into the dining room told him that everything was in readiness. He visualized their meal down to its last detail, and the various dishes materialized on the table, their savory aromas drifting up to his nose and making him smile.

He was just about to go search for Leila when she appeared at the entrance to the dining room. Clearly, she hadn't spent all her time away watching films, because she had changed into one of the dresses Fatima had included in her wardrobe, this one a simple gown in a dark plum color, made of finely pleated silk with a wide beaded belt that enhanced her slender waist. Her only ornament was a pair of long, heavy earrings of gold set with amethysts, but that was all she required.

No woman of the djinn had ever been as beautiful. Malik was certain of that.

After clearing his throat, he said, "Your timing is perfect, Leila. I have just put dinner on the table."

"I know," she said with a smile. "I could smell it as I was coming downstairs. That's why I headed over here instead of going back to the screening room." A pause as she looked down at the gown she wore. "It's too much, isn't it?"

"No," he replied. "It's perfect. As are you. Please—come and sit down."

She did as he requested, taking the seat to the right of the one at the head of the table. He almost protested—he'd intended to give her the place of honor—but then decided it mattered little where they sat, as long as they were next to one another. Instead, he pulled out the chair to her left and sat down.

"This all looks incredible," she said. "And it smells even better. Are those quail?"

His gaze followed hers to where their main course rested on a silver platter, garnished with greens. "Yes. Have you had them before?"

"Once, at some fancy restaurant in Santa Monica. Although these look even better."

Malik didn't know whether that was true or not, but he decided to take her remark at face value. If she was telling a white lie to make him feel more confident about the meal, he couldn't hold it against her.

He lifted the bottle of rosé from the silver ice bucket where it had been resting and filled her glass, then his. Should he offer a toast? He didn't know whether she would appreciate the gesture, that she still obviously carried the burden of her parents' deaths with her, was still mourning everyone else she had lost.

However, Leila surprised him by raising her crystal wine goblet. She tilted her head at him. "To new beginnings."

"To new beginnings," he echoed with some gusto, relieved beyond measure that she had been the one to make the gesture. By doing so, she seemed to have signaled to him that she was willing to accept what had happened in the past, since she knew she could do nothing to change it. At least, he hoped that was what she meant by making such a toast.

They clinked glasses and each took a sip. Yes, that was good, dry and smooth without a trace of residual sugar, but still with a hint of fruit. Leila seemed to approve, because she nodded and sipped again.

"That's good," she said as he carefully lifted one of the quails from its serving platter and set it on her plate. "I'd been avoiding rosé because it was suddenly the trendy thing to be drinking, but I really like this one."

"I'm glad," he replied, wondering what "trendy" had to do with wine. Either it was good, or it wasn't. Then again, there had been many nuances of modern human life he hadn't been quite able to grasp, mainly because he'd only been an observer and had never been able to truly participate in mortal society. However, he would also admit that there had been a great many things he'd never wanted to learn about humans. While some of them could be admirable, a great many did not seem concerned with much else beyond making sure they profited while others suffered.

The problem was, he knew of quite a few djinn who suffered from that same strange mental malady.

A small silence fell as they began to eat, but Malik did not find it uncomfortable. He tried to watch Leila without having her notice that he was watching her—he did not wish to make things awkward, of course, and yet he wanted to see her reaction to the food, like seeing the warmth the flickering candlelight lent to her smooth skin, or the way those same candles awoke glints of umber and russet in her dark hair.

"Have you had a lot of human food?" she asked, after she'd had several mouthfuls and then drunk some more wine to wash everything down.

"Some," he said. "This was a dish I had many years ago in Paris. But I will also admit to a certain fondness for cheeseburgers."

"Ah." Her eyes closed for a moment, lashes thick and dark against her cheeks. "It's been so long since I've had a cheeseburger. Maybe we can barbecue tomorrow night, if the storm clears out by then."

"It will," he told her, even as he reached out with his senses and felt the pattern of the storm, how it would pause over much of the coast and the Los Angeles basin for most of the night before finally moving on to the south and east. "We should wake to sunshine."

"I'd like that," she said, but there was something almost shy about the way she uttered the words, and her gaze wouldn't quite meet his.

Of course—she'd probably thought that he'd meant they would awake together. He hadn't intended to say such a thing, but he could not deny that he would enjoy it very much if they fell asleep in one another's arms, and spent the night that way.

Should he try to clarify? One glance at Leila's downcast eyes told him it was better if he let the matter alone. He would have to allow the evening to progress naturally and see where it took them. Naturally, he would like to have it guide them directly into Leila's bed, but he vowed he would allow her to take the lead. She needed to know that their becoming intimate would be her decision, and not something he had forced her into.

"I saw a fancy built-in barbecue off to one side from the pool," she went on. Clearly, she was determined to brush past the awkward moment and focus on their plans for the next day. "It might need some cleaning, but otherwise we should be in business. It's only fair that I return the favor by cooking for you."

"You barbecued a great deal?" he inquired, somewhat amused. While he knew it was a mode of cooking that many Americans enjoyed, somehow he couldn't quite imagine Leila tending burgers at a grill. Perhaps it was simply because, at the moment, she looked far more as though she should be attending an elegant party or perhaps the opera, rather than someone with experience at backyard grilling.

"Well, not lately," she admitted. "We didn't even have a barbecue at the house Tracey and I were renting. But my dad was kind of obsessed with it—he liked to grill pretty much every weekend the weather was nice. He taught me the tricks of the trade." Her expression sobered, the light in her eyes going out. She was silent for a moment, her fork toying with some bits of rice on her plate. "It's the little things like that, I guess. Knowing I'll never be going back to my parents' house for their big Memorial Day barbecue—they always kicked off summer that way. Realizing I'll never get to hear my mother laugh again, or have my father tease me about buying another pair of shoes."

"Did you have so many?" Malik asked, genuinely curious. Or rather, he asked the question because he preferred to have Leila focus on something frivolous rather than the very real losses she'd suffered.

A self-deprecating grin as she reached for her wine glass. "More than I should have, considering how much I earned as a waitress. Still, I suppose there were worse vices."

"You can have as many shoes as you like," he said. "Isn't there a place in Bel-Air that had very good shopping?"

"Beverly Hills," she corrected him. "Rodeo Drive. Is that part of your djinn community?"

"It is close enough that taking you to shop there should not present any problems." Which was true enough. While the djinn and their Chosen must have their permanent residences within the confines of Bel-Air, they were still allowed to venture forth from time to time to procure any necessary supplies. Whether the elders had had expensive shoes in mind when they included such an exception to their rules, Malik wasn't sure, but at least he knew they did not need to worry about too many restrictions on their foraging, as long as they did not abuse the privilege.

Rather than looking pleased by this prospect, Leila let out a small sigh. "I'd give up all the shoes in the world if it meant I could have my family back."

His fingers clenched in the napkin that covered his lap. "If I could make such a thing happen for you, I would. But even a djinn cannot change the past."

"I know," she said. "What the other djinn did —that's not your fault. I'm not even going to get on my high horse and say that you should have done something to stop them, because it sounds as though those of you who protested the whole thing were grossly outnumbered. Better to save some than none, I suppose."

He had thought that very same thing, although it did not sound quite as noble when uttered in such a brittle tone. And unfortunately, he could not think of what to say to Leila now that would help to heal the emotional wounds she'd suffered. Only time could do such a thing. How the other djinn managed their Chosen, Malik wasn't entirely certain. A hint of glamour, perhaps a subtle suggestion that their losses weren't quite as dreadful as they thought they were? He believed that was more than possible, but he would never do such a thing to Leila. It would be cruel to take her hurt from her, to make it seem less than it truly was. All he could do was be a companion to her, let her know she was not as alone as she perhaps thought she was.

"I wish I could have done more," he said simply, then returned to his food.

Leila's mouth tightened, but then she appeared to push the thought away, for she also picked up her fork and took a few more bites of quail. As they ate, the rain pattered against the glass, and every once in a while Malik heard a particularly strong gust of wind blow around the eaves, although overall this house was very solid and well built, and did not allow much sound from outside to enter.

After a moment, Leila laid down her fork. "I'm not sure I could eat anything else."

"Not even crème brulée and raspberries?" he

asked, relieved that she appeared willing to leave their previous topic of conversation behind.

She smiled and shook her head, pushing her hair back so her shapely shoulders were revealed in the sleeveless gown she wore. "Oh, now you're fighting dirty."

"I?" he asked, eyes widening in mock innocence. "I am merely offering a dessert. If you don't want any—"

"It's not a question of not wanting any," she cut in. "More that I'm not sure I can fit it in anywhere."

"Oh, you'd be surprised. It is quite light."

Leila sighed, apparently in surrender. "Oh, all right. I can always start running a few days earlier than I'd planned, if it comes to that."

"You're worried about your weight?" he asked, wondering how such a thing was possible. "But you are so slender."

"If only those casting agents had agreed with you," she remarked. Then she looked down at herself, at her almost impossibly tiny waist in its casing of beads. "Well, they might agree now—if they were still alive to see me. The apocalypse diet is a great way to lose weight."

Malik wondered what on earth had been wrong with those casting agents she'd mentioned. Even when he had observed her before the Heat changed the world and she'd become a fugitive, she'd still been very slender. Now she was downright thin, except for the curve of her breasts, which didn't seem to have suffered the same changes as the rest of her body.

However, he decided it was best not to argue with her. At least she hadn't declined the dessert. He waved a hand, and two ramekins of the creamy custard appeared before them, the crusts of both darkened to a perfect caramel brown, each garnished with a trio of raspberries.

"Oh, that looks wonderful," she said with a sigh. "Crème brulée was always one of my favorites."

Her words relieved him somewhat. He'd still been worried that she might have preferred chocolate, but she sounded sincere enough. "I'm glad to hear that."

She picked up her spoon and tapped against the crust of her dessert, cracking it slightly so she could get to the custard underneath. A mouthful, and then she sighed. "Oh, that's incredible."

Malik ate a mouthful as well. Yes, it was good. But then, any food he conjured would be good, because he was drawing on all the memories of his long lifetime to bring to life the dishes that had impressed him the most. But something seemed to be lacking.

Ah, of course.

He tapped his fingers against the tablecloth, and a pair of cordial glasses half-filled with a golden liquid almost the same color as the crust on the crème brulée appeared. Leila lifted an eyebrow at him.

"What's this?"

"Cream sherry. It goes very well with the crème brulée."

She reached for the petite glass, lifted it to her lips, and took a small sip. Her eyes widened slightly. "That's really good. I thought sherry was only for Victorian novels and old men drinking in stuffy-looking studies."

"Perhaps it was more popular in the past, but it does pair well with certain desserts."

Leila sipped again, then sent him a speculative look. "And you know all about that past, don't you?"

"Not all of it," he said, suddenly cautious.

"How much, though?"

Which was her way of asking, *How old are you?* Malik did not find himself particularly eager to give her an answer, though. Not because he cared how old he was, but because he feared she would.

Many, many lifetimes of men.

But he had also promised himself that he

would tell her the truth as much as was possible. Lying to her now about something that was, in the grand pattern of the world, not terribly significant would not be a good idea. Besides, she might only have a quarter-century to her name now, but she would also eventually look at centuries the way her people tended to look at decades.

"I am approximately one thousand and seventy-five years old," he said calmly before helping himself to another swallow of cream sherry. "Perhaps a little more. I have begun to lose count."

Her eyes widened. "A thou—you're joking."

"No. My people are very long-lived." He set down his cordial glass and regarded her for a moment. "Surely you already knew this about us."

"Well, it was part of the stories and legends, but—" Leila broke off there, her fingers playing with the handle of her spoon, which she'd left resting in the crème brulée ramekin. "It's just hard to believe that you're really that old. You only look around thirty, if that much."

"That is how it is with my people. Our childhoods are not so very different from those of mortals—we are born, we must go through a maturation process. Once we reach our second decade, however, we age very little. We are able to allow ourselves to age a bit more, if we prefer to look more mature, but we never grow old, not like mortals do."

She was silent for a moment, appearing to digest that information. "And it'll be the same for me, right? Isn't that what you said earlier?"

"Yes. Our Chosen will not age, and they will never get sick. They can be injured, but they can also heal far more rapidly than any mere human could possibly hope to."

"Wow." Again a small silence, and then she smiled. "Well, I suppose if I had to choose an age to get stuck at, twenty-five is a pretty good one."

He returned her smile, relieved that, after her initial moment of shock, she hadn't belabored his age, hadn't asked too many questions. True, she might still do so later on, but for the moment, she appeared willing to let the matter go.

They had both nearly finished their desserts. A subtle wave of his hand, and their glasses of cream sherry refilled themselves. Apparently the movement hadn't been quite subtle enough, though, for once again Leila cocked an eyebrow at him.

Without blinking, he said, "I thought, since we were almost finished, we could go into the living room. There's a good fire going in the hearth."

"There is?" she asked, looking surprised. "I

didn't notice it when I came past there before dinner."

"I just started it."

"Another djinn trick?"

"A talent, I suppose."

That response only brought forth another smile, followed by a shake of her head. But she set her napkin on the tabletop, then rose from her seat, gracefully snagging the cordial glass of cream sherry with her other hand as she did so. Once again Malik allowed himself to admire the graceful shape of her body in the slender silk dress she wore, one which followed all of her delicious curves without clinging to them.

They went into the living room, where indeed a fire crackled in the enormous hearth. It wasn't as though he'd had to exert himself to get it going— the fireplace was gas, after all, which meant all he'd had to do was flip a switch while he sat at the dining room table. Still, the effect was cozy enough, especially with the rain beating against the west-facing windows, moving down the glass in small rivers and rivulets. The landscape lights shone up into the palm trees, showing how they were being whipped by the wind.

Leila noticed as well; he saw her gaze slip toward the trees and then move back to the living room, warm and fire-lit. A few discreet recessed lights overhead provided some illumination, but even so, the space was dark, intimate. Without speaking, she went to sit on the couch, then lifted an inlaid marble coaster from its caddy on the coffee table and set her glass of cream sherry down on it.

Malik hesitated for a moment before he took a seat next to her. They had been nearly this close when they were sitting at the dining room table, and yet she felt far closer to him now, so close he could detect the sweet herbal scent of the shampoo she'd used, could feel the warmth radiating outward from the bare skin of her arms.

"I like this," Leila said, but her tone was thoughtful rather than confiding. "There was a fireplace in the house I was renting, but it needed to be repaired, so we could never use it. I know it's sort of an affectation in a place with a climate like Southern California's, but I always liked it when my parents would have a fire."

"I don't know if it's that much of an affectation," Malik replied. "Surely this night is cold enough to warrant one, even though it is warmer here than many places on the globe."

"You're probably right." Once more her gaze strayed toward the window. "I wouldn't want to be out in that."

No, neither would he, even though water was

his element. He preferred the warmth of the swimming pool, or even the rough waves of the Pacific, to standing out in a rainstorm and getting soaked through his garments.

It was much better to be inside with Leila.

She seemed to have noticed that his attention had moved toward her, because even in the softly lit room, he could see how pink touched her cheeks, how her breasts rose and fell as she took in a quick breath. However, she did not attempt to move away, or to utter some kind of hasty remark intended to place some distance between them.

He bent toward her, pressed his lips to hers. At once she responded, her mouth opening to his, letting him taste her. Sweet and rich and warm, just like the cream sherry they'd been drinking. Heat flowed through him, the desire he'd been doing his best to hold back flooding through him. He needed her, wanted her.

Her fingers moved through his hair, then traced their way down the back of his neck. "It's all right," she whispered. "I want—" And there she broke off, as if she thought that saying the words aloud would make them all too real.

Malik had no intention of leaving matters there, however. He kissed her again, then stroked her bare arm. A shudder went through her as he said, "Tell me what you want."

"You," she replied, eyes opening wide as her gaze met his. "I want you, Malik."

That was all he needed. Now there was no reason to wait any longer. He took in a breath, then blinked them away to her bedroom before either of them could change their minds.

NINE

It all happened so quickly, Leila was barely able to grasp what Malik had done. One moment they were sitting on the couch, and the next they were upstairs in her borrowed bedroom, with the gas fireplace there coming to life, even as the tapers in their candlesticks of inlaid ebony lit themselves. She lay on the bed, Malik's weight on top of her, and yet that weight was far from unwelcome. He felt solid and real. Could a being born of myth and legend be so very real?

He had to be, because she doubted a myth would have kissed her like this, strong and passionate, those kisses moving from her mouth to the sensitive skin of her throat. She gasped and arched against him, felt one hand touch the bare flesh of her thigh as it slipped through the slit in her dress. God, his skin was so warm…or was that only her reaction to him?

She didn't know for sure, just as she couldn't pinpoint the exact moment when he'd slipped the strap of her gown down one shoulder, exposing her breast. The dress's slender straps and low back hadn't permitted her to wear a bra under it—not that she'd hunted too hard for a piece of lingerie that might work. Maybe she hadn't been consciously planning this moment, but deep down she'd known that she and Malik would make love tonight, and so she'd left off the unnecessary undergarment.

A gasp escaped her lips as he took her nipple into his mouth, while at the same time his hand moved up her leg, found the silky edge of her panties, and slipped under them. He stroked her and she moaned, pressing against him, wanting as much of her body to be touching his as possible.

"You were ready for this, weren't you?" he murmured, fingers moving deeper.

"Ye-es," she gasped. So ready, she found herself somewhat surprised. True, it had been a while since the last time she'd had sex, but it also wasn't anything that had interested her in the slightest lately. She'd thought that part of her must have gone dormant, pushed down into oblivion after all those weeks of running and hiding. And yet it seemed that all she'd needed to come alive again was Malik's touch. Was this part of being Chosen, to have such a connection to him, or was this something else, her soul awakening to the realization that he was the one she'd been waiting for all along?

She didn't know. Did it really matter, as long as it felt as good as this? She didn't protest when he took hold of her gown and pulled it up over her head, leaving her naked before him except for the pair of black silk and lace bikini underwear she wore.

"So beautiful," he murmured, then began to trail a line of kisses from her breast down the center of her stomach, pausing so he could press his lips against her mound, breath hot through the fabric of her panties.

Leila hardly dared to breathe. Was he…?

It appeared he was, because in the next moment, he'd pulled her underwear down and flung them off to one side of the bed. Then his tongue was touching her, tasting her, and she arched her back and cried out, her fingers knotted in the heavy waves of his dark hair. Oh, God, she'd never imagined—

The orgasm came as quick and wild as the storm that raged outside the windows. Leila lost herself in that spasm, body convulsing while the waves of exquisite, agonizing pleasure rolled through her. She wouldn't try to remember how long it had been since she'd come like this, mostly because she was pretty sure she never had.

Malik kissed her again, and she could taste herself on his lips. For some reason, that only further ignited her desire, and she ground herself against him, legs wrapping around his hips. Those silk pants he wore weren't all that heavy, and she could feel his arousal, sense his need.

"One moment," he whispered, and before she could even blink, the pants were gone, along with the open robe he'd worn with them.

How magnificent he was, the heavy muscles of his arms and chest and back outlined in firelight, the candles only adding to the warmth of his smooth brown skin. However, Leila didn't have much opportunity to admire him, because at once he had pulled her against him, was pushing into her.

He was big. She felt that rather than saw it, but that was all right. In that moment, all she wanted was him buried deep inside her, their bodies joined. She needed to experience him like that, connected to her in the depths of her core, because then she knew she wouldn't have to feel alone any longer.

Their bodies rocked together, the rhythm

coming to them as naturally as if they'd been doing this for years. Leila buried her face in his shoulder and breathed in the warm, enticing scent of his skin. She didn't think he wore any cologne; that was just the delicious aroma of his flesh. Had she ever experienced anything like this before, a joining far beyond mere sex?

She didn't think so.

The rain fell and the wind howled, but in here all was heat and fire. Another climax was building within her, and she knew it was going to hit hard, possibly even harder than the first orgasm. She pulled in a breath and rode out her release, cresting it like one of the surfers who used to ride the waves on the beach somewhere outside the window. Malik shuddered and then came as well, pounding into her as the orgasm took him, too.

At last they lay quiet, still entwined, neither of them wanting to move. Finally, though, Leila kissed her djinn gently on the cheek, then slid away to the bathroom to get cleaned up. Her hair was a mess and even the minimal makeup she'd been wearing had managed to get horribly smeared, but the reflection that looked back at her from the mirror managed to be radiant anyway, still alight with the afterglow of their lovemaking.

She found a packet of makeup remover towelettes in one of the drawers and repaired the damage, then ran a brush through her hair. After that, she went into the closet and got out a fresh pair of panties from the lingerie chest before slipping into a short black silk chemise she found in one of chest's other drawers.

When she returned to the bedroom, she saw that Malik was now sitting up against the headboard, a stack of pillows protecting him from the wooden surface. His hair was tousled, but he wore a broad smile as she walked over to the bed and slipped in. At once his arm went around her, pulling her close. She leaned her head against his shoulder and let out a contented little sigh, glad to feel his warmth, his strength.

"Happy?" he asked.

There was a question. Yes, she was more than satisfied by the lovemaking they'd just shared, but after everything she'd seen in the recent past, could she truly say she was happy?

"Mostly," she replied, which was the only way she could answer his question and still be telling the truth.

To her relief, he didn't look put out by her response, but instead gave a thoughtful nod. "I can understand that. Grief fades over time, I suppose, but it never leaves us entirely."

Leila shifted slightly so she could look into his face, try to get a read on his mood from his expression. Right then he appeared thoughtful, but not in the least sad. What kind of losses could a djinn suffer, when their people were supposed to be immortal?

"We are long-lived," he said in answer to her unspoken question. "But we cannot say we are immortal, not when we can be killed. It is much more difficult to kill a djinn than it is to kill a mortal, but it is not impossible."

"You lost someone who was killed?"

"Not precisely." He played with a lock of her hair, wrapping it loosely around his forefinger and appearing to study the dark, silky strands. "We can be so long-lived that at last we can grow weary of our existence. When that occurs, a djinn may drink the *aljar al-nawim*—the draught of the dark sleep—a kind of poison that brings a gentle death with no suffering. It is hoped that by dying, one of our kind may pass into the next world, and thus begin a new life there."

For a moment, Leila was silent, doing her best to process what he had just told her. She hadn't stopped to think that long life might be a burden, something to be laid down when it could no longer be supported. "Who was it?" she asked at last.

"My father," he said. "Unlike many djinn, my parents remained together for some time after

Fatima and I had grown to adulthood and their obligation to their children was finished. But eventually the two of them drifted apart, and although my mother went on to have other companions, my father appeared to have no desire to do the same. In the end, he decided that all he wanted was to drink the *aljar al-nawim* and move on from this world."

Possibly it was too personal a question to ask, even after the intimacies they'd shared, but Leila found herself saying the words anyway. "Did you try to stop him?"

"No. It was his choice, and I would not stand in his way. But still, it was…difficult."

"I'm sorry."

He bent and kissed her, but softly on the top of her head. It seemed clear enough that, for the moment at least, he had no desire to rekindle their passion. "It was always a possibility. And if my father is now free of the burden of this world, who am I to blame him? I can mourn his absence without wishing for things to be different."

Leila wasn't sure if she could maintain that kind of calm about the situation if her father had decided to commit suicide because of an enormous world-weariness, an overwhelming ennui. But then, Malik, with all his centuries of experience, probably had had a lot more time to develop a sense of perspective.

"Is that part of the reason why the djinn only number twenty thousand or so? Because some choose to 'move to the next world,' as you put it?"

"Some," he said. "And our families are small. We only have children when we wish—there are no such things as 'accidents' among our kind… which is why I did not bother to mention any kind of protection when we made love. There was no reason for it."

It hadn't been much of a concern to her, either. Being Chosen, she figured she'd be protected against any kind of djinn STDs that were out there—if such a thing even existed. And because she'd had her last Depo shot at the tail end of the summer, only a few weeks before the Heat struck, she knew she was protected against unwanted pregnancy, as long as Malik didn't have some kind of super-sperm that rendered such safeguards useless.

"Well, that's good to know," Leila said. Should she tell Malik about the birth control she'd taken? No, better not to mention it for now. It seemed highly unlikely to her that they would decide to start a family in the next few months anyway. No need to rush, not when they apparently had all of eternity to look forward to.

A horrible thought crossed her mind. What if a djinn who had claimed a Chosen eventually decided he or she had tired of existence, and drank the *aljar al-nawim* in order to be free? Would their Chosen die at the same instant, losing the protection they'd been given all that time? Or would they linger for some time after, until they'd died of old age?

Neither prospect seemed terribly appealing.

"You have no need to worry," Malik said quietly, again with that disconcerting way he had of being able to read her thoughts, or at least her expression. "I would never abandon you in such a fashion."

"You're sure?" she asked, hating the way her voice trembled slightly.

"Very sure," he told her. This time he kissed her on the mouth, but with a wonderful tenderness that couldn't quite hide the passion behind it. "How could I ever think of leaving this world, now that I have you?"

Leila nestled into his arms and shut her eyes, willing herself to believe what he was saying.

After all, what else could she do?

The morning sun touched Malik's face, bright but

not harsh. He opened his eyes and took a quick glance at his surroundings, reminding himself of where he was. This was Leila's bedroom, with the ocean sparkling bright and clear outside the windows, all trace of the previous night's storm now gone. Next to him, she still slept, turned over onto one side with her hair spilling in its shadowy glory across the pristine white of the pillowcase.

He breathed deeply, content. Yes, their conversation had taken a darker turn the evening before, but he was still glad of it, glad that he had told her of his own losses and that she hadn't turned away. In djinn society, for all their outward acceptance of those who took the *aljar al-nawim*, there was still an unspoken prejudice toward those who were left behind, as though somehow there must be something wrong with them, if their loved ones could walk away so easily.

No need to think of that now, though. He had Leila beside him, and she had proved the night before that she was willing enough to be his companion, now and forever. Their bodies had sealed the compact he'd made with the universe when he claimed her as his Chosen. And they had only reaffirmed their connection when they awoke in the depths of the night and made love again, quickly and urgently, as if they had both needed to know for certain that the other one was still there.

Their joining meant they would need to leave this place soon. With their love secure, they could move on to their permanent home and begin to make their life there. What such a life would entail, he wasn't altogether certain; an existence planet-bound here on Earth would be quite different from the one he'd lived in the otherworld. Still, he supposed the djinn of Bel-Air and their Chosen would all find their way together, would begin to grow their own crops and raise their own livestock, rather than taking it from the four corners of the world. Lesser structures would be razed to make way for farmland, and with the earth elementals and the water elementals and the air elementals working together, this land would become far more fertile than its previous inhabitants could have ever dreamed.

He was smiling at this thought, imagining the green fields and the trees heavy with fruit, when his sister's voice broke into his mind.

Malik! I have need of you!

What is it, Fatima? he responded, trepidation already growing in his heart. He knew that his sister would not have contacted him in such a way, and at such an early hour, if the matter was not one of some urgency.

It is Adam, she said. *My Chosen. Every morning he goes out to run, but he has not returned, even though it is far past the time when he would normally do so.*

You cannot sense him? Because once a djinn had bonded with their Chosen, they usually had some feeling as to where that person might be, as long as it was not too far away.

No, she replied, her mental voice sounding almost as though she was going to burst into tears. *Several of us went out looking for him, thinking that perhaps he had simply run beyond the borders of our territory and was late in returning because he had so much farther to go. But we saw no sign of him, nothing at all. That is why I have reached out to you, Malik. I would feel so much better if you would come to assist in the search.*

He could not blame her for that; because of the manner of their father's death, he and Fatima tended to be closer than many djinn siblings would otherwise be. And yet going to aid his sister would mean leaving Leila alone here at the house, for of course she could not travel in the manner of the djinn unless he held her, and that would be a distraction, one Fatima would probably not appreciate. True, he could bring Leila along and have her wait for him at Fatima's home, or perhaps at the home of one the other djinn and their Chosen. She would have to get to know them soon enough.

Yes, that sounded like the best plan.

I will be there shortly, he told Fatima. *It is early, and I am still in bed and will need to get dressed. But it will not be too long.*

Thank you, brother, she said.

The contact ended there; he was not sure what it felt like for other djinn, but when he spoke to his sister in this manner, it was almost as if she stood next to him. As soon as the mental conversation stopped, however, he lost the sense of Fatima's presence.

Would it be the same with Leila? He supposed he might as well find out now.

Leila, he said softly, using his interior voice. *Dearest.*

Her eyes fluttered open, bewildered and perhaps a touch frightened. "Did—did I just hear you in my mind?" she asked aloud as she pushed herself to a sitting position.

Yes, my love, he replied, still speaking to her mind to mind. *This is how djinn and their Chosen can speak to one another. I can do much the same thing with my sister, for we are blood, but you are the only two I can converse with in such a way.*

Wow, she said, then paused, her expression an

endearing mix of confusion and wonder. *This is all I have to do? Just think at you?*

More or less. We are connected now, which is why we are able to converse in such a way. He hesitated, then made himself go on. *My sister just reached out to me for assistance. Her Chosen is missing, and she needs my help. I promised her I would go to her as soon as I could.*

Oh, no—what's happened?

Fatima doesn't know. I'm sure it is something as simple as Adam wandering much farther on his morning run than my sister is willing to believe he would go, but the more of us who can help, the sooner we can find him.

Of course you must go help her.

You should come with me. I do not like the thought of leaving you here alone.

Rather than agreeing that this was a sensible plan, however, Leila only shook her head. *Why can't I stay here? Isn't it safe?*

Malik knew that it was; Fatima was the only person who knew where the Malibu house was located, and so Leila was certainly at no risk of being discovered by marauding djinn. Besides, this neighborhood had been swept weeks ago, and there was no reason for those who were intent on cleansing the world of humans to come back here. Even if they did, Leila was marked as his Chosen, and any djinn who tried to bring her harm would be forfeiting his own life. No point in that, not when there was so much easy sport to be found elsewhere.

I believe it is as safe as it can be, he replied. *But why would you not wish to come with me?*

I don't want to get in the way. Besides, she went on, a faint flush coloring her cheeks, *I think I'd rather wait to meet your sister on a day when I hadn't been banging her brother for most of the night before. Call me old-fashioned.*

He could not help but chuckle at this display of modesty. *I don't think Fatima would care one way or another, except to be glad that we had formalized our relationship. But if you truly wish to stay—*

I do, Leila said. *I'll get some breakfast, maybe go lie by the pool. I'll be fine. You need to go help your sister and not worry about me.*

If you're sure—

"I am," she said aloud, giving him a playful push that scooted him an inch or so toward the edge of the bed. "So get going. I'm sure Fatima is waiting for you."

That remark was only the truth. With some regret, he climbed out of bed, for he had hoped—before Fatima reached out to him, anyway—that he and Leila might be able to make love again this morning. Well, they would be able to do so soon enough. He would be back once Adam was found, and then perhaps it would be time to fall into bed again.

Malik summoned fresh clothing to him and got dressed, running his fingers through his hair in an attempt to tame it somewhat. During these preparations, Leila watched him from the bed, clearly content to remain where she was.

"I've left coffee going, and there are eggs in the refrigerator and a loaf of bread in the pantry."

"Thank you, Malik," she said as she finally climbed out from under the covers. Seeing her in the short silk chemise she'd put on the night before, noting the way it slipped over the curve of her breasts and revealed her long, lightly muscled legs, he wished more than ever that he might stay here.

But duty called, and he could not ignore it. Instead, he went over to Leila and kissed her briefly but passionately, trying to ignore the sensation of her body pressed against his.

"I'll be back soon," he promised, and then was gone.

Strange how knowing Malik wasn't here could

suddenly make this oversized house feel positively cavernous. Leila showered and got dressed, then went downstairs, trying to ignore how echoey the place felt without him. At least it was a bright, sunny day, with light pouring in through all the windows. No shadows here, nothing she needed to jump at.

As Malik had promised, coffee was waiting for her on its warming plate. She poured herself an oversized mug, then went into the pantry to look for the bread he had mentioned. Yes, there it was, a heavy multigrain loaf wrapped loosely in a linen tea towel.

She took it out to the counter and cut herself a couple of slices, then popped them in the toaster oven. How exactly Malik was able to get the electricity to function when he wasn't even here, she didn't know, but she was definitely glad of it. Sometime she'd have to ask him how that all worked.

Once the toast was done, she put it on a plate and generously buttered it, then took the plate and her mug of coffee over to the round table where she and Malik had shared breakfast several days earlier. That morning, which felt so long ago now, she still hadn't been sure what she planned to do about the djinn who had brought her to this place, but their lovemaking of the night before seemed to have settled that question. Now she couldn't imagine not going to bed with him, not allowing him to become her lover. They had fit so perfectly together, were more in tune than she'd ever been with any of the other men in her life.

She also appreciated that he'd been honest with her, had let her know about some of the tragedy in his own life. Before he had confided in her, she'd still had a difficult time seeing the djinn as anything more than an amorphous, undifferentiated mass of otherworldly beings, most of whom were intent on mankind's destruction. Now, though, she realized they were all individuals, each of them with their own hopes, fears, and dreams. She could still hate many of them for what they'd done, but she had to recognize that each one of them did so because of their own choices, their own motivations.

The toast and coffee tasted so good, she thought she'd have a second round. No real harm in that, especially since she didn't know when Malik would be back. That toast might have to last her a good long time, although she supposed she could always whip up a couple of eggs if necessary to tide her over. There were also last night's leftovers, now neatly packaged in a set of Pyrex bowls with locking lids. How all that had happened, when she and Malik had had an uninterrupted transition from the dining to the living room, Leila didn't know for sure. Djinn magic, she supposed.

Even the most leisurely of breakfasts couldn't last forever, though. Once she was done with the second batch of toast and coffee, she rinsed off her plate and mug and put them in the dishwasher. Then it was upstairs to brush her teeth and get rid of her coffee breath, preparing for whenever Malik would get home. Leila opened the French doors and stood on the balcony, breathing in the fresh salt air. Yes, it was sunny and beautiful, but the air had enough of a bite to it that she decided against looking for a bathing suit somewhere amongst the clothes that had been provided for her. She could still sit by the pool and soak up some sun, maybe read a book if she could find another one that looked interesting. During her days of solitude, she'd plowed through quite a few of them.

She selected one of Stephen King's more recent books, a novel she'd kept intending to pick up but never seemed to find the time for, then took it with her downstairs. A quick glance in the kitchen to make sure she'd left everything neat and orderly—something about this house seemed to demand cleanliness—and then she was out the French doors that led to the flagstone walkway. The koi pond sparkled, the water level an inch or so higher than it had been the day before, thanks to the deluge of the previous evening. She smiled down at the fish as they swam languidly through the water, glimmering graceful shapes in pale gold and white and deep copper.

The wind was stronger down by the pool than it had been when she first exited the house. Leila's hair whipped around her face, and she frowned, thinking that she probably should have grabbed a barrette or a hair tie from one of the bathroom drawers before she headed out here. Well, if it got too bad, she'd just go inside and fetch one. It wasn't as though she was on any kind of a schedule here. The thought was almost exhilarating. For so long she'd had to make sure she was always on time—for work, for auditions, even get-togethers with friends. And even after the world ended, her life had been regulated by the sun, which had governed when to hide, when to run. Now she had all the freedom in the world.

At some point she supposed she'd figure out what to do with it.

She sat on the same chaise longue where she'd rested several days before and let the sun shine down on her. The book rested on her lap; she would open it when she was ready, but for now it felt good to lie here in the wind and the sunlight, to revel in the sense of well-being that seemed to have flowed out to every limb, every extremity. She closed her eyes and breathed in the salt air, and marveled at how the afterglow from last night's lovemaking had lasted all the way to this glorious morning.

A shadow blotted out the sun. Leila blinked and then gasped. Standing over her was a tall djinn in cornflower blue robes, his eyes almost the same brilliant cerulean shade as the sky overhead. Gold-streaked brown hair rippled with the wind, echoing the golden borders of his clothing.

"Hello, Leila," he said. "I'm so glad I could catch you alone."

TEN

A GROUP OF SOME TWENTY DJINN WERE gathered in the living room of the mansion Fatima had taken for her own. These were all the air elementals in the Bel-Air group, called here by their leader because they would be of the most use in the search for her missing Chosen. All djinn could travel instantly from place to place, and all of them had the ability to rise into the air when the situation required, but only the djinn who controlled the air could actually fly.

Malik knew a few of the assembled djinn by name, more of them by sight, but some of their faces were completely unfamiliar to him. The djinn population was much smaller than the human one—or at least, what the human population had once been—and yet it was still rare for one of them to know all of their kind. He supposed the elders must, for all djinn were their charge, but otherwise it was not terribly feasible, even given his people's long lives.

Fatima came to him, dark eyes bright with worry. If she had wept, however, he saw no sign of it in her face; the kohl that ringed her large eyes was perfect and unsmudged, as was the reddish stain she wore on her lips. "I have called everyone here," she said. "We waited only on you."

He heard the faint accusation in her voice, but chose to ignore the rebuke and instead say, his tone mild, "I came as quickly as I could."

"You did not bring your Chosen with you?" Fatima inquired. "I would have thought you would take this opportunity for her to get to know those from the community who aren't involved in the search."

Luckily, Malik had expected a comment such as this, and so he had a ready answer. "I asked, but Leila chose to stay home. I believe she was feeling somewhat shy, and so I did not wish to press her. She will have all the time in the world to become familiar with you all, for I think we will be moving here very soon."

Those words provoked a small smile, as if that was all Fatima could manage to muster right then. "I am glad to hear it. Well, since we have no one

else we need to wait for, we might as well get started." She turned away from him and addressed the
watching djinn, both men and women. "You all
know the area you've been assigned for your
search. Go forth, and see if you can find Adam. I
fear that he might have fallen and injured himself,
for I cannot think of another reason why he
would not have returned home by now."

The assembled djinn murmured their assent,
then headed outside, where they launched into
the skies and fanned out, all of them moving in
different directions. Fatima waited until they were
gone, then said, "Now we can join in the search."

"How exactly do you want to proceed?" he
asked. "For while we can blink ourselves from
place to place, if we don't have a good idea of
where we are going, we could end up precisely
where we don't want to be."

"Oh, no," she replied, moving away from the
living room so she could head down a long hallway, "I have a better idea than that."

Malik followed her, somewhat mystified, but
forbore from asking any questions. He supposed
he would discover their destination soon enough.

Which he did, for after a moment she brought
him through a door that opened into the garage.
Housed in the closest of the four bays was a large
black SUV of some sort, but Fatima ignored that

vehicle and continued past it, pausing so he could get a glimpse of the automotive glory before them.

It was very sleek, a shimmering acid-green shade. The wide-mouthed grille was adorned with a Mercedes-Benz emblem, one of the few car logos he could recognize on sight.

He looked down at his sister and raised an eyebrow.

"I couldn't resist taking this toy for myself," she said. "It is very fast."

"As fast as elementals searching in the sky?"

"Well, no," she admitted. "But definitely more efficient than blinking ourselves all over Bel-Air and Beverly Hills."

He decided not to argue that point. It had always been the air elementals who served as scouts, while those who belonged to the other three elements fought on the ground. Not that this would be a fight, of course. Rather, it would be a weary drive from place to place, hoping that they might find Fatima's wayward Chosen some- where rather nearer than farther away.

"I am not sure I will fit in that thing," he said dubiously, eyeing the vehicle's low roofline.

"Oh, it's bigger on the inside than it looks from the outside," she replied. "Come and see. We need to get on our way."

Repressing a sigh, he walked over to the

passenger side of the vehicle and opened the door. He had to bend himself nearly in half to get in, but somehow he managed to fold his way into the passenger seat. Luckily, the controls that operated it were easy enough to locate, and he immediately pushed the seat as far back as he could.

In the meantime, Fatima had made a much more graceful entrance on her side of the car. However, she still looked rather incongruous sitting in the leather seat, her fitted coat of figured silk brocade, billowy silk pants, and armfuls of golden bangles in stark contrast to the smooth black upholstery. Despite all that, she started up the car matter-of-factly enough. It came alive with a low, grunting roar that made the hair on the back of Malik's neck want to stand up. As a djinn he commanded more power than mortals could comprehend, and yet something about the primal sound of that engine made him think that perhaps climbing into the car with his sister had not been the wisest idea.

Too late, however, for at once Fatima put the Mercedes in gear and backed it out of the garage, handling the vehicle with far more skill than Malik had expected. Then again, although they were close, they did not spend every waking hour together. Perhaps she had spent her time here on Earth indulging in a love of fast cars.

She turned to the left, heading toward the hills. They barely slowed down as she took them around a curve, and Malik found himself gripping the door handle to keep himself from sliding toward the center console.

"Where did you learn to drive like this?" he asked.

Her eyes were fixed forward, both watching the road and, he supposed, scanning the area for any sign of Adam. "I took one of those driving courses they offered for people who wanted to drive like a secret agent in the movies." A smile touched her red-rouged lips as she took another curve at speed, making Malik glad he had not yet eaten anything that morning.

"Any particular reason why?"

"I thought it would be a useful skill to have."

Perhaps it was. More likely, though, Fatima had been looking for something new and novel to amuse herself. She had always been inclined toward more physical pursuits, had once spent nearly a year in Buenos Aires so she might learn the tango, and another time lived in Gstaad for the greater part of the winter season in order to master the black diamond slopes there. Malik supposed that taking a workshop in learning how to drive like James Bond was par for the course, to use the human phrase.

However, once they were traveling along some truly winding roads that climbed into a western spur of the Hollywood Hills, Fatima slowed to a respectable rate of speed. The Mercedes' engine sounded almost wounded, as if it thought crawling along in such a fashion was beneath its dignity.

They were silent as they drove, Malik studying the side of the road next to him, Fatima watching the walkway to her left. The homes here were also massive, but more difficult to see, as they tended to be set far back on gated drives, surrounded by trees.

Fatima's fingers tapped on the steering wheel in annoyance. "I don't know why Adam keeps up with this silly ritual anyway. I told him that since he is Chosen, he will always be as fit and healthy as he is now, and will never get ill or grow old. But he just smiled and told me that old habits die hard. Mortals can be foolish sometimes."

Malik gave a small lift of his shoulders. "I don't think you should be too annoyed with him. I have heard that some mortals used running as a kind of meditation, a way to focus within. If he was used to running as a means to clear his mind, then I can see why he would wish to continue with it, even if there is no real physical reason why he needs to do so."

"Perhaps." However, her fingers still moved restlessly on the wrapped leather of the steering wheel, rubies and topaz glinting in the bright morning light. "I know it is just worry that has made me so irritable."

"I understand." Malik kept watching their surroundings, but there was nothing here to suggest that anyone had passed by recently. Everyone who had lived in these magnificent houses was long gone, and even if there had been one or two survivors in the area, they would have been hunted down by now. Unlike other parts of Southern California he'd observed, it seemed these people had died as they had lived, hidden behind high walls. There were no abandoned cars blocking the road, no sign that this street had once been populated at all.

What a waste. A tragic waste, and yet he knew there was no point in dwelling on what his fellow djinn had done. All he could was continue, and hope that the community of djinn and Chosen in Bel-Air—and other communities like it elsewhere—might one day build a world that was a worthy successor to what had gone before.

They came to a dead end. Fatima let out a hiss of annoyance from between her teeth, then slowly turned the car around so they were pointed back down the hill. Malik refrained from commenting that perhaps she should have consulted a map before setting out. Djinn could see much, but they were not omnipotent. Unlike their creator, they were all too prone to making mistakes.

At the first intersection they encountered, she turned the car left, heading west. Again, Malik wondered if his sister knew at all where she was going, or whether she was driving purely as the mood took her, possibly allowing her instincts to guide their route. From the way she had spoken, it sounded as though she had some idea of the normal routes her Chosen took when he went out running, but those had already been searched and had turned up nothing.

She zigged when they came to another intersection so they were headed south once again, back toward the neighborhoods the djinn had taken over.

"Have you been here before?" he asked.

"I believe I passed through once while prospecting for houses, but I decided that where we ultimately settled was a better fit for our group." A small sigh, followed by a resigned shrug. "Truly, I do not know where I am going. I believe I told Adam of this area before, and so I thought we might as well cut through here, just in case. But I fear that all we are doing is going in circles with nothing to show for it."

"It is far too early to despair," Malik said, hoping that he sounded calm and reassuring. In truth, it was too early to give up hope, but he had to admit that Adam's disappearance was more than a little puzzling. Where on earth could he have gone? And why? "After all, we have no idea how the other searchers are faring. It is very possible that one of them has already located your Chosen."

"If that were the case, he would have reached out to me," Fatima said. "We are not so far away from home that if Adam had been brought back there, he would not have contacted me."

Of course. Malik realized he should have thought of that. Still, just because Adam had not been found within an hour of beginning the search, it certainly did not mean that he wasn't somewhere in the vicinity.

They turned left, now going east and, it seemed, heading back toward the house. Was Fatima giving up already?

Then she came to a sudden stop, tires squealing. Malik put out a hand to stop his forward movement, although the seatbelt still caught him by the throat, nearly strangling him. "What is the matter?"

With one shaking hand, she pointed forward, through the windshield. "What is that?"

He had been watching the sidewalk rather than the road, and so she had seen the item in question first. Sitting in the middle of the pavement was a white oblong object. Was that…?

Fatima was already fumbling with her door handle. Before he could finish the thought, she was out of the car, leaving the Mercedes idling as she hurried forward. Malik undid his seatbelt and climbed out as well, cursing the way he had to hunch over to extricate himself from the low-slung vehicle. Weren't Germans supposed to be tall?

His sister already had the object in her hand as he approached. With a sinking sensation somewhere in his midsection, he realized what it was.

A white running shoe.

Tears glittered in her dark eyes as she held out a piece of paper. "This was attached to it."

Malik took the paper from her. Only one line was written on it, in heavy black ink. The words and letters weren't English, but a form of ancient Sanskrit that had already been dead before he was born.

"What does it say?" Her voice shook as she asked the question, but she held herself calm as she waited for him to reply.

He could read the words; unlike his sister, he had spent a great deal of his long life in more scholarly pursuits, and could read and write ten living languages and just as many dead ones. Right then, however, he wished he could claim ignorance, could tell her that he had no idea what those gracefully shaped words actually meant.

"Malik!"

No point in delaying, he knew. After pulling in a breath, he told her, "It says, *You will get him back…as long as you do not interfere.*"

"Interfere with what?" she demanded. "What else does it say?"

"That is all," he replied, heart heavy. Whoever had taken Adam, it appeared they enjoyed playing games. Deadly ones, at that; for to kidnap a Chosen, to promise bodily harm if certain conditions were not met…such antics would not sit well with the elders, if they should ever learn who was behind this.

"But…." Fatima let the word trail off, as if she'd realized that any protests she made would be for naught. "What are we to do, if they give no other conditions, if we do not even know who they are?"

"We wait," Malik said, his tone heavy with misgivings. "I fear there is nothing else we can do."

Leila sat frozen in her lounge chair, all of her instincts screaming at her to run, even though she knew doing so would be useless. She'd seen far too many of her companions hunted down and killed to believe for one second that she had any chance of outrunning a djinn.

Instead, she set the book on her lap aside as calmly as she could before saying, "What do you want?"

"So hostile!" the strange djinn said. His appearance was disconcerting to her, because most of the djinn she'd seen so far were dark like Malik, dark as her ancestors in Iran. This man, with his light brown hair and blazing blue eyes, hardly looked like a djinn at all to her.

Well, except for his outward perfection; his skin appeared tanned from the sun, but possibly that was its natural hue. However his skin tone had been achieved, it definitely helped to accent the strongly defined muscles of his chest and stomach.

His appearance wasn't the issue here, though. It was the way he'd conveniently showed up almost as soon as Malik left the house.

"Sorry," she said, telling herself she needed to play it cool if she wanted to survive this encounter. Then again, if the djinn had been intent on murder and mayhem, he could have simply descended on her and ripped her limb from limb rather than bothering to engage in conversation. Or maybe he was the kind of sick bastard who liked to toy with his victims before he killed them. "I suppose I was startled—I wasn't really expecting company. And you are...?"

"My name is Omar al-Tariq," the djinn replied. "Malik al-Mazin and I share a long acquaintance."

Despite the bright sun beating down on her, Leila felt as if she'd suddenly been encased in ice. Omar al-Tariq? He was the one who had originally wanted her, the djinn who had only backed down when Malik made it clear he was willing to fight for her.

A cold, sadistic, gas-lighting waste of oxygen, if what Malik had told her was true. And so far, Malik had given her no reason to think he was a liar. The exact opposite, actually. He'd been far more open and honest than she'd had any right to expect.

However, there was no need to let Omar know that Malik had already provided her with an accurate description of his character. The only thing Leila could think to do was make him believe she knew nothing about him. Maybe that way, she'd be able to survive this encounter.

Okay, girlfriend, she told herself, setting her

fear aside and doing her best to change mental gears. She'd done it hundreds of times in auditions, and now her performance might just save her life. *Time to put your acting shoes on.*

She assumed her best slightly confused smile, cocking her head to one side as she did so. "So you're a friend of Malik's?"

"Exactly right," Omar replied, smiling back at her with very white teeth. For some reason, though, the effect was less toothpaste commercial and more great white shark on the hunt. "He was concerned about leaving you here alone, and so I offered to come check on you."

"You're not helping to look for his sister's Chosen?"

"They already have plenty of people to assist with that task," Omar returned easily, his smile never wavering. "Besides, Fatima, I fear, does not have much use for me, not since we had a dalliance some time back which did not end all that well. I wanted to remain on friendly terms, but you know what they say about a woman scorned."

Leila took in a breath, reminding herself that she didn't dare fling this pack of lies back in the djinn's face. Not until she knew what the hell he was up to, anyway. "Oh, I'm sorry to hear that," she said, knowing that she must sound like a complete ditz—which was the whole point. She'd gotten the sidekick part in that one comedy pilot because she could manage the ditz thing fairly well, although trying to act that way eight hours a day made her want to bash her head into a wall. It was probably a good thing the pilot never got picked up.

A shrug. "These things happen. Because we djinn live so long, we need to learn to live together harmoniously, even when relationships don't work out. But Fatima, I fear, is one to hold a grudge. The best thing for me to do is try to stay out of her way."

"You're with the Bel-Air group?" Leila asked, her tone all confused innocence. "Is your Chosen back there with everyone else?"

This question aroused a flicker of irritation on Omar's smooth features, as though he'd just realized that the only logical explanation for him being part of that group was that he also had a Chosen tucked away somewhere. "Yes," he replied, after a hesitation so brief, Leila doubted she would have noticed if she hadn't been looking for it. "Actually, she's part of the reason why I came here. She said it was too bad that you'd stayed here alone, because everyone was looking forward to meeting you. That is why I volunteered to come here, to see if you would come back with me."

Oh, great. Leila had no doubt that Omar wanted to take her with him someplace, but she highly doubted it would be anywhere near Bel-Air and its new community of djinn and Chosen. If she refused, how would he react? Right now, he was all smiles and pleasantries, but she doubted that would last for very long, not once she'd done her best to thwart his plans.

Probably the best thing to do was stall for as long as she could. Malik hadn't said how long he would be gone, but she had to hope that the search wouldn't take too much time. If he arrived while Omar was still here, then he should be able to drive off the other djinn. From what Malik had said, Omar was a bully, not one who had much stomach for physical confrontations. If he'd run before, he most likely would run again.

Once more she tilted her head to one side in what she hoped was a charmingly bemused way. "Oh, didn't he tell you? I decided I really didn't want to go to Bel-Air today, and that's why I stayed home. I thought I'd just be in the way, what with everything that's going on, and besides, the thought of having to meet all those people felt a little…overwhelming, I guess."

"But they all want to meet *you*," Omar replied, his tone what he probably thought was ingratiating. Unfortunately for him, Leila heard the impatience behind it and knew he was not very happy about being contradicted.

Too bad. She gave a little laugh, then pushed herself up off the chaise longue. Obligingly, Omar stepped backward to allow her room to stand up, but she didn't trust that small show of chivalry. He was still close enough to grab her if he wanted to.

To her relief, though, he didn't move, only stood there, watching her and clearly waiting for some kind of reply.

"Oh, I know," she said. "And I want to meet them at some point. Today just didn't seem like the best time. Everyone would be distracted by looking for Adam. Is there any word on that, by the way?"

"Not that I'd heard," Omar replied, his voice a little tight. His gaze shifted toward the house, as though he feared Malik might be coming home at any moment.

With any luck, he would be. However, Leila knew she couldn't rely on luck to get her through this. Her body tensed as she realized she'd have to do what she could to keep Omar occupied until her djinn returned.

"Oh, wow, that has to suck for Fatima." She glanced toward the sky briefly, as if noting the position of the sun, then said, "It was getting too hot for me out here. Do you want to come inside?

I can get you a glass of water or some iced tea or something."

Omar's mouth thinned. She could tell she'd put him on the spot—if he refused, then at best he'd seem rude. At worst, his refusal would make her wonder why he wasn't willing to accept her hospitality if he'd really come here to check on her as a favor to his "friend."

The pause was more noticeable this time, but then he said, "Of course. Something to drink would be a good idea. It is quite a warm day for this time of year."

As casually as she could, Leila bent to retrieve her discarded book from the chaise longue. "This way," she said as she began walking toward the house, toward the large glass doors that opened on the backyard.

This time, Omar didn't hesitate. If anything, he was following her a little too closely, as though he wanted to make sure she wouldn't slip inside the house and lock the door against him. Again, that wouldn't slow him down for very long, but it was just one more complication he probably had no desire to deal with.

More than anything, she hoped she would see Malik's tall form as she made her way to the kitchen, but no such luck. The house was almost achingly empty, her footsteps on the travertine floor far too loud, echoing up into the twenty-foot ceilings. Still, she knew she had to act as though nothing was strange about this visit, that nothing about Omar's presence was anything too unusual.

At least there was a pitcher of iced tea in the fridge. Malik must have conjured it there, maybe thinking that she would go sit outside at some point and would like a cold drink to keep her hydrated. That was just the sort of thoughtful gesture he would make.

Now if only he could provide more evidence of his thoughtfulness by coming home to make sure she was okay....

All too aware of Omar's bright blue gaze on her, she went to one of the cupboards and opened it. No glasses there, only a variety of serving bowls. "Oops," she said, shutting the cupboard door. "I still haven't figured out where everything's located in this kitchen. It's bigger than my first apartment!"

"It is rather large," the djinn agreed, although his eyes narrowed slightly, a sign that he wasn't too thrilled by the further delay.

The next cupboard she opened turned out to hold the glasses she was seeking, and she took out two of them, then went to the refrigerator to get the pitcher of iced tea. As she filled both the glasses, she said, "Your Chosen is from L.A.?

That's what Malik told me—that you're all here because you picked someone from the area."

Once again she spotted that flicker of irritation, come and gone so quickly that most people probably would never have noticed it at all. But part of acting was training yourself to observe other people's expressions, their reactions, and so Leila was fairly certain about what she'd just seen. Omar was annoyed because she'd forced him to concoct another lie. However, he answered without missing a beat, "Yes, from Santa Monica."

"Oh. Is she going to miss the beach, living in Bel-Air?"

"She can still visit the ocean. Bel-Air is our new home base, but we are still free to visit where we like, as long as the location hasn't been claimed by another djinn. We can't settle elsewhere, true. However, we can still come and go mostly as we please."

Interesting. Was that really true? Malik hadn't seemed concerned about taking her to Irvine, so maybe Omar was telling the truth now. She'd have to ask Malik when she saw him again.

With any luck, that would be very soon now.

She took one of the glasses of iced tea and walked over to Omar, then handed it to him. He took it from her, being careful not to touch her fingers. Why, she wasn't exactly sure, although maybe his reticence had more to do with not wanting to tip his hand too soon than out of any respect for her personal space.

"That's great to hear," she said. "Not that I was really a beach person before"—she waved a vague hand in the general direction of downtown Los Angeles—"but I've liked being here, being close to the water."

"You like the ocean?"

"Well, like I said, I never got to live too close. Even where I grew up in Irvine, we were still about twenty minutes away. But it's nice—the sound of the waves is really soothing."

Leila realized she was babbling like an idiot, but maybe that was a good thing. For one thing, she was using up time, which meant the chance of Malik coming home soon was increasing. Also, if Omar thought she was little more than a pretty face with a vapid brain behind it, then he wouldn't have any reason to suspect that she was doing everything she could to keep stalling.

"My element is air, but I, too, find it sooth-ing," Omar said. He sipped some of his iced tea, then took a step toward her. "Perhaps we should go outside and take a walk. Does this house have access to the beach?"

It did, of course; she and Malik had used that long stairway just the day before to walk down to the shoreline. Not that Omar really needed the stairs, since he could always blink himself down to the beach.

"I think so," she replied, cocking her head to one side. "The property is so big, I don't know it very well yet, but I thought I saw some stairs going down somewhere."

"That's good to know." Another step closer, still wearing that shark grin of a smile. "Why don't you show me?"

A chill worked its way down Leila's spine, but she put on what she hoped was a guileless smile of her own and said, "You haven't finished your tea—"

"It will be waiting for me when we get back."

"I—"

She wasn't given the chance to say anything other than that, because in the next instant, Omar had let go of his glass of tea so it shattered against the travertine floor, sending shards of glass and ice everywhere. Cold liquid splattered against her bare toes, even as his arms went around her, pulling her against him. A shocked gasp escaped from her lips, but before she could protest, the kitchen disappeared around her and they were gone.

ELEVEN

THE OTHER DJINN HAD BEEN SENT HOME TO be with their Chosen. Fatima sat on one of the velvet-upholstered couches in the living room of the home she shared with Adam, the fateful note still clutched in one hand, even though she couldn't read a word of it.

"Who do you know who could have written this?"

"I'm not sure." Malik had found himself too full of nervous energy to sit down, and so he stood by the room's marble fireplace, staring grimly out into the backyard. Off to one side, a fountain played, bright water splashing in the sunlight, and yet he still thought he had never looked upon a drearier scene. "There are many of us who can read and write the old languages. If you are hoping to narrow this down to a small group of suspects, I fear you will be disappointed."

"But still, not everyone can write ancient Sanskrit."

"No," Malik admitted. "But when you have three or four thousand people who can, you still have far too many possible candidates. There has to be something more."

Fatima turned the note over in her hands, as though she hoped to find some piece of incriminating evidence in the very paper itself. Unfortunately, the sheet she held was nondescript in the extreme, the kind of smooth white paper mortals had once used in their computer printers and copy machines. "All right, if the use of Sanskrit is not enough on its own to single out someone, then let us think. Who in the world would have a grudge against me and Adam?"

"A former lover, perhaps?" Malik ventured, although he knew that suggestion was not a very likely one. She had always taken care to part amicably from her romantic partners, with nary a hard feeling on either side.

His sister seemed to have the same idea, for she let out an annoyed huff of breath and said, "No, of course not. No one was ever so hopelessly enamored with me that they would go to such lengths for revenge, especially knowing that they would bring down the wrath of the elders by acting in such a way."

Malik had thought as much. Very well, not a former lover, but perhaps someone who had a point to prove. Although the other djinn had grudgingly acceded to the elders' wishes when it came to saving a token group of Chosen, they still were not happy that any mortals at all had been allowed to continue breathing. Possibly whoever had kidnapped Adam thought it was worth risking the wrath of the elders to steal the Chosen of the Bel-Air community's leader, although Malik had to believe such a stunt would turn out very badly for them. The elders preferred to stay out of the day-to-day affairs of the djinn, but if they were crossed, they would be implacable foes.

Because he had few words of comfort to give, Malik offered the only ones he could think of right then. "At least they left a note, which means they are willing to deal."

"A note as cryptic as they come," Fatima retorted, tossing the now-crumpled piece of paper onto the shining glass surface of the coffee table. "It would help if they had told us precisely what it is they don't want us to be interfering with!"

"I agree," Malik said. He came over to the couch and sat next to his sister, took one of her hands in his. "But if they are setting conditions, then it seems to me they will be back in contact soon enough with further instructions. In the meantime, I think it best that we reach out to the elders."

Rather than agreeing with him, Fatima appeared utterly alarmed by this suggestion. She snatched her hand from his grasp and snapped, "I think that might be the worst possible thing we could do! Surely whoever has taken Adam will look on such an action as interference from the very beginning."

Perhaps she had a point. Although if they couldn't take their problem to the elders, they had very few options. "What do you propose we do, Fatima? Merely sit and wait?"

"Yes, if that is what these kidnappers want," she replied. "I don't like it any better than you do, but what choice do we have?"

Malik let out a breath and ran a hand through his hair, finishing the damage the wind had already done. He hated to feel so thwarted, as though there was absolutely nothing he could do to help his sister. And yet…that was their current situation. Until the kidnappers made some sort of contact again, they had nothing to go on. Fatima had said she couldn't reach Adam with her thoughts, which meant he had to have been taken out of range. With djinn involved, he could have been removed to any of the four corners of the world. Malik feared there were plenty of djinn who would be willing to shelter Adam from anyone who might try to seek out his location. Yes, those who participated in such subterfuge might be risking retaliation from the elders, but the elders, though strong, were not omnipotent. They could not see everything, were still in their palace in the otherworld, as far as he knew. And he guessed there were probably plenty of djinn who would be willing to risk the elders' wrath in order to enact some form of revenge on a helpless human.

"We have no choice at all," he said, his words heavy with resignation. "But if that is the case, then I should get home to Leila. I can do you no more good here, and I would feel better if I knew she was all right."

"Why shouldn't she be?"

"A few hours ago, I would have said there was no reason not to worry. But now…." Malik stopped himself there, knowing there was no point in borrowing trouble. After all, Adam's whereabouts were public knowledge among the djinn, especially with the way he would go running every morning, a very visible figure on Bel-Air's empty streets.

But no one except Fatima knew where her

brother and his Chosen were currently dwelling. Malik knew he could trust his sister with his life, which meant Leila was quite safe. Still, that niggling sensation in the back of his mind was only growing stronger. He needed to get away from here.

"Very well," Fatima said, sounding resigned. "You are right—there is little you can do here at the moment, except keep me company and stop me from having my fears continue to chase one another around in my brain, like cats after rats. But there are plenty of others here in our community who would be happy to do the same for me." She rose from the couch and added, "Go on, Malik. I know you will not be content until you have reassured yourself of the safety of your Chosen."

"Thank you, sister," he said, getting to his feet as well. He bent and kissed her on the cheek. "Reach out to me as soon as you hear anything."

She nodded. Her dark eyes had a suspicious glitter to them, but Malik knew she would not allow any of those tears to fall in his presence, for she had never been the kind of woman who made her grief public. "I will."

After offering her an encouraging smile, he blinked himself away from her house, back to the mansion in Malibu. Because the day was so fine, he went straight to the patio by the pool, thinking that Leila was probably outside, enjoying the sun. But the patio was empty, although he noted that one of the chaises had been shifted slightly, making him think she had been out here earlier. Perhaps she had decided she'd gotten enough sun and had gone indoors.

He did not bother to climb the path that led up to the house. Instead, he blinked himself into the living room. The couches there were soft and luxurious, a good place to put up one's feet and read. However, the living room was empty. Frowning, he called out, "Leila!"

No reply, which didn't necessarily mean anything. If she'd gone for a swim in the pool, it was very possible that she'd gone up to her room afterward so she could take a shower and wash off the chlorine.

But there was no sign of her in the bathroom. The towels on the rack were still faintly damp from the shower she'd taken earlier that morning, but if they had been used recently, they would have been much wetter.

The opulent miniature movie theater in the east wing of the house was also empty. Fighting a growing apprehension, he walked back toward the kitchen. He supposed it was possible that she'd gone in there to fix a snack, but if that were the case, she surely would have heard him calling her name.

As he entered the room, he stopped dead, cold dread filling his heart. Scattered on the floor not too far from the refrigerator were broken bits of glass and puddles of liquid that he thought were spilled iced tea. Sitting on the counter across from the refrigerator was a glass nearly full of tea, looking as though only a few sips had been taken from it.

Two glasses? Had she dropped the one somehow, then fetched herself another? Perhaps, but Leila would never have left such a mess behind. She would have cleaned up the broken glass and the spilled tea, and then fetched herself another.

Which meant…what? That someone else had been here? Malik did not want to think such a thing was possible, but he could come up with no other reasonable explanation. She must have been stolen while he was off trying to help his sister.

The words of that cryptic note came back to him, words that now carried an even more sinister meaning.

You will get him back…as long as you do not interfere.

Now the terms of that "interference" were becoming painfully clear….

Bright sunlight dazzled her eyes. Leila blinked, then pushed herself away from the brutally strong arms that held her, forgetting in her fury that she was supposed to be acting ditzy and confused and completely harmless.

"What the *hell?*" she spat.

Omar stood a pace away from her, looking incredibly smug. She wished she could reach over and wipe that nasty smile right off his face, but she knew her chances of coming out ahead in a physical fight with a djinn were basically nil.

"I am sorry about that," he said, not sounding contrite at all. "I couldn't think of a way to explain while we were there in Malik's house, so I thought I'd bring you here."

"And where is here?" she demanded, giving the room where they stood a quick once-over. Softly modern, with cream-colored sofas and pale wooden floors and equally pale wooden furniture. Expensive abstracts on the wall, including one above the huge, angular plaster fireplace at one end of the space. French doors stood open, letting in a sea breeze. From what she could tell, the house backed right up to a beach, with a wide deck the only thing separating it from an empty white expanse of sand.

Which didn't tell her a whole lot. There were miles and miles of beaches in Southern California, stretching from San Diego all the way up to Santa Barbara. Maybe someone who knew real estate better than she might have been able to look at the house and the beach outside and make an educated guess as to their location, but since Leila had never been in a position to own oceanfront property, she had absolutely no idea where they were.

If they were even still in California at all. This could be Florida, for all she knew, but she didn't think so. It wasn't nearly humid enough.

"This is…a safe place," Omar said. "We can talk here."

"That doesn't tell me anything."

His smile faded slightly. "It tells you that you're safe. Please, sit down."

He gestured toward one of the couches. Leila hesitated for a second, wishing she could tell him exactly what he could do with his "safe place." Unfortunately, she knew she didn't have a lot of bargaining power here. Better to slip gradually back into ditz mode, see what he had to say. Maybe he'd let down his guard enough to offer information she could use to figure out an escape.

"Okay," she said with a sigh. "But really, Omar, if you wanted to talk, you could've just said something instead of scaring a girl half out of her wits."

"I am sorry about that." He reached out with both hands, and a pair of glasses appeared in his grasp, both of them filled more than halfway with pale yellow wine. "Perhaps this will help to settle your nerves."

"Oh, wow, thanks," she said, inwardly praying that the wine wasn't drugged in some way. She sort of doubted it, because she could tell Omar was the type who believed he could talk his way through anything, but still....

Unfortunately, there wasn't any way to refuse the wine without giving away her suspicions. She needed him to think that, while she might be confused and a touch annoyed by the way he'd brought her here, she certainly didn't believe he was up to no good.

Although she feared that was exactly what he was up to.

She took the glass of wine from him and went to stand next to the French doors, pretending to look at the view. It was a gorgeous day, no doubt about that, and yet the sight of that wide, empty beach dismayed her. There didn't seem to be a single landmark to identify where she was, definitely not a big stone jetty like the one at Newport Beach. Maybe that was a lifeguard tower a few hundred yards away, but one lifeguard tower pretty much looked like another.

Omar walked over and stood near her, although not so close that she could accuse him of crowding her personal space. But he was definitely near enough to reach out and grab her if she tried to bolt.

No fear. She knew that her escape couldn't rely on something so simple and obvious. Right then she really couldn't think of how she might get away from him, but the most important thing was not to tip her hand, to keep making him think that she was completely harmless.

"Great view," she commented as she lifted the glass of wine to her lips and took a sip. Chardonnay, a little too buttery and oaky for her taste, but she knew better than to criticize. At least she couldn't detect anything particularly off about the wine, nothing that would seem to signal it had been doctored in some way. Then again, would djinn drugs or poisons even be detectable to a human?

There was still so much she didn't know.

"I'm glad you like it," Omar said. "I do find something soothing about the sound of the ocean, just as your Malik does." The smile he'd been wearing faded then, and he assumed an expression of some concern, one that Leila guessed was patently false. "But I fear it is Malik I need to speak to you about."

"Oh?" she asked, trying to look innocently confused. "Is he all right? Did something happen while he was searching for Adam?"

"No, not at all. As far as I know, Malik is fine. However, I realized today when I saw him that I could not allow this to go on. It would not feel right."

He almost sounded sincere. Problem was, he most likely didn't know that he was dealing with someone who'd spent a lot of time around actors, whose bullshit detector was pretty refined. Leila had to hope his wasn't nearly as well-tuned, because she knew the only way she would survive this was to do some serious b.s. slinging of her own.

"What is it?" she asked, allowing a faint tinge of alarm to enter her voice. "What can't you allow to go on?"

"You and Malik. You see, you were my original choice, Leila. I knew from the beginning that you were meant to be my Chosen. But Malik interfered, and I backed down because I had no wish to fight him. There had already been enough violence, enough death."

Omar's bright blue eyes sought hers as he delivered this little speech. It almost had the ring of truth, but that was only because parts of it were in fact true. But not all. Not the important parts, the most important of which was his role in this whole thing. Now that she'd bonded with Malik, she knew instinctively that he was the one she'd always been meant to be with.

She let her eyes widen in mock surprise. "Oh, my God. I had no idea."

"Of course you didn't, because Malik made sure to lie to you from the very moment you met."

"But…." Leila let the words trail off into nothing, then shook her head before taking another sip of chardonnay. "Didn't you tell me that you had a Chosen?"

"I told you that because otherwise I knew you would wonder why I was living in the Bel-Air community but had no human partner." He shrugged and looked away from her to the white sands beyond the deck. Sunlight glinted, warm and gold, in his streaky brown hair. "They took pity on me, for they knew I could not spend my time among the djinn who are doing everything they can to rid the world of humans. What they are doing is anathema to me. So I live with the Bel-Air djinn and their Chosen, albeit alone."

"I'm so sorry." Should she reach out and touch his arm? No, that didn't feel right. Even if she needed to pretend as though she was sympathetic to Omar's plight, that kind of physical contact might seem forced. Besides, the longer she could put off touching him again, the better. "I had no idea."

"Well, now you do. That is why I brought you here. You needed the chance to hear the truth in a place where Malik could not prevent me from telling it."

"I—I'm not sure what you expect from me, Omar." There. She'd put just the right amount of quaver in her voice...or at least, she hoped she had.

"Expect?" His shoulders lifted again, and he turned away from the French doors so he could face her directly. "I am not sure I 'expect' anything. I wanted to give you the truth so you could decide what to do with it."

"I don't know!" she flung back at him. Perhaps that outburst had sounded a touch melodramatic, but Leila could already tell that Omar was one for grand gestures. A subdued response wouldn't please him at all. She stepped away from the French doors and went over to one of the couches, where she sat down and put her glass of wine on the coffee table so she could knot her fingers together, then glance up and give him a pleading look. "I'd just barely gotten used to the idea of being with Malik. But now you're telling me that our being together was a lie?"

"Not a complete lie, perhaps," Omar responded. He moved toward her but did not sit, and instead remained standing a foot or so away from the sofa. "Of course he wanted you, too, or he would not have stolen you from me in the first place. But I suppose he lied by omission. He had no real desire to take a Chosen at all, but when given the chance to thwart me, he was all too eager to step in."

Again, a tiny bit of truth mixed in with all the lies. Because Malik had admitted that at first he was not sure he wanted to take a Chosen at all, and had only intervened when he knew he could not allow her to be claimed by Omar. He'd been protecting her, not trying to steal her.

Leila bit her lip, her gaze avoiding the djinn's. She had to hope he saw the gesture as one of vulnerability and confusion, while in reality she was desperately trying to come up with the best response to this apparent "revelation."

To stall for time, she drank some more of her wine. She hadn't eaten much that day, and so she could already feel a tiny bit of a buzz coming on. She needed to be careful, or she could end up in worse trouble than she already was. If any situation had ever called for a clear head, this was it.

Omar spoke again. "I know this must be difficult for you. Believe me, I had no wish to compound the tragedies you've already suffered. But neither would it have been right for me to stand by and allow an evil man such as Malik to take someone as good and pure as yourself."

Those words made her want to burst out laughing. Good and pure? That was laying it on a bit thick. To hide her reaction, she pulled in a breath and did her best to look worried and bewildered, and perhaps just the slightest bit weak and tragic. Whether the performance was Oscar-worthy or not, she didn't know. Then again, it didn't have to be Academy Award material. It just had to fool the djinn who stood there and watched her.

"He—he didn't seem evil to me," she objected, knowing she was taking a calculated risk. However, she guessed it wouldn't seem very realistic for her to not make at least a token protest when it came to defending Malik. Omar had to know that the two of them had been intimate, or, if he didn't know for sure, he probably would have made an educated guess. "In fact, he was very kind to me, very thoughtful."

"Of course he would *seem* that way," Omar replied, his tone patient, almost indulgent. "He would want to make you think that he had only your happiness, your welfare, in mind. I have known Malik al-Mazin for a very long time. He is quite good at being charming when he wishes to. But his only purpose was to make you fall in love with him so he might take his own sport later when he played at breaking your heart."

A small gasp escaped her lips, and she said, "I can't believe that."

"You don't want to believe it. Those are two very different things."

With a hand that shook a little, she reached out for her glass of wine and took a large swallow. *Nice touch, Leila,* she told herself, proud of the way she'd been able to bring out the tremor on cue. *But too many more gulps like that, and you're really going to be feeling it.*

In a way, she could almost admire Omar's technique. Malik had told her what to watch for, and so she knew she had no chance of falling for the other djinn's lies. Still, once again he was taking his own truth and using it against her, projecting his own nefarious methods onto Malik. It all sounded so plausible because it was true…if applied to Omar himself.

"I need some time to sort this out," she said. "Is it all right if I walk on the beach for a bit?"

"Certainly," he replied with a smile.

That response told Leila there was no one

around who could help her. Then again, who would there be? Most of humanity was dead, and certainly no djinn would care much about her fate.

Well, except Malik. But if he'd had even the faintest inkling of where she was, he would have already hurried here to rescue her, and brought with him the fight Omar had done so much to avoid.

Which meant she probably needed to get to work on rescuing herself....

TWELVE

"I DON'T UNDERSTAND," FATIMA SAID, looking up at her brother. "Why would anyone take Leila from you?"

"Clearly, as a pawn of some sort," Malik replied. He had spent his rage already, shouting at the universe—or at least into the empty rooms of the house he shared with Leila—and now he felt weary and strangely hollow, as if some essential part of himself had been taken away, and he was only now beginning to realize it. "I have to believe that Adam's disappearance and her kidnapping are connected somehow."

"You know for sure she was kidnapped?"

Malik wanted to retort that he didn't know what else it could be, with that glass broken on the floor and all trace of his Chosen gone. As he looked down into his sister's weary face, however, he reined in his impatience. She was suffering as well, and venting his rage and frustration on her would do neither one of them any good.

"I can't think what else could have happened. Leila would not have left such a mess behind, and there was the matter of the second glass, the one that was still sitting on the countertop. I am almost sure she had someone with her."

"This is where it would be good to have some of mortal society still functioning," Fatima said, her expression thoughtful. "Did they not have police who would look for fingerprints or bits of hair, that sort of thing?"

"Yes, they did," Malik responded, the words coming slowly as an idea began to take hold. No, he was no forensic scientist—he would not know what to do with a strand of hair even if he found one that did not look like Leila's—but it should be easy enough to check for fingerprints on the glass that had been left behind. If they were too large to belong to his Chosen, then he would know for sure someone else had been there. Even if they turned out to belong to Leila, at least he'd know she'd been holding that glass and could put the kidnapping theory aside. Not for the first time, he chafed at the limitations of his people, that they had no easy way of tracking one another, unless they were blood relations. "And I believe I can utilize some human technology to get a little more information. Thank you, Fatima, for the suggestion."

"I'm not sure I suggested much of anything," she protested, but he smiled and bent to give her a quick kiss on the cheek.

"Oh, yes, you did, even if you were not aware of it at the time. Now I must go so I can follow up with this idea, but of course you must reach out to me if anything changes."

Her big dark eyes looked up at him, surrounded by shadows and kohl. "I fear nothing will change at all, but yes, I will let you know."

He did not bother to give her a reassuring smile—they knew one another too well for that—but he did tilt his head in her direction before blinking himself away from her house, over to a place he had seen but never had any need to visit before this.

The Beverly Hills police station.

It was quite an impressive building, given its former function. But then, he supposed that in an upscale area such as this, the residents wanted all of their public structures to fit in, to give an impression of wealth.

The front doors were not locked. Indeed, one

of them stood slightly ajar, so that a few fallen leaves had blown inside. The sight made Malik raise an eyebrow. There was not much he feared, and so he did not immediately go to the conclusion that someone might be lurking inside. No, he surmised that during the last hours of the Heat, someone in the station had allowed any surviving prisoners in the holding cells to go free, rather than perish alone and locked away. It would have been a final act of compassion, albeit a futile one. Then again, perhaps one of the men or women who'd been locked up here had been immune.

In a way, that possibility was even worse. They would not have survived for very long on the outside, not with so many djinn hunting down anyone who survived the fever.

He pushed the door open all the way and went inside the lobby. Here were a few piles of the ubiquitous gray dust, some of them rather disarranged by the draft that had come in through the partly open front door. Because there was little else he could do, he ignored them and paused near the reception desk so he might read the directory in the glass case off to one side. Forensics was up on the second floor.

With no electricity, and with no clear idea of where he was going, Malik was forced to take the stairs, but he didn't mind. Being occupied with some sort of physical activity, even something so mundane as walking up a flight of stairs, allowed him to think he was actually doing something to help Leila, rather than merely sitting at home and wallowing in worry.

The forensics lab was at the end of the hallway. This door proved to be locked, and had once been accessed by some sort of key card system, but all he had to do was lay his fingers on the latch to have the door swing inward before him. Darkness greeted him, and so he touched a light switch and willed the ugly fluorescent bulbs overhead to come to life for the first time in nearly two months.

Off to one side was a laboratory, equipped with microscopes and many other pieces of equipment he couldn't identify. However, he was here for one specific thing, and so he ignored the lab and went in search of the supply room.

Which he found down near the end of the hall, in the last door on the left. It, too, was locked, but opened to him with just a touch. Inside were a number of shelves and cupboards, all stocked with all manner of arcane supplies. As he scanned the offerings, his gaze fell on the item he'd been seeking, a metal box that was clearly labeled.

Fingerprint Kit.

He reached out and took it, then glanced around. Perhaps there were other items here he might use at some point, but for now it was best to file them away for future reference.

A blink, and he was back in the kitchen of the Malibu house. The glass still waited on the countertop, and the broken bits of the other tumbler were still scattered on the floor, although the spilled tea had begun to dry.

Mouth set, Malik opened the fingerprint kit and pulled out a small container of dark powder. Although he'd never used such a thing before in his life, he had observed enough television dramas that he thought he could muddle his way through the process. After unscrewing the lid, he sprinkled some of the contents over the surface of the glass, being careful to hold it by the lip. If he'd been thinking, he would have gotten some latex gloves to prevent himself from leaving his own prints behind, but it was too late for that.

Next came the brush. He began to whisk away the powder and was gratified to see a series of smallish fingerprints around the center of the glass. Next, he took out the tape that had been provided in the kit and carefully laid it on top of one of the prints, lifting it from the surface of the glass. After holding one of his own fingers up to the print to compare sizes, he was almost certain that these prints had been left behind by Leila. They seemed far too small for a man. Or rather, while a mortal man of small stature might have left such prints behind, Malik knew they could never have come from a djinn.

It seemed clear enough Leila had held this glass. But what of the other one, the one that had broken on the floor?

He crouched down and took a closer look at the pieces scattered across the title. There were several at least an inch across; luckily, the tumbler had not shattered into dust. Gingerly, he reached for the largest piece and brought it up so he could set it on the counter. A quick dust with the fingerprint powder, another whisk of the brush and lift of the tape, and sure enough, another print was revealed for his inspection.

Unfortunately, this one seemed to be the same size as the prints he had noted on the unbroken glass, which meant Leila must have held this one as well. Perhaps his theory that she had dropped the first glass and then replaced it with the second was correct after all. But surely if the explanation was that innocuous, then she would still be somewhere on the premises. A single dropped glass wouldn't be enough to send her into hiding.

A frown pulling at his brow, he bent again to retrieve another piece of broken glass, this one a little smaller than the first. Once more he went through the ritual of dusting the piece and taping it off, not really expecting to find much.

But there it was—another print, much bigger than the first. When Malik held his own thumb next to it, they were almost identical in size. It seemed obvious enough that a man—or a djinn— close to his stature much have held this glass at some point.

The print wasn't his own, though. Peering more closely at the print, he could see that it had a distinctive double-whorl pattern, while his own thumb possessed only one.

Someone else had definitely been here. And because so few mortal men still breathed in the metropolis they had once called the City of Angels, Malik was almost positive the print must have been left behind by a djinn.

Rage flared up in him at the thought of some other elemental entering this house and taking Leila away. He supposed he should be glad that at least he saw no signs of violence, no indication that a struggle had taken place during her abduction, for the thought of her being hurt in any way made him ache with frustrated fear and worry. However, he couldn't ignore the very obvious fact that someone had come here for the express purpose of kidnapping her.

His thoughts immediately went to Omar al-Tariq, as Malik couldn't think of anyone else who bore a grudge against him…or who had shown any interest in Leila. He was certainly the most likely suspect.

The problem was, Malik had no idea where he could find Omar. The other djinn had gone out of his way to avoid his former adversary, which suited Malik very well. He had had no wish to cross paths with al-Tariq. Now, though, it was vitally important to discover where he was holed up. No place around here, probably; the air elemental would make sure to set up his base of operations in a location that couldn't be easily discovered by Malik or any of the Bel-Air community. And that meant al-Tariq had taken Leila far enough away that Malik couldn't reach out to her through their telepathic bond.

Jaw tight with tension, he left the kitchen and went to look out the enormous windows in the living room. Not because he thought he would be able to see anything that might jog his memory, but because gazing at the water helped to soothe him somewhat, allowed his racing thoughts to calm themselves so he could think clearly.

If al-Tariq truly was behind Leila's disappearance, what was his end game? Did he think the elders would sit back and allow him to steal another man's Chosen away from him? No, surely Omar could not be that naïve. Perhaps he had gained enough confidence to force a confrontation, although that seemed out of character as well. Omar al-Tariq had never met a fight he didn't enjoy running away from.

Then...what? Was this all an elaborate scheme to torture him? Malik wouldn't put it past the other djinn, for he knew all too well how much Omar delighted in cruelty, casual or otherwise. Indeed, his mental tortures had once even sent a lovely djinn woman to drink the *aljar al-nawim* in order to free herself from his abuse. Yes, he thought he could see how al-Tariq might torment his foe by stealing the woman he loved, only to murder her in the end. Then he would have his own sick form of revenge. The elders would punish him, but it was not their way to put transgressors to death. Instead, those who had violated the law in some way were banished to the outer circles, a hellscape where even a djinn would be hard put to survive, and where a human would perish within moments.

Were a few hours or days of petty torture worth facing such a terrible consequence? Of course Malik would never say such a thing out loud, but he had long been of the opinion that Omar al-Tariq wasn't entirely sane, at least not in the way most rational beings measured such things. Achieving some form of revenge might be enough for him, even it meant he would pay for that revenge by spending the rest of his days in the outer circles.

Sick fear rose up in Malik's heart then, but he pushed it away as best he could. Panicking would not help Leila. He needed to find a way to track her down.

And he thought he might know whom to ask.

The wind caught at her hair, wild and salty, and Leila breathed it in, hoping that its fresh tang would help to give her the courage she needed to face her immediate future. Although her back was to him now, she thought she could sense Omar watching her as she walked along the water line. He'd remained standing in the open French doors, allowing her enough freedom to come here to the water's edge and pretend to be deep in thought.

Actually, she wasn't pretending. She was thinking...hard. Only she wasn't thinking about everything the djinn had told her, because she knew it was all lies. No, she was wondering how in the hell she could get manage to get herself out of this mess.

Large houses like the one he'd taken for his clandestine hideaway marched their way down the sand, all of them clearly empty. There was no one here who could help her. She had her wits, and that was about it. No weapons at all, and now she keenly felt the loss of her .45, the one she'd left behind when she'd had to flee her basement hiding place nearly a week earlier. Funny how wishing for a gun now seemed like the most natural thing in the world, when a few months earlier, she'd barely known how to shoot one. She'd gone to the range once with a friend just so she could familiarize herself with how to hold a pistol without looking like a complete idiot while auditioning for a part on an action-adventure show, but that had been the extent of her knowledge...until the Heat came along.

Didn't get the damn part, either, she thought, bending down to pick up what she thought was a shell but which turned out to be only a shiny rock. The skirt she wore didn't have any pockets, so she set the rock back down and kept walking—but not too fast. She didn't want to alarm Omar or make him think she was trying to make a break for it. Yes, at some point she would try to escape, but now wasn't the time. Despite the panic that lay coiled within her, ready to strike when she least wanted it, she knew she had to plan.

All right, houses all around, but no real place to hide. This beach was wide open, flat and level. No wonder it had been so heavily developed. But maybe inside the garages attached to those houses were cars left behind by the people who had once lived there. It probably wouldn't be that hard to find the keys, assuming their owners had died in their homes.

Would a car start after sitting unused for nearly two months? Leila had to hope so; battery technology had gotten pretty good before the world ended. Whether or not a car could outrun a djinn was an entirely different proposition, but if the stars aligned and the opportunity presented itself, she'd still take that chance. The group of survivors she'd traveled with had avoided using any kind of motorized vehicle because they tended to be loud and attracted attention, and also because so many streets were still choked with abandoned cars. It would have been far too easy to get trapped in a dead end. The same thing could happen here, she supposed, but it might be worth the risk.

She half turned toward the house, then lifted her hand in a wave and smiled at Omar. He smiled back, teeth flashing in the sunshine.

Bastard.

But she had to keep up the act that she was

seriously weighing whether to be with him, that she did believe at some level that he was the good guy. How far she'd have to take that charade, she wasn't sure.

What if she had to kiss him? God forbid, sleep with him?

Her thoughts didn't want to go there, but despite her fear and disgust, she knew she had to make herself consider the situation coldly. Going to bed with someone you hated was still better than dying. Or at least, she had to think it was. She'd heard plenty of horror stories from friends about the so-called "casting couch," about the subtle and not-so-subtle threats and coercion used to get beautiful, desperate women into bed in exchange for supposed favors, whether that meant giving them parts outright, or merely luring them along with talk of arranging a meeting with the "right people." For whatever reason, Leila hadn't experienced that sort of harassment, although she'd always wondered whether it had something to do with an off-hand comment she'd made at one Hollywood party about her Uncle Amir—who wasn't really her uncle, but a sort of second cousin—being an arms dealer and in with the Iranian mob. She'd meant the remark as a joke, but really, she'd never been able to figure out where her uncle got his money. It could have been guns, or drugs, or some judicious money-laundering, or merely spectacular luck at day trading. Her parents had always studiously changed the subject whenever it arose, which made her think she was on the right track when it came to theorizing where Amir got the funds for his fairly ostentatious lifestyle.

At any rate, she'd never had to ponder the prospect of trading her virtue for favors. If she slept with Omar, it wouldn't even be for favors, but only to stay alive. Surely Malik would forgive her for that…wouldn't he?

Maybe she was borrowing trouble. However, she knew she had to come to that decision at some point, even if the worst-case scenario never happened. Right then she wished she could have been more like some of the women she'd known —acquaintances, really, not close friends—who could fall into bed with a man without batting an eye. A night of pleasure, some fun, and then it was over with and done. No strings, no worries, no attachments. If she'd been more like that, she could have coldly contemplated having sex with Omar to keep him happy and not had to worry about her own emotional repercussions.

But she'd never been into casual sex. For better or worse, she had to have feelings for anyone she slept with, even if things hadn't gotten to the stage where she could call it love.

For that matter, did she love Malik?

That's a hell of a question, she thought, moving toward the water so she could let some of the waves come up and tickle her toes. That water was damn cold, telling her she had to be somewhere in California still. It would have been much warmer in Florida or one of the Gulf States…or in Hawaii.

How can you love someone you've only known for barely a week?

Maybe it wasn't love, but it was definitely something. She knew she'd never met anyone like Malik al-Mazin before, and even being away from him this long made her ache at his absence. Or was the uneasy feeling in the pit of her stomach merely fear at being here alone with Omar?

For a long moment, she stood there on the sand, feeling the cold water barely kiss her toes. Very soon she'd have to turn around and go back toward him, put on a false face once more and do whatever it took to survive.

Because damn it, she'd survived this long. She wasn't about to let a sociopathic djinn get the better of her. She needed to live, if only because she really, really wanted to watch Malik pound the crap out of her kidnapper once he caught up with him.

Yes, that would be satisfying.

Still wearing a smile, she turned and began to walk slowly back toward the house where Omar was waiting.

THIRTEEN

The penthouse was an impressive one, situated at the top of a building recently constructed in downtown Los Angeles. From here, one could see all the way to the Pacific Ocean when standing on the west side of the enormous apartment, while the windows that faced east showcased the San Gabriel Mountains, now with a faint dusting of snow from the last storm that had passed through. Malik doubted the snow would last very long, not with the mild temperatures that had followed.

This was exactly the sort of place he had expected to find Amaal al-Tariq, Omar's younger brother.

Not that tracking down the other djinn had been precisely easy. Amaal was not one who had taken a Chosen, and so he could not be found in any of the human/djinn settlements that sprang into existence after the Heat had done its terrible work. However, he had been spotted in the Los Angeles area by one of the Bel-Air djinn, who had gone downtown to recover some personal effects for his Chosen from her apartment there.

Malik did not know Amaal well, but he was acquainted with him enough to know that if he was frequenting the area, he would be doing so from a hideaway that suited his particular tastes, which had always tended toward luxury. His palace in the otherworld had been quite lavish, and far larger than he truly needed, as he lived alone and had no partner or children. Indeed, Malik wondered whether the other djinn had experienced some ambivalence at having to leave such a magnificent abode behind him, even if Earth was so much more appealing in almost every other measurable way.

Then again, this view could compensate for a good many things.

Amaal came toward Malik now, a martini in either hand. Not precisely Malik's preferred alcoholic beverage—and, he guessed, not Amaal's, either. No, he had probably chosen the martinis because the angular glasses and the clear liquid they held suited the aesthetic of the penthouse better than a few glasses of wine might have. The dwelling was hard-edged, stark, masculine, with its black marble floors and steel and glass furniture. Even the canvases that adorned the pure white walls were spare and cold, done in shades of black and gray and dark blue.

Because he had more important things to spend his energy on than argue over his host's choice of beverage, Malik accepted the martini. After glancing around the penthouse, he said, "Is this where the elders have settled you?"

"Oh, no," Amaal replied. He sipped at his own drink, then added, "It is someplace to the east of here, in the foothills of a mountain range. Beautiful country, if not precisely to my taste. I am not quite sure what I want to build there, and so I am making my temporary residence here."

"Ah." Malik was not entirely certain what to make of that remark. Each djinn who was not among the One Thousand had been given his or her own plot of land to do with as they wished. He had not stopped to consider what the elders might do if the djinn who was given a certain bit of territory was not particularly eager to settle there. It was entirely possible that they would not do anything at all. If no one else had been given downtown Los Angeles to live in, then there was not much point in worrying about the way he appeared to be neglecting the land that had been bestowed upon him, for there would be no one to contest Amaal's presence here.

Amaal sipped at his martini again, watching Malik with amused blue eyes. In appearance, he resembled his older brother, with the same bright sky-colored eyes and sun-warmed skin, although Amaal's hair was much darker. When he spoke, his tone was equally amused. "Come, Malik. I do not think you came here to discuss real estate. What is it you want?"

Such a question was not unexpected. Although Amaal and Malik were not open enemies—Amaal had done what he could to distance himself from his brother's questionable antics—it was still strange that Malik would come to seek him out unless he had a very specific reason in mind. "I fear that your brother has taken my Chosen," he replied, not bothering to soften the words. Amaal needed to know what Omar had done.

Amaal didn't blink. "You're joking."

"I fear I am not."

Another swallow of the martini, a larger one this time. "My brother can be rash sometimes, but I cannot believe he would do something so mad. Surely he must know that the elders will not ignore such an obvious flouting of their authority."

Malik feared that Omar knew such a thing very well, and still didn't care. It was the other djinn's very recklessness that worried him the most, for he knew it only increased the danger Leila was in. "I would like to believe the same thing, Amaal, but Leila is missing, and I know of no one other than your brother who would have stolen her away. If I can locate her, then perhaps I can stop all this before the elders learn anything about what Omar has done. It can be our secret."

For this was his hope, that by persuading Amaal to help him, Malik might convince the other man that no harm would come to his brother. Indeed, Malik was not bent on revenge. He only wanted to rescue Leila before Omar hurt her, or she suffered some other harm. Most likely Omar would not believe he was motivated only by a desire for Leila's safety and nothing more, because in general he tended to think the worst of people, but Amaal was of a different temperament, somewhat indolent, given to pleasure-seeking. As far as Malik knew, Amaal had never participated in hunting down humans, not because he cared one way or another whether they lived or died, but because chasing after them and killing them one by one involved entirely too much effort. Better to let others do the hard work so that he could enjoy life in his newly acquired penthouse.

One of Amaal's eyebrows lifted, but otherwise he did not seem to react to Malik's proposal, except to say, "Your offer assumes that I even know where my brother is. We haven't spoken in months, not since well before the Heat was loosed on the human population. I fear I can be of little help to you."

Damn. Malik had feared a response such as this. It was not so very unusual for djinn siblings to fall out of contact with one another for long periods of time, simply because in a race as long-lived as theirs, what might seem to a mortal to be an extended absence would feel like only a day or so to a djinn. A few months really wasn't that much to speak of...unless it was a few months that involved life-changing events such as the Heat and the djinn beginning to settle here on Earth.

"You have no idea where his new lands are located?"

"No," Amaal said. "Just as he does not know where mine are, either. We did not think it terribly important, for we knew we could reconnect whenever we chose, merely by calling out to one another across the miles. I wish I could give you better information, Malik. It must be very trying to have your Chosen disappear in such a way, and if I knew where Omar was, I would send you along to see him—if for no other reason than to clear his name, as I still find it difficult to believe he would do something so rash as to steal your woman from you. But I have nothing to offer in terms of my brother's whereabouts."

For the first time, Malik lifted the martini to his lips and allowed himself a swallow of the harsh liquid. The taste made him want to shudder, but he forced back the reaction. At least he could feel the alcohol when it hit his stomach, making him experience a brief burst of heat. "I am sorry to hear that, Amaal. You know why I had to ask."

"Of course." A shrug, one that made the late afternoon sunlight streaming through the windows shimmer along the copper-colored robes he wore. A fire elemental, he tended to dress in those warm colors, just as Malik favored the blues and greens of the sea. "And if Omar should happen to drop in, I'll make sure to ask whether he has your Chosen."

"I doubt he would give you an honest answer," Malik remarked.

"Perhaps not. But I like to flatter myself that I would be able to tell if he did." Amaal moved toward the window, gazing down at the empty streets some fifty stories below. Perhaps he wondered what they had been like when they were full of cars rushing past, and how those sidewalks must have appeared to the previous occupant of this penthouse when they were still filled with people hurrying about their daily tasks.

Or perhaps not. Amaal had never seemed overly concerned about anyone other than himself. In that way, he was somewhat like his brother, albeit without the malice.

"I have taken enough of your time," Malik said. "If you see or hear anything, you can contact me or my sister Fatima, who now has the charge of the Bel-Air settlement."

"Ah, the lovely Fatima." Amaal went quiet for a moment, as if recalling the last time he had seen her. "She was entirely too good for my brother, although I must confess I was rather surprised to hear that she had taken a Chosen."

His tone short, Malik replied, "Well, *she* always had a kind heart."

Amaal raised an eyebrow again, clearly catching the implication. He let out a not very convincing chuckle, then said, "That is true. Give her my regards."

"I shall. Have a good day, Amaal."

As the other djinn bowed in farewell, Malik blinked himself away from the penthouse, back to the mansion in Malibu. The warmth of its high wood-beamed ceilings and indoor atrium was an abrupt contrast to Amaal's coldly decorated penthouse, enough to make Malik pull in a breath and realize he was glad to be here, even knowing that Leila was gone.

Not for much longer, if I have anything to do about it, he thought, although he knew he was no closer to discovering her location than he had been when he left to speak with Amaal.

Something about that conversation didn't ring quite true, though, now that Malik stopped to think about it. Amaal and Omar weren't nearly as close as Malik was with his own sister, but they still had spent a good deal of time together, possibly because Amaal's palace was so much more luxurious than Omar's. Malik supposed it was conceivable that they hadn't spoken for months, true. However, it wasn't terribly likely; their kind tended to be solitary creatures, but despite that—or perhaps because of it—they often communicated with their family members, if only via thought rather than in person.

Which meant Amaal had probably been lying. Malik wasn't even sure whether he could blame the other djinn for doing so. Blood ties tended to count for more than any kind of loyalty to other djinn, or to a mortal woman Amaal didn't know at all.

So perhaps Amaal wouldn't tell Malik outright where Leila was being held.

That didn't mean Malik wouldn't be able to track her down in the end…even if he currently had no idea how to do so.

"I thought you could stay in here," Omar said, opening a door to reveal a large bedroom furnished with more of the pale wood pieces Leila had seen in the living room. A duvet cover in a soft Tiffany blue covered the queen-size bed, and she could see a well-appointed *en suite* bathroom through the partially open door on the other side of the room. No, it wasn't the master suite—unlike Malik, Omar probably wasn't the type to offer the best room to anyone other than himself —but it was still lovely. And, she thought with relief, clearly not the same room where the djinn was sleeping, which worked for her. At least he wasn't proposing that they immediately shack up.

"It's very nice," she responded.

"Good. I'd hoped you would think that." He went past her into the space, heading toward another door, one that opened onto a walk-in closet. It wasn't empty, but had a decent complement of clothing hanging from its racks. "Here are some changes of clothes, and the bathroom has plenty of toiletries." Omar paused, then added, "I wanted to make things comfortable for you here…if, of course, you intend to stay."

Why was it that when Malik had done much the same thing for her, it had only seemed thoughtful, while Omar supplying her with a wardrobe and bathroom supplies felt positively creepy, as if he'd been speculating on what size underwear she wore and whether she was a maxipad or a tampon kind of girl?

Leila repressed a shudder, and instead did her best to smile in gratitude. Then she said, "I'm glad you gave me some time to think. And well, I still don't know exactly what I should do. But I realized I gave Malik a chance without stopping to think about it too much. I suppose what I'm trying to say is that I need to give you a chance, too. Just…try to be patient with me, okay?"

"I completely understand," Omar replied, giving her another one of his oily smiles. "In the meantime, it is getting on toward dusk, and so we should think about having something to eat. I hope you won't mind sitting down to dinner with me."

"No, that sounds great." Actually, it sounded

the complete opposite of great, but Leila knew she couldn't exactly refuse him. It was going to be hard to remain civil, especially when she thought of the lovely meals she and Malik had shared, and yet she knew she had to play nice for now. She had to pretend to be happy about being with Omar, would have to eat the food he gave her and drink the wine. At least she was a little less worried about him trying to drug her; he could have done that with the glass of chardonnay he'd provided earlier, but nothing adverse had happened as a result of drinking the wine. "I'd offer to help, but Malik already showed me how you djinn put a meal together, so I know you don't really need an assistant."

Omar's eyes narrowed slightly at the mention of Malik, but he only said smoothly, "This is true. However, that doesn't mean I wouldn't appreciate having you there as I get things ready. Come along."

He led her out of the bedroom and back downstairs. This house was big, although nowhere close to the square footage of the Malibu house she'd been sharing with Malik. Too bad, because it felt as though it would have been easier to avoid Omar if the place had been a little bigger. But then, if she became too obvious about trying to avoid him, then he'd know in a heartbeat that every smile she'd offered, every word of understanding, was a complete lie.

About all she could do was keep up the act for as long as possible, and hope like hell that either Malik would find her and take her away from this place, or she'd come up with a way to escape.

The kitchen was large, but not quite as cavernous as the one in the Malibu house where Malik had made her breakfast. Omar pointed out where the dishes and glasses were kept in their separate cupboards, then suggested she could set the table if she wanted to help. Leila agreed eagerly, mostly because that way she could stay out of his immediate presence for a few minutes. Even so, she couldn't help experiencing a flare of resentment as she took the dishes into the dining room. Omar could have taken care of all of this with a snap of his fingers, but he hadn't. Most likely he'd wanted to see if she would argue with him about performing this task, and because she hadn't, had meekly gone about setting the table as he requested, he would now know that she was likely to do his bidding.

Dream on, she thought as, after a bit of searching, she found placemats and cloth napkins and silverware tucked away in a drawer in the sideboard in the dining room, then set them on the table. *I'm only doing this so you'll think I'm cooperating. If you really knew me, you'd know what a joke that is.*

But he didn't know her at all. Otherwise, he would have seen right through the ditz act, would have realized that she was only saying what he wanted to hear in order to keep herself alive. Clearly, when he'd first selected her as his Chosen, he'd only considered her appearance. He hadn't spared a thought about the woman behind the face, and obviously hadn't been paying any attention to who she really was.

Fine by her. Leila wanted him to be fooled. That way, he wouldn't see it coming when she got the hell out of here, one way or another.

The dining room table was long, with space to seat a dozen people. As much as she would have preferred to put their place settings at opposite ends of that table so she could sit as far away from him as possible, she knew that sort of ploy probably wouldn't go over too well with Omar. Instead, she put one place setting at the end of the table and the other to the left, knowing that the djinn would want to pretend he was the master of the house and sit at the table's head.

He came out to survey what she was doing, then nodded in approval. "That all looks very good. This is a fine room."

As much as she didn't want to be here, Leila

had to agree with Omar's observation. A large seascape covered one wall, and the opposite wall wasn't really a wall at all, but a bank of windows with French doors set into them, offering a nearly uninterrupted view of the ocean. Now, with the sun setting and sending a flare of golden light into the room, it really was spectacular. Of course, the sunset would be just as beautiful when viewed from the Malibu house, but she knew better than to point out that particular fact.

A wave of his hand, and the tabletop was suddenly filled with dishes, the kind of feast she might have had once upon a time at her grandparents' house—lamb kebob and roasted vegetables and large bowls overflowing with fragrant rice. True, she'd given up lamb years ago, but Leila sort of doubted that Omar would care to hear why she no longer included lamb and veal in her diet, especially since she doubted he would respect the scruples that had made her exclude those foods from her meals.

"That smells great," she said instead, inwardly hoping she'd be able to get at least a few bites of the lamb down. A few days ago, she might not have hesitated at all, she'd been so hungry, but now that she didn't have to worry about scrounging every bite that went in her mouth, all the old objections had come rushing back.

"I think you will enjoy it." A decanter appeared on the table as well, and Leila couldn't quite prevent her mouth from tightening as she looked at it. Decanted wine spelled trouble, in her book. If she couldn't watch it get poured directly from the bottle, she had every reason to suspect that it might have been tampered with. Unfortunately, she wasn't in any position to complain. Perhaps noting her hesitation, Omar went on, "Go ahead, sit down. There's no need for you to keep hovering like that."

Leila wasn't aware she'd been hovering at all, but she didn't bother to protest. Forcing a smile onto her lips, she took the chair to the djinn's left and sat down, then carefully spread the napkin over her lap. Omar remained standing for a moment, ostensibly to pour some wine into his glass and then hers. However, Leila couldn't help wondering whether he'd also continued to stand so he might point out how much taller he was than she, how he loomed over her.

Go ahead and play your petty power games, she thought as Omar finally took his seat. *You think I don't see right through them?*

Even as the scornful thought crossed her mind, though, she couldn't help wondering if she would have been so quick to pick up on Omar's games if Malik hadn't already warned her about the other djinn's psychological issues. She wanted to think so, because God only knew that Hollywood had been a hotbed of mind games on a truly Olympic scale, but....

"To giving things a chance," Omar said, raising his glass and thus forcing Leila to lift hers as well.

"To giving things a chance," she echoed, inwardly reflecting that his toast could have several different meanings, depending on how you looked at it.

Moment of truth. Leila took in a gulp of air, prayed to whatever gods might be listening that the wine wasn't drugged, and then allowed herself a very small sip. It seemed to taste all right, but that didn't necessarily mean anything.

Omar drank as well, and she felt herself relax slightly. He could have doctored the wine, but Leila doubted he would have been able to drink from the same decanter and not be affected. Then again, she didn't know that much about djinn physiology. She supposed it wasn't outside the bounds of possibility that one of them could consume drugs or poisons that would stop a human in their tracks and yet be unaffected.

Putting aside her worries, she had to admit the wine was very good. She couldn't really identify it, except that she was fairly certain it was probably a

Rhone blend of some kind, a good match for the lamb and vegetables.

"I like that," she said with a smile.

"Good," Omar replied. "I tried to choose something I thought you would enjoy. If I may?"

At least he did her the courtesy of dishing up some food for her—a lamb kebob, a healthy portion of vegetables, a rather smaller pile of rice.

Afraid I'm going to get fat, Omar? Leila thought with some amusement as she took the plate back from him. While she'd watched her weight back before the world changed, it had been more out of habit than because she really needed to. At any rate, she couldn't help but contrast his behavior with the way Malik had treated her, how he'd made sure she got plenty to eat, not seeming to care at all about the calories involved.

"Thank you," she said, then watched while he gave himself a good deal more food than he'd given her. Which was fine. Being in his company was a damn good appetite-killer, and she knew she'd have to force herself to eat even the modest portion on her plate. What she really wanted to do was push her chair away from the table and go up and hide in the room that had been provided for her, but she guessed that idea was a non-starter.

Instead, she lifted a forkful of vegetables to her

mouth and ate them with what she hoped appeared to be a decent appetite. Omar appeared pleased by this—or maybe he was only happy that she'd gone for the veggies first—because he smiled at her before going on to spear a piece of lamb with his fork. They both ate in silence for a moment.

Then he said, "I hope you will see that I mean you no harm—indeed, the very opposite. It is distressing to know that Malik did his best to turn you against me."

He didn't bother to waste the time. I doubt he spared two thoughts for you. These words passed through Leila's mind, although she knew better than to say them aloud. She gave an offhand shrug. "Oh, I can tell already that he wasn't being truthful. You've been nothing but a gentleman to me."

Omar opened his mouth to speak, but whatever he'd intended to say was abruptly cut off by an odd whistle of air, followed by the appearance in the dining room of another djinn. His features were similar enough to Omar's that Leila guessed he must be family, although this new djinn had darker hair, and his looks lacked something of Omar's hardness.

Clearly, this visitor hadn't been expected, because Omar actually rose out of his seat, his eyes narrowed in anger. "Amaal, what are you doing here?"

"Why, brother, you don't look pleased to see me." The newcomer glanced over at Leila and gave her an appraising look, followed by a swift grin. "Although I can see why you would not wish to be interrupted."

Rather than being irritated by the once-over, Leila had to do her best to repress a grin of her own. There hadn't been anything malicious about his smile, just a flash of appreciation. Although Amaal's eyes were the same shade as his brother's, they were friendly and open, almost teasing, rather than cold and flinty.

"To what do I owe the honor of this interruption?" Omar inquired, clearly not thrilled by his brother's presence.

"A certain…matter…has come up. I thought I had better speak with you."

Whatever this "matter" was, it clearly caught Omar's attention. He gave a brief, exasperated glance at the food on the table, his full wine glass. Then he said, "My apologies, Leila, but I must have speech with my brother. Perhaps it would be best if you took your plate up to your room."

"I—" she began, then paused, knowing that Omar would cut off any protests. "Um, sure. Give me a sec."

Somewhat awkwardly, she piled her cutlery on top of her plate, then grabbed a napkin and her wine glass. The two djinn were silent as she left the room and headed down the hall to the staircase. She had a feeling they wouldn't say anything else to each other until she was safely out of earshot.

Not that she had any intention of going meekly to her room and finishing her food. Once she reached the landing at the top of the stairs, she carefully set down her plate, although she kept the wine glass clutched in one hand. Back when she was in high school, she'd done much the same thing when she wanted to listen in on the adult conversations her parents hadn't wanted her to hear.

If Omar caught her —

No, she wouldn't think about that. Those boots he wore made enough noise on the tile floors that she should probably be able to hear him coming toward the staircase once he was done talking to Amaal. Unless he decided to blink himself into her bedroom.

She took a quick gulp of wine and strained to pick up the thread of the conversation. Both of the djinn had deep enough voices that they carried well enough, but sometimes they were almost too deep, and lost themselves in unintelligible rumbles.

"…knows something." That was Amaal, more baritone than bass.

"Which doesn't surprise me." Omar, sounding unconcerned. "After all, I am the most likely suspect. But does he have anything more than….?"

Leila couldn't quite catch the last word, although she guessed it was probably "suspicions." Which made sense. Malik wasn't stupid—Omar must have been his first choice when it came to figuring out who had absconded with his Chosen.

"No," Amaal said. "He thought I might know where you were. I said I did not."

"And…believed you?"

"…doubt it. But he has no way of finding this place. Even so, I thought it…warn you."

"And I thank…for that." A long pause, during which Leila hardly dared to breathe. Had the brothers finished their conversation? More likely, Omar had taken a brief break to drink some wine. "Things…going well. But…more time."

"I   understand.   If   I   learn anything…you know."

"I…you will."

After that came a prolonged silence. With a start, Leila realized the conversation had probably ended. She grabbed her plate and hurried down the hallway to her bedroom, then set the wine glass and plate on one of the nightstands. She was just lifting a forkful of rice to her mouth when a knock came on the doorframe—only a courtesy, since the door still stood open.

Omar peered inside, and smiled slightly as he saw her eating her meal. "He has gone. You can come back downstairs now, so we might finish our meal together."

"Mine's getting a little cold—" she began, but he shrugged.

"It is no matter. I can heat it up for you when we are sitting at the table."

She'd seen Malik do the same thing, although she decided it was probably better not to mention that. "Oh, great. Just a sec, then." Once again she gathered up her plate and her wine glass, then went to meet Omar at the door. "I'm glad we can still have our dinner. Is everything okay?"

"Oh, yes, everything is fine. Come along."

Leila followed him downstairs, mind working furiously. Amaal had clearly come here to give his brother a heads-up, so now Omar would be even more on his guard. However, it also sounded as if Malik didn't have any way of tracking her here. He'd said once that djinn weren't omnipotent or all-seeing, and the current situation seemed to bear out that statement. But she wouldn't let herself lose hope. If there were absolutely no chance of Malik finding her, then she doubted that Amaal would have come running over here to let his brother know what was going on.

So…some cause for hope. In the meantime, she'd try to hang on and see if she could break herself out of this place. Djinn might have come out of some old fairytale, but that didn't mean she was going to sit here like a princess in a tower and wait for her hero to rescue her.

Sometimes you just had to rescue your own damn self.

FOURTEEN

Malik invited Fatima to dinner at the Malibu house, partly because he hated the idea of having to sit down to eat by himself, and also because he knew his sister was in a similar predicament, her own Chosen gone as well. He thought it better for the two of them to be together so they could commiserate. Anyway, it wasn't healthy for her to sit by herself in her big empty house and wait for word about Adam, word that might never come. If, by some grace of God, a new development arose, the djinn in the Bel-Air community could reach out to her and have her come home quickly enough.

She seemed to have recognized the dinner invitation for what it was, and did her best to be animated as they ate their food and drank some wine and attempted to discuss everything except the kidnappings of their respective partners. But then her gaze strayed to the empty chairs at the table, and she let out a small sigh. "It was good of you to ask me here, Malik," she said. "If only it could be the four of us sitting at this table, though, and no worries about the fate of those we love."

He could not agree with her more. With any luck, the happy scenario she had just described would come true sooner rather than later. "Yes, that would make for a much happier time. The hours stretch when we are separated from our Chosen, but I try to remind myself that it has not been so very long, and certainly not long enough to give up hope."

"You have learned something?" Fatima asked, wine glass partway to her lips.

"Not as much as I would have liked. I paid a visit to Omar's brother Amaal, who did not offer anything I could work with."

"Even if he knows something, I doubt he would share it with you."

Malik nodded; he couldn't argue with his sister's assessment of the situation, not when he had thought the same thing himself. "No, and I suppose it was foolish of me to believe otherwise. Amaal—unlike his brother—is not a bad man, but he would also not do anything he thought might harm Omar, or risk bringing his activities to the elders' notice. No doubt he is wishing he had nothing to do with any of us, and is a bit angry at his brother for dragging him into it. But that irritation, I fear, is not sufficient for him to betray Omar's confidence."

"No," Fatima said. "I cannot claim to know Amaal well, but his life has always been as easy as he has been able to make it. Complications do not suit him."

Malik gave her a wry smile and sipped at his own wine. "That is only the truth. In a way, it would be easier if we were all mortals—then I could merely lurk near Amaal's residence and follow him the next time he drove off. That sort of scheme seems to work well enough in the movies and television shows I have seen, but unfortunately, it will do me no good when it comes to following a djinn."

A small laugh as Fatima set down her wine glass. "You are correct in that. It has always been easy for us to slip away if we do not wish to be found. However...." Her words trailed off there, and her elegantly arched brows drew together in a small frown.

"'However'?" Malik prompted her. Did his sister know something he did not?

"Oh, it could be nothing." She waved a hand. "It is only that I remember how Yasir, from whom I parted ways many decades ago, said he had figured out a way to track a djinn's movements. I did not pay that much attention at the time, for Yasir was always researching something, always meddling with spells and charms."

For all Fatima's dismissal, Malik could not prevent a rush of hope from moving through him. If her former lover really had come up with a way to track a djinn.... Trying to keep his voice calm, he asked, "Do you know where Yasir is now?"

"Oh, yes," she replied. "He is one of the One Thousand, and is settled with the group in San Diego. His Chosen was a graduate student at one of the universities there, I believe." A small chuckle, and she added, "This does not surprise me at all. I can see how Yasir would want a woman of learning at his side, for, as I said, he had a most undjinn-like scientific bent."

"I must speak with him," Malik said, and began to rise from the table.

At once, Fatima put a hand on his wrist, preventing him from moving any further. "I can see why you would want to talk to Yasir, see if he can help you, but can you not finish your meal first?"

Malik offered her a sheepish smile, then

settled himself back in his chair. "My apologies, sister. My enthusiasm got the better of me."

She gave a small lift of her shoulders and said, "It is fine. I understand. Indeed, despite my worry for Adam, I would have told you to let it wait until morning, for the dinner hour is not the best time to intrude on strangers. But I doubt you would have listened to me."

"No, I could not wait that long." Even the few minutes it would require to consume the rest of their meal seemed excruciatingly long. Still, it would be better to wait a little. For all he knew, this Yasir would also be dining, and would not appreciate being interrupted. "I will just have to hope that he does not mind having an uninvited guest drop by this evening."

"Once you have explained why you need to speak to him, he will most likely understand. Yasir is not the type to worry about conventions."

That was good to hear. Although he and Fatima were close enough, the subject of her lovers—past and present—was one they generally avoided. She had clearly not been sufficiently smitten with any of them to start a family, and therefore Malik had never pressed her for more information than she was willing to give freely. He wondered why she had not found Yasir suitable for a more long-term relationship, since the few tidbits she had dropped during this conversation seemed to indicate that his was a much more amiable personality than Omar's, but he supposed that was none of his business, either.

"And you know the location of the San Diego settlement?"

"Yes," Fatima replied. "It is information the elders shared with all of us who would lead these groups, just in case we ever had reason to contact one another. They are in a place called La Jolla. I can show it to you on a map."

"Thank you, sister." Such information would make his journey much easier. Djinn could travel to places they had never been or seen, but it was a tedious process that involved "blinking" to the farthest point in their sightline, and then making another jump from there, and so on. It was certainly faster than walking, or riding a horse, or even using a car, although that was about all which could be said for that particular mode of travel.

But if Fatima had a map she could show him, then he could send himself directly to this La Jolla place, which must be somewhere in San Diego's environs, although he had never heard of it before. With any luck, Yasir would have been working on his tracking spell in the time since he had parted from Fatima, and hopefully had perfected it by now.

If not, well, Malik would have wasted some time, and nothing more. Without any other good leads to follow, he wouldn't have known what to do with that time anyway.

He ate quickly while Fatima watched him with a halfway amused expression on her features, as though she knew precisely why he was hurrying through his dinner. At least she did not tease him over his behavior, for of course it also served her purpose that his trip to La Jolla be a fruitful one.

Soon enough they were both finished. He waved a hand to clear away the dishes, and then he accompanied her to her home in Bel-Air, so she might show him La Jolla's location on the map. Yes, there it was—some fourteen miles north of what had once been the downtown San Diego area, and directly on the coast, with a large bay and a forested area to the north. It seemed like a fine location; he could understand why that particular group of djinn had settled there.

"And here is Yasir's home," she said, finger tracing on the map to a street right next to a bluff that overlooked the beach, clearly a prime location.

"Perfect. That will be easy enough to find."

Then he was kissing Fatima on the cheek and

promising her he would come and report on what he found. She touched his arm briefly and said, "Good luck, brother."

Good luck, indeed. He could use some of that about now. With every moment that passed, he feared something terrible might be happening to Leila, something he was powerless to prevent. If Omar caused her any hurt, Malik knew he would never forgive himself for his carelessness in leaving her alone.

The office of Fatima's Bel-Air home disappeared, and in the next moment Malik stood on a sidewalk in front of a large Spanish-style home, two-storied and sprawling, surrounded by palm trees and beds of flowers. Lights gleamed from most of the windows, telling Malik that its current residents must be home. Then again, where else would they be at this time of evening?

Solar lamps lined the walkway of reddish sandstone, guiding him up to the front door. Once there, he hesitated for a moment, wondering whether this mission was as harebrained as it suddenly seemed it might be. But no, he was doing this for Leila...and for Adam. Fatima had told him Yasir might be able to help. It would be foolish to throw up his hands and walk away now.

Jaw set, Malik knocked on the door. For a

moment, there was no answer, and then it opened, and a djinn he had never seen before stared out at him in some confusion.

Before the moment could grow too awkward, Malik said, "I am Fatima's brother, Malik al-Mazin. You are Yasir al-Barak?"

The djinn blinked again, although this time more in comprehension. His eyes were gray, an unusual shade for a djinn, and he had dark brown hair that he wore pulled back in a ponytail, also somewhat unusual, since djinn men tended to leave their hair loose. "Yes, I am Yasir. Do come inside. How is Fatima?"

"Very well," Malik answered politely. Whatever the reason her sister had not continued her association with this man, it did not seem as if they had parted on bad terms. That should make asking for a favor a bit easier.

"She is the leader of the Bel-Air community now, is she not?" Yasir asked as he led Malik farther inside the house, which seemed warm and welcoming, with its parchment-hued walls and Spanish tile on the floors.

"Yes, she is."

From elsewhere in the house came the low hum of voices. Yasir glanced down the hall and said, "My Chosen, Radha. She is watching a movie."

That seemed to be Yasir's way of letting Malik know they were not likely to be disturbed in the near future. "Ah. I do want to apologize for intruding on your evening, but Fatima told me something that made me think you might be able to offer some assistance."

"Assistance with what?" Luckily, the other djinn seemed more curious than anything else, and not at all concerned about having someone he'd never met suddenly appear on his doorstep.

"My Chosen, Leila, and Fatima's Chosen, Adam, have both recently disappeared. I have my suspicions as to who might be involved, but I fear that without being able to follow the possible suspect, I will not be able to prove my hypothesis."

"Ah." Yasir reached up to rub his chin, which was covered in a neatly trimmed beard. "Fatima told you about my tracking spell?"

"She mentioned that you had been working on something like that, yes."

"I haven't done anything with it for a while," the djinn said, then added, as though he'd seen Malik's face fall, "but only because it did work well enough as it was, and I have had no reason to use it."

"But it worked."

"Oh, yes." Yasir paused for a moment, giving

Malik a curious look. "May I ask on whom you intend to use it?"

"I'd prefer not to say," Malik replied. "All I have are suspicions, and I do not wish to name names until I am certain. It is no one in your community here, however."

Yasir chuckled. "No, I was not thinking that, not at all. Everyone is present and accounted for, and we do not have any extra Chosen visiting us." His expression sobered, and he went on, "I am sorry to hear that your own Chosen is missing, and Fatima's as well. That is a grave matter. But come with me—I will take you to my workroom."

He waved with one hand, indicating that Malik should follow him out of the living room where they'd been standing and talking, and down a hallway that passed the family room. In there a pretty young woman with long blonde hair lay on the couch, watching something on the large flat-screen television that dominated the opposite wall. She flicked a curious glance in their direction but didn't speak, apparently content to let Yasir explain things to her once he was done talking to his guest.

Through the kitchen, and then down another short hallway, one that ended in a door which opened on the garage. It was large, with room for four cars, although one section proved to be exactly what Yasir had said it was—clearly his workroom, with a large table on one side, and a metal cabinet filled with tools, and bins of various objects Malik couldn't quite identify. He'd never had much of a mechanical bent, and so was unfamiliar with mortal gadgets.

Yasir went to the workbench and opened one of the drawers of the metal cabinet that sat off to one side. From within he extracted what appeared to be a compass of some sort, along with a small leather bag.

"The principle is quite basic, really," he said, holding up the compass, which was bright brass with a fine pattern etched into its case. "Compasses point north, and are little more than magnets, pulling toward the Earth's magnetic field. In this bag is a powder I made from filing down several small magnets. Sprinkle the powder on the doorstep of the person you want to track. It will stick to their shoes, and the compass will point you in the direction they've gone—and will continue to do so until you catch up with them."

"That sounds simple enough," Malik said, already plotting how he might arrange to place the powder at the entrance to Amaal's penthouse.

"It is." Yasir turned the compass over in his palm. "It took some time to figure out how to enchant the compass so it would always point to the filings, but once I got that part of the problem solved, the spell worked without fail. Here," he said, then handed the round brass object to Malik. "Take care with it, for it is the only one I have. I could probably make another if necessary, but since I have had little need to use this one, I do not quite see the point. Still, I would prefer that it be kept safe."

"I will be careful," Malik promised. The brass casing felt warm against his skin, but perhaps that was only because Yasir had recently held the device. It certainly did not feel magical in any way, which Malik supposed was for the best. Most djinn did not dabble in this kind of magic, since the native powers they possessed were enough to see them through almost any situation. He had to admit he was somewhat uneasy about working with this kind of enchanted object. But he would do what he must in order to rescue Leila.

"And the powder." Yasir gave the pouch to Malik, who slipped the drawstrings over his wrist. "Use as much as you need, for this is easier for me to make."

"I hope I will not need to use much. I have only the one person to track, and if this works as you say it does—"

"It does. It will."

"Well, then, only a small amount should do the trick."

Yasir nodded, his features suddenly grave. "I hope so, for your sake. I cannot imagine losing my Chosen."

Losing Leila was something that Malik wished could have remained only a product of his darkest nightmares. Unfortunately, Omar al-Tariq had made her disappearance a very upsetting reality.

"She will be recovered," Malik said, hoping he sounded confident, rather than worried that this all might be for naught. It was entirely possible that Amaal had had no recent contact with his brother, and so Malik would be tracking an innocent man. But he had to know. He had to be sure. "And the one responsible for stealing her from me will be punished."

"From your mouth to God's ears," Yasir responded, using the human phrase.

"Thank you for this. If ever I have a chance to return the favor—"

"It is nothing. I am glad that it can be of some use to someone."

Malik smiled in gratitude. "Peace be upon you, then."

"And on you."

He whisked himself away…but he did not go

home. No, he headed toward downtown, where Amaal's borrowed penthouse lay.

He had some reconnaissance to do.

Dinner wasn't quite as excruciating as Leila had worried it might be, mostly because Omar seemed preoccupied, not as focused on attempting to charm her as she'd feared. She did her part by talking about the beach, and the weather, and asking how he'd decided on this house.

"It pleased me," he said before taking another sip of wine. "I cannot say precisely why—I suppose it was the high ceilings, and all the windows. I am a creature of the air, after all, and so I am drawn to places with this sort of space and light."

"It's gorgeous." She drank some wine as well, but in sips smaller than Omar's, tiny little swallows that weren't much more than a taste. Wine didn't affect her the same way as the hard stuff, thank God, and yet she didn't want to be stupid about this. She didn't think she could ever get drunk enough to actually welcome this djinn's attentions, but no point in losing any kind of control. After setting her glass down, she said, "That was your brother?"

Omar's jaw hardened slightly. "Yes. Amaal."

"Is everything okay?"

"Yes," Omar replied, still with that same tension in his jaw line and neck, so it seemed as though he had to work hard to force out that one syllable. However, his tone was mild enough as he went on, "He only wished to consult with me on a minor matter."

Should she push it, or let it go? Leila decided it would seem more out of character not to respond, so she said, "It didn't seem minor."

A huff of breath, and Omar helped himself to a noticeably larger swallow of wine. Leila tensed in her chair, wondering if she'd made the wrong choice by continuing to comment on Amaal's visit, and what in the world she would do if Omar decided to retaliate against her in some way.

But apparently he was still more interested in smooth-talking his way into her pants than engaging in any power plays, because he said, "Amaal tends to be overly dramatic. While the situation seems important to him, it is of no real consequence. The elders gave him lands to settle on, but he does not care much for them and has instead taken up residence someplace else. He needed reassurance that they would not punish him in some way for not following their wishes."

"Would they do that?" Leila inquired, genuinely curious. It sounded as though these elders had a lot of power, all things considered. After all, they'd somehow managed to make the hardliners play nice and keep away from the other djinns' Chosen.

"I doubt they would expend the energy to intervene." Omar ladled some more rice onto his plate, then added another kebob. Clearly, he wasn't too worried about his waistline. "Oh, I suppose at some point one of them might go and speak to him, let him know that he needs to live where his designated lands are located, but I cannot see that happening anytime soon. Until the world is completely cleansed, they have more important things to worry about."

The wine Leila had just swallowed seemed to lodge somewhere in her esophagus. Omar had spoken so casually of this "cleansing," as though it didn't matter at all to him that human beings might be dying right now at the hands of his fellow djinn. But then, he probably didn't care one way or another. He'd only chosen her because he'd wanted a human to torment. Was keeping her alive so he could abuse her any better than killing her outright?

Not really, except that prolonging her torture might provide more opportunities for escape. As her father had liked to say, *Where there's life, there's hope.*

But Leila knew she couldn't allow Omar to see how upset she was. Although the thought of eating anything else made her stomach curdle, she forced down a piece of lamb and another sip of wine before asking, "Are the elders involved in the cleansing?"

"No. Not directly, anyway. I suppose such activities would be beneath their dignity. It is more that they will want everything to be over with so the true settling in, so to speak, can begin."

"So they're going to come live here, too?"

That query elicited a cold, sideways glance. "You ask a great many questions, Leila."

"Sorry," she said quickly, then gave a nervous giggle, one carefully calibrated to ease his suspicions. It seemed to work, because he relaxed slightly and leaned back in his chair, one hand lying on the tabletop as he regarded her. She took a breath and went on, "I guess it's just all so *interesting,* you know? Like, just a totally different culture. All these questions keep bubbling up in my head."

And, holy hell, did it hurt to say that. Just please God, let him have bought it.

Apparently God was listening—or her acting

skills were better than she thought, after all those failed auditions—because Omar gave her an indulgent smile. "I suppose I hadn't thought of it that way. But I can see your point. This is all new to you, so of course you would have a great deal to ask. I will tell you what I can, but when it comes to the elders...." He let the words trail off, then gave an indifferent shrug she didn't believe for one second. "Their ways are often quite inscrutable, and so I can't really say with any authority what prompts their decisions and their motivations. They claim to rule with a light hand, which I suppose is true enough, for they do not tend to interfere with our day-to-day lives. And that is why I told Amaal he did not have anything to worry about."

Well, that was something, she supposed, although right then Leila would have preferred a little more in the way of hands-on governing. A *laissez-faire* approach worked just fine when everyone behaved themselves and didn't break the rules, but it would have been nice to believe that the elders would descend from the otherworld and inflict some serious ass-kicking on Omar as soon as they found out what he'd been up to. Malik had made it sound as though they would dispense justice once they had evidence of wrongdoing. Unfortunately, someone had to present that evidence to them—it didn't seem as though they intended to go out of their way to find it for themselves.

"It does seem a silly thing for them to worry about," Leila said. "If Amaal isn't bothering anyone, what does it matter where he's living?"

"Precisely." Omar seemed to have noticed that she hadn't eaten anything for a few moments, because he asked, "Have you finished?"

"Yes," she said, relieved that he didn't expect her to continue eating. It had been getting more and more difficult to shove the food down her throat.

"Well, then." He waved a hand, and her plate disappeared, as did his. The wine glasses, however remained. Luckily, Omar seemed more interested in filling his own glass than attending to hers, although possibly that was because she still had barely touched the glass. "Let us go out and watch the last of the sunset, shall we?"

Leila didn't know whether that was a particularly good idea, but she also guessed that any demurrals would be met with some hostility…and possibly suspicion. "Sure," she said. "As long as you think it won't be too cold."

Another negligent wave of his hand, and this time a soft, warm pashmina shawl in a dark red shade to match her skirt appeared, wrapping itself around her shoulders. She couldn't help startling a bit, but then she laughed.

"Well, that's handy," she remarked, then cast a quick glance at Omar, at the open robe he wore. "Don't djinn get cold?"

"If the conditions are extreme enough," he replied, rising from his chair. "But I have nothing to fear from the weather outside this house."

Since it didn't seem as though she'd be able to stall any longer without appearing painfully obvious, she got up from her seat as well. Omar came over and took her by the arm, guiding her out of the dining room and through the French doors so they could stand on the deck. She wished she could have pulled her arm from his grasp, but that kind of behavior was certain to invoke his ire. Instead, she drew in a breath and told herself to pretend this was all an audition, that none of it was real. It wouldn't be the first time she'd had to act opposite someone she didn't like. If she'd managed to muscle through it before, she could do the same thing now.

All right, the stakes were a lot higher now, but she thought it probably better not to dwell on that particular aspect of the situation. If she allowed herself to really think about what was going on here, she knew the panic would rise up and overwhelm her. She couldn't let that happen. She needed to hang on, no matter what, so Malik would have enough time to find her.

The wind from the ocean was cold and sharp. The shawl Omar had given her helped a little, but she could still feel the chilly air penetrating the silken skirt and thin knit top she wore, and her toes in their beaded sandals were nearly numb. Well, this would pass. The conditions were uncomfortable, but it wasn't as though she was standing outside in sub-zero temperatures or something.

Out to the west, only a brooding glow lingered on the horizon. The skies were clear, turning a deep sapphire shade. Once again Leila was struck by how alone they were here, how the house behind them was the only source of light, floating like a diamond on a bed of deep blue velvet.

If she'd been here with Malik, she could have taken some comfort from his presence, from knowing that she was safe with him. But he was God knows how many miles away, and she still didn't know what Omar intended for her.

"It's really beautiful," she said, keeping her gaze fixed on the faint band of orange light that lingered to the west. She thought that was safest.

"You're beautiful," Omar said. He moved

closer to her, took a lock of her wind-whipped hair and ran it through his fingers.

From someone else, that might have been a caress. As it was, she could only think of how easy it would be for him to yank on her hair, use it as a means to pull her toward him.

"Oh, wow…um, t-thank y-you," she replied, letting the words stammer a bit. It actually wasn't that difficult, since her teeth wanted to chatter from the cold anyway.

"It is no idle compliment." Omar's voice had lowered, become more intimate, almost caressing. "You are exquisite, Leila Donovan. All Chosen are attractive, but you are something else, a rare jewel. Why else do you think Malik al-Mazin and I would both challenge one another to be your protector?"

She felt it then—that strange, hazy quality to her focus, the sensation that part of her mind wasn't quite hers. The glamour, Malik had called it. He had attempted to use it when they first met, but only to quell her fear, not to bend her to his will. This time, though, she knew exactly why Omar had employed that particular piece of djinn magic. He didn't want to give her the chance to choose him. No, he wanted to make sure she had no choice but to become his.

Deep within, her soul rebelled. And yet she

knew if she defied him openly, he would retaliate. What form that retaliation might take, she didn't know—she didn't want to know. Better to give him a little of what he wanted, and hope he was willing to wait for the rest.

"I—" she began, then broke off, as though she didn't know what she'd intended to say. Instead, she looked up at him with what she hoped were appropriately glassy eyes. She desperately needed him to think that the glamour had worked on her.

Apparently, he did, because in the next moment, he bent and pressed his mouth against hers, hard. In fact, he came at her with such force that she found herself pushed backward a few paces, until her body touched the glass doors.

Well, at least he didn't taste bad, only of the wine he'd drunk before they came out here. Leila found it best to detach herself from the moment, to look at it clinically and decide whether she should put her arms around him or let them dangle at her sides, as if she was so overcome her body still didn't know quite how to react. Whether to open her mouth wider, or allow Omar to push it open with his tongue. Really, it wasn't that different from analyzing a performance, trying to see how it could be improved, even though underneath it all she wanted to scream and push herself away.

But if she remained clinical about it all, she could tell herself this was survivable. Just another role with a leading man she didn't particularly care for.

And it did end...eventually. He pulled away, watching her with his hard blue eyes, which picked up an odd, glinting reflection from the lights inside the house. On cue, Leila put a hand to her head, feigning dizziness.

"Oh...wow," she gasped. "I didn't expect that."

"Did you mind it?"

"No—no," she replied. "It was—it was fine. More than fine," she added hastily as she saw the way the djinn's eyes began to narrow at what he apparently considered faint praise. "But I feel so odd. Kind of dizzy." To emphasize her words, she put one hand flat against the glass panes of the French door. "I think—I think I need to go upstairs. Is that okay?"

A long pause, during which Leila felt her heart began to beat harder. What if he didn't allow her to escape? What if he threw the glamour at her again in order to push her into bed? She'd tried to steel herself against that possibility, but now with it looming....

Then Omar said, "It is fine. You have had a

long day. And there's always tomorrow, isn't there?"

She smiled up at him. "Yes, there is." Before she could lose her nerve, she went up on her tiptoes so she could kiss him quickly on the mouth. "I'll see you tomorrow, then."

And she put her hand on the latch for the French door, worried that he would reach out and grab her as she opened it. He didn't, though, only stood there and watched as she let herself inside and did her best to walk calmly over to the stairs.

Her heart was hammering away with such force, she thought it might beat its way right out of her chest. As she climbed the stairs, one thought consumed her entire being.

I have got to get out of here.

FIFTEEN

THE NEXT MORNING, MALIK TRAVELED TO downtown Los Angeles. Not too early, because he knew Amaal was not much of early riser. Actually, his greatest fear was that Amaal would have no reason to leave his penthouse today, that he would stay the entire time holed up in the coldly luxurious residence he'd taken for his own.

Well, if that happened, then Malik would return the next day. And the next, even though the thought of having to wait that long felt as though it would kill him. Sooner or later, Amaal al-Tariq would have to venture out. And if he did not, well, Malik would concoct some kind of ruse to get the other djinn to leave his home. In that moment, Malik vowed to himself that he would do whatever he must in order to track the fire elemental to his brother's hiding place.

The other difficulty would be in getting the powder on Amaal's shoes. Djinn were not like mortals; in most cases, they had no reason to cross the threshold of their homes, not when they could blink themselves out of a location without a second thought. Therefore, sneaking onto the top floor of the building and sprinkling the magnetic substance on the mat in front of the penthouse door would not do much good. Malik would have to go inside the penthouse itself and spread the powder around without getting caught. Logistically, this should not have been that difficult, simply because Malik could also blink himself inside. That sort of behavior was considered very rude among their people, unless permission was explicitly granted to enter someone's residence. Still, he cared little for conventions at the moment. This was not a social call, but rather his only chance to locate Leila.

As he lurked on top of the high-rise opposite the building where Amaal's penthouse was located, Malik briefly considered waiting for the other djinn to leave so he might enter the penthouse without fear of being detected. He immediately abandoned that notion, however, for what if the reason for Amaal's departure was to go to his brother's hiding place? If that were the case, Malik would have given up his only chance at being able to track his prey.

He raised a pair of binoculars to his eyes and focused them on the penthouse. No doubt the architect who'd designed the place hadn't considered it might be surveilled from the neighboring building's roof, or perhaps he—or she, Malik supposed, although the penthouse had seemed almost comically masculine in design—would not have had its walls composed almost entirely of sheet glass. As it was, he had been able to observe Amaal rise from his bed and put on an ostentatious red and gold silk dressing gown, then wander into the kitchen in search of his morning coffee, which he brewed using the complicated equipment that had come with the apartment, rather than conjuring it himself. After that came an elaborate breakfast, also made from scratch. It seemed clear to Malik that the other djinn rather relished utilizing all the accoutrements that had come with the penthouse apartment.

It also seemed clear that Amaal was in no particular hurry to do much of anything, and his extravagance in wasting time made Malik want to grind his teeth in frustration. However, since there was little he could do except watch and wait, he told himself that patience was often rewarded, and that he certainly did not have the luxury of being able to walk away.

At last Amaal went back to his bedroom and disappeared into the attached bathroom—which, thankfully, did not have glass walls.

That appeared to be his opening. Malik could not think of a better time to infiltrate the apartment than while Amaal was showering, especially since he would probably make that into just as much of an event as brewing a pot of coffee or cooking an omelette. After hanging the binoculars by their strap around his neck, he blinked himself into the apartment, then hastily spilled some of the magnetic filings on the floor just outside the bedroom door, and again in the kitchen. Since the flooring was black marble with pale gray veining, the dull gray of the powder material did not show up too badly.

Besides, who would be staring down at the floor when they had that spectacular view outside their windows?

Malik blinked himself away just as he heard the water in the master bath shut off. Once again lurking by the enormous air conditioning stacks on top of the neighboring high-rise, he brought the binoculars up to his eyes. No sign of Amaal yet, but he probably spent an inordinate amount

of time grooming himself, just as he did everything else.

Eventually, however, he did emerge from the
master suite, today in robes in a dark brick-red
shade. He strode right over the filings Malik had
left behind, and then went into the kitchen to
pour himself another cup of coffee, thereby
adding to the magnetic powder that had already
collected on the bottom of his boots. For a few
excruciating moments, he only stood there,
drinking coffee and staring meditatively off into
the distance, although at what, Malik had no idea.
Then Amaal set down the mug he was holding
and promptly blinked out of sight.

The compass, which had been resting in a
pocket in Malik's robes this entire time, began to
vibrate. Hurriedly, he pulled it out, saw that the
little red needle was pointing due east.

East it was.

He did a short hop at first, into the same
neighborhood where he'd finally located Leila,
since he knew it well. A quick glance down at the
compass told him the needle was still pointing east,
so clearly Amaal had traveled farther than this.

The next jump took him into Pasadena, where
he'd lost Leila's trail altogether for a time, thanks
to the way she and her fellow survivors had taken

refuge in the steam tunnels under Caltech. It would have been a strange symmetry that brought her back here, but another hasty survey of the area told him it was completely empty of anyone, human or djinn. Besides, there was the needle on the compass, still drawing him eastward.

This brought him into unexplored territory. The best he could do was travel to the freeway, then use its wide-open expanse to eat up large chunks of distance by transporting himself to the farthest point he could see, pausing to take his bearings and consult the compass, and then traveling another three or four miles in the blink of an eye.

Soon enough he was very far inland, with the San Bernardino mountain range looming ever closer. Was this where Omar had taken Leila? In a way, bringing her to such a remote spot made a good deal of sense, for the only djinn out here would be those who had been granted lands in this area, and so they would be scattered widely.

Mountains made good hiding places.

His next jump was shorter, for by this point he was forced to leave the freeway and take a smaller two-lane highway that wound its way up into the foothills. Because he could only see a mile or so ahead, that was as far as he could travel with each blink. At least the compass continued to point reassuringly to the east, telling him he was still on course.

If Yasir had been telling the truth about the efficacy of his spell, that is.

Malik jumped again, this time down a private road that branched off the highway, which by this point was only a single lane in either direction. Pine and oak and sycamore crowded on either side, but the private road was in good shape for such a remote area, covered in fine gravel that didn't appear to have been disturbed for some time.

The final blink brought him to the end of the lane, which opened out into a large clearing dominated by a wide, sturdy house on a raised stone foundation, with sharp eaves and a wall of windows on one side, and a deep porch on the other.

Standing on that porch was Amaal al-Tariq.

His eyes widened in alarm when he caught sight of his visitor, but Malik gave him no time to react, immediately blinking himself onto the porch so he could reach out and grasp the other djinn by both arms, shoving him up against the front door.

"Where is she?"

"Where is who?" Amaal responded, looking more confused than anything else.

"Leila!" Malik thundered. He was inch or so taller than the fire elemental, and he pulled himself up to his full height, praying that he looked sufficiently menacing that Amaal would feel compelled to answer.

Despite that maneuver, Amaal only shook his head. "I don't know what you're talking about!"

Malik tightened his grip. "I think you do. And I think you had better tell me…unless you want to explain yourself to the elders."

Amaal paled slightly. Perhaps Malik's threat had worked, or perhaps it was simply because the djinn couldn't seem to figure out how in the world Malik had managed to track him here, and so he'd decided that running wouldn't do him much good. Whatever the case, he blurted out, "She's not here. She's never been here."

Malik's fingers tightened on Amaal's arms. "You're lying."

"No, I'm really not. This is my house—the house and the land the elders gave me. Omar didn't bring her here. It would've been too easy for them to figure out."

After brief examination, this did seem like a plausible explanation. "Then where are they?"

"At—at a house he's occupied in Pacific Beach. That's just north of San Diego," Amaal added helpfully, as though hoping his continued cooperation might serve to dissuade Malik from breaking him over his knee like a sapling.

Actually, that particular feat might be fairly difficult to accomplish. Amaal was not as heavily muscled as Malik, but he was far from scrawny.

Pacific Beach. North of San Diego. He had probably been very near to the house in question last night when he'd gone to visit Yasir, never knowing that the woman he loved was being held barely a stone's throw away. Why Omar had taken a house so close to the community of Chosen and djinn in La Jolla, Malik could not say for sure. Very possibly it was merely his way of thumbing his nose at those who had made the choice to follow the rules. His chances of discovery were not so very great, because the inhabitants of such communities generally did not travel too far afield. Perhaps the potential risks involved had made the situation that much more thrilling to Omar, the possibility of discovery giving his illicit activities an extra fillip of excitement.

The situation was so absurd, Malik wanted to laugh. However, he decided it was better not to waste his energy.

"Where in Pacific Beach?"

"Just off Mission Boulevard and some side street—I can't remember what it's called. There's a line of houses, though. If you go too far north, you'll run into a restaurant." Amaal grimaced, then added, "You can let go now. You have the information you wanted."

Slowly, Malik released his grip on Amaal's biceps. "You had better be telling me the truth."

"I am." The other djinn shrugged, doing his best to appear nonchalant. "I tried to warn Omar that this would not end well, but he never listens to me."

"No, nor to anyone else, from what I've been able to tell." Malik turned away, preparing to jump back to the Malibu house, where he could consult a map and be on his way, but Amaal's voice stopped him.

"How did you do it?"

"Do what?"

"Find me here. No one knows about this place."

Malik gave him a grim smile. "I had some magical help. In the future, though, you should think twice about aiding and abetting a kidnapper. The elders will not be happy about what you've done."

Another lift of the shoulders, this one almost resigned. "Perhaps not. I think most of their ire will be focused on my brother, however."

That was probably an accurate assessment of the situation. However, Malik had no more time to spare for Amaal, or to worry about his possible punishment.

Leila was waiting, in a house in Pacific Beach.

To her surprise, she'd slept far better than she'd expected. Possibly that was because of the murmur of the waves only a few yards from the house, or maybe it was only that she'd been so damn tired. Besides, if Omar had decided to come to her room and force himself on her, there wasn't that much she could have done.

Close your eyes and think of the apocalypse.

Leila shuddered, then pushed herself out of bed and stood silently for a moment, listening to the sounds of the house around her. There was the ever-present roar of the surf, of course, and the cry of seagulls. But then she also heard a clatter coming from the direction of the kitchen. Omar, she guessed, making coffee or breakfast. Or rather, using his powers to conjure eggs benedict or what-have-you.

At any rate, it sounded as if he was occupied for the moment. She went in the bathroom and searched through the drawers, at last locating a clip she could use to get her hair up and out of the way. Since she'd washed it the day before, there was no point in wasting the time today.

Besides, the less time she was naked and vulnerable in the shower, the better.

She was out in less than five minutes. Towel wrapped around her, Leila went back into the bedroom and located clean underwear in one of the dresser drawers, a fresh bra in yet another. The clothing Omar had selected for her must have been djinn-wear—close-fitting long jackets in sumptuous brocades, to be worn over filmy blouses and baggy pants in lighter-weight silks. Beautiful, but not very practical…and neither were the little jeweled slippers that went with them.

Still, baggy silk pants were probably marginally better for escape attempts than long, flowing skirts. Now that the sun was out, bright and cheerful, and apparently caring not at all that the world had changed hands in the past few months, she could see once again how closely the houses in this stretch of shorefront were set next to one another. In fact, she thought it pretty likely that she'd be able to jump from one roof to another, if the opportunity presented itself.

Then again, she'd never been very good at heights. She should probably come up with an alternative escape route.

"Leila!" Omar's voice traveled up the stairs, loud, commanding. "Are you awake? I heard water running."

She went to the door and opened it. "Yes, I'm awake. I'll be down in just a moment."

"Good."

There hadn't been any time to put on makeup —if Omar had even provided any—but maybe that was for the best. He could see her without a speck of mascara or lip gloss and then decide for himself whether she was really as beautiful as he claimed she was.

Taking a breath, she made herself go downstairs. Sunlight poured through the windows, and the Pacific Ocean was deep, deep blue, sugar-frosted with whitecaps.

Despite her current dire situation, Leila could feel her spirits lift. It was hard to feel too dour on a morning such as this. Surely Omar wouldn't try anything with the sun shining down so brightly. It was hard to escape light like that. The sorts of things he probably had planned were far better carried out in the dark.

She passed the dining room and saw that the table was as clean and bare as they'd left it the night before. Apparently, her "host" thought it too lofty a setting for breakfast. When she entered the kitchen, she saw that her guess was right, because two place settings had been laid out on the island in the middle of the room. Omar himself was over by the counter, pouring coffee into some mugs. Without turning around, he said, "Good morning."

"Good morning," she replied, hoping she sounded cheerful and looking forward to a day with him, when in fact the exact opposite was true. What was the best way to play this? They'd exchanged a kiss—or at least, he'd forced one on her—so their relationship had changed subtly. Probably the smartest thing to do was be friendly but also act just a little bit awkward and embarrassed, as if she didn't quite know what to do after sharing that one intimacy with him.

Omar came over to her, mugs in each hand. "I assumed you'd want some coffee."

"Dying for some, actually," she replied, employing a hesitant smile, a brief downward glance, intimating that she was having a hard time meeting his eyes.

He didn't exactly smile, but she detected a twitch at one corner of his mouth, a glint in those bright blue eyes. Oh, yes, he'd noticed her reaction, and appeared to be pleased by it.

Good. She wanted him to think she'd softened toward him, while at the same time being confused as to what she should do about her transfer of affection. She lifted the coffee to her lips, blew on it gently. Omar hadn't asked her whether she wanted any cream or sugar; the coffee was black, just the way she liked it, but of course he couldn't have known that.

Arrogant. Luckily, she'd had plenty of experience dealing with arrogant men.

"It's a gorgeous day," she offered.

His gaze flicked toward the window, then returned to her. "Yes. Perhaps we can walk on the beach after breakfast."

"That sounds like a great idea."

A nod that seemed to indicate he was pleased by her apparent acceptance of the situation. "You slept well?"

"Like a baby. The sound of the ocean is so comforting, you know? I used to have one of those white-noise generators that sounded like the surf, but it's not really the same thing."

"Then I'm glad I chose a place where you could enjoy the sound of the waves." He set down his mug and snapped his fingers. Immediately, a set of plates appeared on the placemats he'd put on the island, both of them heaped with eggs and fruit and toast. "I believe this is the sort of food your people enjoyed eating to break their fast."

"Oh, yeah—that looks great." Smiling at him, she took her mug and went over to the island, then pulled out a stool and sat down. He followed, taking his seat next to her.

Today he wore a robe in a deep cobalt blue shade, trimmed in silver. It brought out the color of his eyes, but Leila didn't care much about that. What she cared about was how he'd expertly maneuvered his long robe out of the way as he sat down on the stool, the careless grace with which he moved. His legs were much longer than hers; it wouldn't require much effort for him to catch up with her.

And that wasn't even counting the way djinn could blink from place to place, and the way some of them could actually fly, like huge birds of prey. Omar was an air elemental, and so he must have that ability. He'd be on her like a hawk swooping on a mouse.

There has to be some way, she thought fiercely. *I just haven't thought of it yet.*

"This is great," she said, after taking a few bites of eggs. "It's so much easier when you can just snap your fingers and get anything you want to eat."

"It does tend to simplify matters," Omar responded. He drank some coffee, then set his mug back down. "Have you given any thought to what we discussed last night?"

"I—" She broke off there and pretended to

look out the window. The kitchen overlooked a small enclosed patio, lush with hanging baskets of fuchsias and petunias. Given the small lots these beach houses occupied, she guessed that patio might be the only "yard" this place possessed. "I did, a little. I mean, I'm still not sure what to think."

"Think only of the truth of the matter," he said softly. "I want what is best for you, and Malik al-Mazin does not. Everything he told you was a lie. Surely you cannot have feelings for a man like that."

Leila thought of the gentle way Malik had held her, of his frankness, his compassion. The blazing heat of his lovemaking, and the way his dark eyes lit up when he laughed. Oh, yes…she could definitely have feelings for a man like Malik al-Mazin. And not little feelings like thinking he was fun to be with, or someone she wouldn't kick out of bed for eating crackers. No, these were big feelings, the kind that made you consider an eternity spent together, and wonder whether that would still be long enough.

Big feelings, like…love.

She reached for her mug of coffee and took a large swallow before setting the mug back down again. The coffee was hot and black, and woke up some desperately needed nerve endings. "I don't—

no, I don't have feelings for him. I mean, I thought I did, but now that I've heard the truth…." A sigh seemed like it would work here, so she allowed one to escape her lips as she toyed with a lock of hair, wrapping it around one finger. "This is hard, Omar. When you kissed me last night…."

His brows drew together as his blue eyes took on a hard, hungry light. "Yes?"

"I—I didn't think I would react like that. I'm really not the sort of person who used to go from one man to another. But you made me feel…."

"Feel what, Leila?"

He wanted to kiss her again. She'd seen that look on too many faces before. The question was, did she dare let him? The last thing she wanted was for him to press matters further than she was willing to take them. This breakfast couldn't end with him trying to get her into bed. That wouldn't work at all—she didn't have a plan yet for fighting him.

"Like I wanted that kiss." She glanced away from him, back down at her plate, although she made no move to touch any of the food there. As with everything she'd done so far, uttering her next words was a calculated risk. However, she had to make him think she'd capitulated, even if she wasn't quite ready to admit it to herself. "Like I wanted you."

"Leila." Her name was barely a whisper on his breath. He bent closer, and she knew without a doubt that he was going to kiss her and that there wasn't a damn thing she could do about it except play along and hope he'd be satisfied with a kiss for now.

He tasted like coffee, but then, she probably did, too. Just like the night before, his technique was decent enough. Even so, she had to force herself not to recoil, not to close her mouth and draw away.

It's all an act, she told herself. *Just go with it.*

His hands were on her shoulders, holding her where she sat, preventing her from pulling away. She made herself sit there while he continued to kiss her, and then when he was done, she forced what she hoped was a besotted smile.

"Wow." Then she giggled and shook her head. "That's what I said last night, isn't it?"

"Yes, but there is no harm in having such a reaction." His gaze roved over her, lingering on the deeply cut neckline of the brocade jacket she wore. Leila didn't move, pretended to be oblivious to the naked desire in his face, although the food she'd eaten turned over in her stomach.

Please God, don't let him touch me again.

Unfortunately, it seemed as though God was occupied elsewhere, because Omar reached out and ran a finger over the exposed skin of her forearm, caressing her. A shudder passed through her body, although, judging by the way he smiled at her, slowly and lasciviously, she guessed he'd thought it was a shiver of desire and not a shudder of repulsion.

"I can think of something better to do than walk on the beach," he said.

"Oh?" she replied, playing the fool. "What's that?"

"I think you know."

Once again, she forced out a nervous giggle. "I'm not sure, Omar—"

At once his hand clamped down on her arm. "What is it you're not sure about?"

"I—" She blinked, wondering how long she could draw out this false confusion, make him think she really was conflicted about sleeping with him. No real confusion there; she'd rather dodge murderous djinn on the streets of downtown Los Angeles again than suffer those sorts of attentions from him. "It's just so fast, that's all. I mean, you only brought me here yesterday."

"Why delay, when you know the two of us were meant to be together?"

Oh, hell. She hadn't delayed very much with

Malik because, despite everything, despite all the pain of loss she'd suffered, she'd also known in her gut that she wanted to be with him. Well, her gut was talking to her now, although it was telling her a very different story from the one it had told about Malik.

Omar's grip tightened. "I hope you are not toying with me, Leila."

Damn it. Clearly, the delaying tactics weren't working anymore. Omar knew what he wanted, and that thing was her. Even as she stared at him, she could feel the muzziness of the glamour descend again. However, if she pretended to give in to it this time, she'd be consenting to a lot more than just a kiss.

No.

Her body rebelled, and instinct took over. She didn't even stop to think about what she was doing, only grabbed her mug of hot coffee and threw it right in his face. Eyes widening in shock, he let go of her arm, and she pushed herself off the stool and ran from the kitchen, hurling herself across the hallway and into the living room, bolting for the French doors.

From behind her, she heard his enraged cry. "Leila!"

Looking back would only waste time. Her fingers found the deadbolt on the door and turned it, and then she was running across the deck and onto the beach. Almost at once those silly bejeweled slippers she was wearing began to slide from her feet, and she stumbled. Without pausing, she kicked them off and kept running, the sand cool against her bare toes.

A shadow loomed overhead. Omar, taking to the air to pursue her. Already she was regretting the way she'd attacked him, but she'd committed to this flight and couldn't stop now.

In the next moment, she realized she had little choice in the matter, because he shot overhead and then lowered himself to the ground in front of her, blocking her path. At first she thought his face was suffused with fury over her attack, but then she realized his skin was reddened and splotchy, thanks to being splashed by that mug full of hot coffee. It would heal, she knew, because Malik had told her djinn had immense powers of healing. In the meantime, though, it would probably hurt like a bitch.

All those months of evading capture stood her in good stead now, for instead of running smack into Omar where he'd planted himself in front of her, she zigged to the right and headed for the property next to the house where he'd been holed up. Its back patio was fenced in, but the gate stood ajar, presumably left that way by whomever had last let themselves in or out of the property. Her plan was fuzzy at best, although she hoped she might be able to get inside and find a vehicle before the enraged djinn caught up with her.

However, she only made it a few steps before a tall shape materialized in front of her, causing her to come skidding to a halt. Terror-fueled adrenaline burst through her—until she realized that the man blocking her path was familiar, and dear.

She ran into Malik's arms, even as Omar descended a few paces away, his face even more red now, red with a combination of pain and fury.

"You will not have her, al-Mazin," he spat.

"Well," Malik returned, his voice harder than Leila had ever heard it. "We will just have to see about that."

SIXTEEN

WHEN HE'D SEEN LEILA RUNNING IN TERROR, barefoot in the sand, her long hair a stream of black silk behind her, a rage filled Malik like none he'd ever experienced before. Yes, he'd known that Omar al-Tariq must have her, and yet the reality of her situation had not come home to him until he appeared on the beach and caught sight of her desperate flight from her captor. Thank God she'd been close enough to run right to him, so he might protect her. And although the fury that pounded through his veins made him want to reach out and rip al-Tariq limb from limb, Malik forced himself to some measure of calm. There was a correct way to do this, one that would satisfy the laws of his people.

"You will face me now, Omar al-Tariq," he

called out. "You ran from this fight before, but you will not run any longer."

Al-Tariq's face twisted in anger. "I did not run," he retorted. "I merely realized that this mortal was not worth the effort."

Leila pulled herself free of Malik's arms, although she remained standing very close to him, close enough that he doubted Omar would attempt to reach out and take her. Anger brought a flush to her cheeks as she snapped, "If I wasn't worth the effort, then why steal me away from Malik? Why try to convince me that I was supposed to be with you rather than him? It seems like a lot of work for no real reason."

"You were a pawn, nothing more," Omar said coldly.

"In that case, you have nothing more to say to her," Malik told him. "I have challenged you to combat, and there is no reason to delay."

Omar's nostrils flared in dislike. "She is not worth fighting over."

When he responded to that weak comment, Malik did not bother to hide his scorn. "Coward. Face me, or your name will be even more tainted than it already is."

"Very well," Omar sneered. "When you have lost, and I have claimed this mortal to use as I please, you will regret provoking me."

Words calculated to anger him further. Malik ignored the taunt about Leila, knowing that a battle between djinn required as much mental effort as it did physical, for these duels were about pitting their powers against one another to see who would prevail. Air against water could be tricky, although he thought he had the advantage, thanks to their current location.

However, there was only one way to find out for sure.

Omar struck first, calling down the shore winds to batter Malik's body. Above the howl of those winds, he could hear Leila's startled gasp, even as she began to move toward him, clearly wishing to help.

He needed to get away from her. While of course Malik knew he would do nothing that might harm her, he could not say the same for his opponent. There was always the chance that she might be inadvertently injured by an attack intended for him.

Without thinking, he blinked himself away, reappearing at the water's edge. Omar's mocking laughter followed.

"Running away already?" the air elemental taunted him. "Why, that was little more than a summer's breeze. Let us see what you think about this."

Air swirled, collected, became nearly solid, a spinning vortex moving toward him at a rapid rate. Malik did not waver, though, knowing he was now close to the source of his own power. Another whirlwind appeared, this one not made of wind at all, instead a water spout that moved up the shore and connected with Omar's tornado. Water sprayed everywhere, but as he watched, Malik saw the water spout overcome the tornado, tearing apart the winds that composed it until it collapsed and was gone.

"Well, that is something," Omar remarked, the sneering note still clear in his voice. He had stopped a few feet away from the water's edge, stance wary as he regarded his opponent. "But I do not think it is enough."

More wind came whistling out of nowhere, pummeling Malik with the force of a thousand unseen fists. He grunted and stepped back into the water, making sure to have his retreat appear as though he could not summon any kind of a suitable defense. Omar came closer, clearly sensing triumph.

Good.

The attacking winds hurt, but Malik ignored them. Whatever injury Omar caused, he knew he would heal from it soon enough. He bent double, wincing as the winds tore at his hair, whipped the sands so it felt as though they were scouring the skin from his flesh.

There. Now both of al-Tariq's feet were firmly planted in the water, little waves rushing over them.

That was all Malik needed.

This ocean was a hungry one, cold and strong and utterly without mercy. The wave came from the depths, growing in power as it reached the shore. All around them, the gentle water that had lapped at their feet receded, rushing out to merge with the force he had summoned, the wave growing in size, looming taller than twice the height of a man...three times higher...four times higher. It came in with a roar like a locomotive, and moved nearly as fast.

Malik's power shielded him, but al-Tariq did not have that same protection...which was exactly what Malik had counted on. Even as the other djinn turned to flee, realizing the danger he was in, the looming wave crashed down with the force of an earthquake, sending out such a booming roar that Malik's ears rang from the sound. The surging water knocked al-Tariq flat against the sand. His fingers scrabbled at the ground, but it was not his element and could not save him. Then the surging water swirled around his body and pulled him out to sea, the bright, shimmering blue of his robes soon drowned in the ocean's vast dark. Malik watched for a long moment, fearing that his adversary might somehow claw himself free of the water despite its immense force, but he saw nothing, no glint of blue robes, no movement besides that of the waves.

Then Leila was running toward him, face white above the gaudy glory of the red and gold clothing she wore. "Oh, my God, Malik! Are you all right?"

"I am fine," he said. In truth, he was weary, winded as if he had just run a footrace. He stumbled his way back onto dry land, going to meet his Chosen so he might take her hand in his. "Come—we should get away from the water line."

"Why?" she asked, clinging to him, clearly wanting to make sure there was no chance of their being parted again. However, she seemed to know she should heed his words, for she kept pace with him as he staggered across the sand, putting as much distance between them and the water as he could.

"You'll see."

The wave came rushing back in, not as tall this time, but nearly as ferocious as it sought to fill the vacuum it had left behind. Water crashed upon the shore, rising higher and higher. Leila's eyes filled with alarm, and she held on to Malik's arm, all but dragging him to higher ground and safety.

It could not reach quite this far, so he stopped, Leila still clinging to him. As he watched, the water pulled away once more, but more gently this time, the normal rhythm of the tide moving out to sea.

"The ocean has great power," he said quietly. "I only had to call upon it to help me. This was something Omar forgot, or perhaps he never knew. Yes, we djinn of the water are sometimes more limited in our powers, for we do not have the source of our strength all around us at all times, as the air and earth elementals do. But when water is nearby, even in the smallest amounts, it can come with a force to drown out all others."

As he spoke, he saw a glint of bright blue on the sand. Once the waves receded, the sea left its victim behind.

"Is he...?" Leila began, then stopped, her voice hushed.

"Yes. We djinn are strong, but our strength is no match for the power of the waves. Omar was too confident...but then, I intended him to think that he had the upper hand."

"So you weren't really hurt?" She tilted her head up at him, dark blue eyes nearly the same color as the glinting sea only a few yards away. "I almost ran to you to try and help, I was so worried."

"I am glad you did not." His fingers tightened on hers. Her skin was cool from the wild sea air, but Malik didn't mind. He could feel the strength of her spirit in the slender fingers entwined with his own, sense the fierceness of her love, and that was enough for him. "And yes, he was hurting me, although not as badly as he thought. He wanted to come close and gloat, and that was all I needed. Once he stood in the water, he was mine."

Leila nodded, although he didn't see any real satisfaction in her expression, only a sort of abstracted worry. "I suppose there was no other way."

Malik's eyes narrowed as he stared down at her. "Surely you do not think he should live, after everything that he had done. You were certainly not his first victim."

"No, it's not that." She drew in a breath, then said, "It's more that I wish you didn't have to be the one who killed him."

Ah, so she was only worried about how the responsibility for al-Tariq's death might weigh upon him. Malik began to pull her close, but then he stiffened and stood up straight, for a group of three figures suddenly appeared before them on the sand. Two men and a woman, her long red hair blowing in the breeze.

The elders.

Leila had no idea who the three people —the three djinn—who had just materialized in front of them were, but she guessed they must be important, judging by the way Malik stopped, then lifted his chin and squared his shoulders. One of them actually had hints of gray in his hair, the only sign of aging she had ever seen in a djinn. The woman was beautiful, with gorgeous copper-colored hair that fell to her waist. The third djinn, another man, was tall and handsome and dark-haired, but it was the first two who caught Leila's attention.

"Elders," Malik said, bowing slightly from the waist.

These were the elders? They sure as hell didn't look like elders, the gray in the one djinn's hair notwithstanding. Was she supposed to bow, too? Leila didn't know what she should do with herself, so she made herself stand quietly at Malik's side and hoped that none of them would notice her sandy bare feet, her complete lack of makeup.

"Malik al-Mazin," said the one with the gray-flecked hair. His gaze flickered toward Omar's body, which lay at the water line a few dozen yards away, although his expression never changed. "It seems your score has finally been settled."

"Only because al-Tariq forced my hand," Malik replied. He seemed more resigned than worried, which Leila thought must be a good sign. Surely these elders weren't going to punish him for acting in self-defense? Given the situation, there hadn't been a whole hell of a lot he could have done except fight Omar. From what Malik had said right before the two of them started brawling, it sounded as though these sorts of "duels" were how the djinn customarily settled their differences.

"Oh, we know," said the redhead. She had a low, calm voice, but Leila thought she noted a hint of amusement in the djinn woman's tone. "For a man who did not wish to fight, he had a strange way of going about his business."

Malik bowed his head. "It was inevitable, I suppose."

"Yes." The female elder shifted slightly, her gaze moving toward Leila. "And you came to no harm, Leila Donovan?"

Leila couldn't help starting a little at the question. How had they known her name? But then, these elders seemed to know a lot, so she supposed it wasn't so strange that they would possess that piece of information. "No, I'm fine," she said. "Omar didn't have me captive long enough to do any real damage. But let's just say there was a reason why I had to bolt this morning."

"I am only glad I came when I did," Malik said, then added, "and sorry that I could not come sooner. Unfortunately, until I received some assistance, I did not have the means to track you down."

She wondered what that "assistance" had been. Well, that was a story he could tell her over a glass of wine…preferably one shared in bed, with a fire going in the hearth and the sound of the waves outside. Yes, that would do nicely. An evening like that, and she might be able to put this whole terrible incident behind her.

"It's all right," she murmured, then added in a slightly louder tone, so all the elders could hear, "I'm all right. Really, I just want to go home."

"Yes, about that," the eldest djinn, the one with the gray in his hair, said. "You will be making your permanent home now, will you not? We were willing to indulge you in this, for you had valid reasons for not immediately settling with the group in Bel-Air, but it seems clear enough to us now that you and your Chosen are comfortable with one another. There should be no further reasons for delay."

"No, there are not," Malik replied, both his voice and his expression resigned. It seemed clear enough to Leila that he still wasn't entirely happy about having to leave the Malibu house behind.

Well, she wasn't all that thrilled, either, but she knew she'd get over it. The important thing was for the two of them to be together. She'd realized, after being taken from him, how much she enjoyed his company, how much she'd allowed herself to care in the short amount of time they'd been together. As long as she was with him, she could muddle through the rest. Besides, it would be good to be part of a community again. After she'd lost the last members of her little group of survivors and she'd had to forge ahead on her own, she'd realized how much it hurt to be entirely alone.

No worries about that now. She had Malik, and they would both have the people in the Bel-Air settlement. In time, she'd probably forget what those days and nights of running had been like.

At any rate, that was her hope. She wanted to put all those horrors behind her.

"Then go to Malibu and fetch your things," the red-haired elder said. "We will check tomorrow to make sure you are safely settled in your new home."

She smiled as she spoke, but Leila heard the warning in her words. The elders might be mostly hands-off, as Malik had said, but Leila had a feeling they didn't scruple at interfering when necessary.

Malik bowed his head and looked as if he intended to reply, but even as his mouth opened, he was interrupted by the arrival of Omar's brother Amaal.

He popped into existence a few feet away from where they all stood. From the strain in his handsome features, and the way his gaze flickered toward the body of his brother where it lay on the sand, it seemed obvious enough that he'd already feared the worst. Still, he lifted his head and stared at the elders, pointedly ignoring Malik and Leila.

"I would like to take my brother's body for proper burial," he said, arms crossed, fire-hued robes blowing in the sea breeze.

The red-haired elder's smile abruptly faded. "There are some who would say he has not earned that honor, but we will not deny you the chance to mourn in the proper way." She paused for a moment and sent a single sideways glance at the elder with the gray-streaked hair. His nod was so slight, Leila didn't think she would have noticed it at all if she hadn't been watching for it.

Could the elders speak to one another with their minds, the way she and Malik could? She had to admit that would be a handy trick, one that would give them the chance to confer while standing right in front of whomever they might be passing judgment on.

"Provided," the elder went on, her tone stern, "that you surrender your own hostage so he might be returned to his djinn. I know that you held him only as a favor to your brother, but continuing to keep him away from his home does you no credit."

"I know," Amaal said. "That is partly why I came here. I wished to give him back, but I did not think it would be a good idea to bring him directly to Fatima. She might wish to retaliate."

"That she would," Malik growled. "For clearly, you seized Adam only as a means to draw me away from Leila, so that Omar had the opportunity to steal her while I was occupied elsewhere."

To his credit, Amaal looked almost contrite. "I told Omar it was not a good idea, but he would not take my counsel. He used the djinn glamour on Adam to obtain the location where you were staying with Leila, but I assure you, he is otherwise unharmed and doing well."

"Where is he?" asked the oldest of the elders.

"At my home in the mountains, the one that was assigned to me. It is a remote spot, and one where I knew he would escape notice."

This admission caused Malik to make an odd little growling noise, something that sounded like a strange mixture of frustration and amusement. Leila sent a quizzical glance up at him, wondering what that was all about; he shook his head and murmured, "I was there and had no idea. I hope Fatima will forgive me that oversight."

"It is good that Fatima's Chosen has come to no harm," the redheaded djinn said. "I will accompany you to your home, so I might return him to Fatima—and also so I may see you safely installed there. For I will tell you the same thing I just told Malik—you will stay at the home you were assigned, and no longer take up residence wherever you please. Do you understand?"

"Yes, my lady," Amaal replied. He looked so hangdog, Leila almost felt sorry for him. Was the land they'd assigned him really so terrible? "And my brother?"

The third elder, the one who had remained silent this whole time, finally spoke. His voice was deep and calm. "I will bring him to you, so you may lay him to rest on the mountainside. Although his was not the power of the earth, we can all hope that his soul might learn some peace in the rarefied air of your new home."

Amaal lowered his head. "I thank you."

The red-haired elder went to him and laid a hand on his arm. "Let us go now and fetch Adam. I do not wish to think of Fatima having to spend a single moment more in worry and torment than she already has."

"Of course." For a second, Amaal glanced over at Malik, although Leila couldn't precisely decipher his expression. Was he looking for forgiveness? Was he plotting some kind of revenge? Or was he only trying to reassure himself that neither Malik nor Leila had suffered any kind of harm at his brother's hands?

She didn't know. There was something appealing about Amaal, a certain quality that made it difficult to hate him. She wished she could go to him and tell him it was all right, that she didn't harbor any ill will toward him because of what he had done. For his brother…definitely. But in the end, Omar was the one who paid the true price for his greed and his spite.

Malik stood straight and still next to her, his mouth compressed to a thin line. Clearly, he wasn't ready to forgive Amaal. Maybe someday he would. In the meantime, it was probably a good thing that Omar's brother wouldn't have any reason to come anywhere near the Bel-Air settlement.

The redheaded elder and Amaal disappeared then, vanishing into thin air with an audible *pop*. The two remaining elders watched Leila and Malik, their gazes stern. It was clear enough what they wanted.

"Come on, Malik," she murmured. "Let's go home."

SEVENTEEN

PACKING UP FOR A DJINN WAS NOT QUITE THE same thing as it was for a human, for all it required was for him to send their things over to their new location. Malik had already decided on the house where they would go; it was a few streets away from Fatima's palatial home, and had a waterfall and pond in addition to the swimming pool and spa. Not the same as the ocean, true, but he hoped Leila would be happy there. At any rate, it was the work of an eye blink to manage the transfer of their belongings. And this house—it showed no trace of their ever being here, for he had done nothing to change the furniture or anything else.

Well, except for one thing. As Leila watched, he went to the fireplace and carefully lifted her cowrie shell from the mantel, then brought it over to her. "I thought you would want to take this with us to our new home."

Her fingers wrapped around the shell, and she sent a tremulous smile up at him. "Thank you. I —" She broke off there and shook her head. "It's silly, isn't it, to feel attached to this place? I mean, I was only here for less than a week. But...."

"I know," he said gently. He bent and kissed her on the cheek, a soft caress, one intended to tell her that he cared...and that he understood. "There is something enchanted about this house, I think. Or perhaps it only feels that way because it is the place where I fell in love with you."

A faint flush tinged her cheeks. "And I fell in love with you," she said, her voice soft. "I didn't know for sure what was going on with me...I'm not the type to fall for someone that fast." A mischievous glint entered her eyes. "Are you sure you didn't use that djinn glamour on me?"

"Positive," he replied, refusing to be baited. "As you recall, I did attempt it, and it didn't work. No, this is something I believe you mortals like to refer to as 'chemistry.'"

"Omar tried the glamour on me, too," Leila said. Her mouth twisted in distaste. "Thank God it didn't work for him, either."

Anger rose in him, but Malik pushed it away.

Omar was dead and could no longer hurt anyone. Besides, Leila had just stated that the glamour was as ineffective for al-Tariq as it had been for him, which only served to support the hypothesis he had formed earlier. Voice musing, he said, "I think you might have a touch of djinn blood in you."

Eyes widening, she stared up at him. "What?"

"I had wondered about it before…in general, djinn cannot use their powers of glamour on one another. That you are apparently immune to it as well…." He let the words trail off, then shrugged. "It makes some sense. Djinn have mingled with humans over the millennia. Not so very often, but enough times that there were still those whose families had djinn blood."

For a moment, she didn't say anything. She looked down at the cowrie shell she held in one hand, then glanced out the floor-to-ceiling windows, eyes fixed on the shifting blues of the ocean beyond. "Was it enough to save them from the Heat?"

Puzzled, he stared at her. "What do you mean?"

A small frown touched her brow as she said, "There was a tiny fraction of humanity that just happened to be immune. But do you djinn know why? Just some quirk of genetics? Or is it that the survivors were the ones with just a smidge of djinn blood, enough to save them from the Heat?"

That was something he hadn't thought of. As far as he knew, there was no way to definitely test whether a particular human possessed any djinn DNA, and so Leila's theory, while interesting, was not something that could ever be proven one way or another. "I don't know," he replied slowly. "I am not sure anyone knows."

Her chin lifted and he could tell she was angry…although he also knew that anger wasn't directed at him. "Maybe one of you should try to figure it out," she said. "Because if that's the case, then it might turn out that all those djinn out there who're so bent on eradicating the last of humanity might be killing some of their own."

Malik also hadn't thought of that. Perhaps this was something that should be mentioned to the elders, although it would be rather like shutting the barn door after the horse was gone. The world was nearly empty of humans now, except for those who were Chosen. He opened his mouth to speak, but Leila shook her head.

"Something to think about," she said. Her free hand took his, clutching his fingers tightly, her touch fierce. "For now, though—take me home."

This place—well, it wasn't a ten-thousand-square-foot edifice perched on the edge of a Malibu cliff, but Leila thought it would do pretty well. Maybe half that size, it had been modeled on a Tuscan villa, with gorgeous stonework and carefully selected antiques and warm-washed walls. And there was the pond outside, with a waterfall and lily pads and flowers blooming everywhere.

She wanted to love it, mostly because she knew Malik had been so worried that she wouldn't. Only a spoiled brat wouldn't love a house like this, and she hoped she wasn't anything like that, especially when you considered that her entire rented house in Highland Park could have fit in the master suite in this place.

Their discussion right before they'd come here still weighed on her mind. Was it even possible that she might be part djinn, going back decades or even hundreds of years? She supposed it might be true; what woman from a small village in Persia would have had the courage to confess to her husband that she'd been visited by a "demon" in the middle of the night, one she feared had given her a child?

No wonder so many cultures had stories about incubi and succubi. Most likely they weren't demons at all, but randy djinn with a taste for slumming.

As for the rest…she didn't know what to say. Maybe there were still some human survivors out there, but would the djinn hunting them even care that they might have a tiny bit of DNA handed down from a long-ago tryst with an elemental?

It was all too much to wrap her head around.

Malik seemed to sense her inner turmoil, because after he'd given her a tour of the house and shown her that all her things had been carefully placed in the master bedroom, he said he wanted to arrange things in the library, thus giving her some time to herself. She walked in the garden and let the breeze ruffle her hair, watched the tiny, perky black phoebes with their proud little crests flutter around the pond, clearly drawn to the water. Yes, it was very beautiful here. She thought she could find some peace in this place, if she'd only allow it into her soul.

Movement on the other side of the backyard caught her eye, and Leila glanced away from the pond to see the red-haired djinn elder standing near the tall hedge that separated their property from the one behind it. The djinn woman lifted a hand, beckoning.

Refusing to come over wasn't really an option. Leila squared her shoulders and walked over to the elder, her heart pounding a little, even though she tried to tell herself that this was probably just the elders' way of checking up on her and Malik, of making sure that they really had come to settle in Bel-Air and weren't lingering in Malibu.

"It is a lovely place," the djinn woman said.

"Yes," Leila replied, then paused, not sure how else to respond.

"And yet your heart is heavy."

A rueful smile tugged at Leila's lips. "Is it that obvious?"

"To those who pay attention, yes." The red-haired elder was silent for a moment. It seemed that she was looking at the house, but who knew for sure? This close, her beauty was even more obvious, and extravagant—the warm copper shine of her hair, the poreless nature of her fair skin. Any director who laid eyes on her would have to cast her as some kind of otherworldly creature, because she was far too perfect to be a mere mortal. She went on, "These things that prey on your mind…let them go. For yes, many hundreds of years ago, before your mother's family even took the name of Khorasani, a djinn loved your many-times-great-grandmother, and she bore a child. There is djinn blood in you, enough that you could resist our glamour."

Leila took in a breath, trying to process this revelation. Yes, she and Malik had discussed it as a possibility, but that wasn't the same thing as having a djinn elder tell you that one of your distant ancestors wasn't quite of this earth.

"And," the djinn woman went on, her tone firm, as though she wanted to make sure Leila would not try to interrupt, "I can also tell you that has nothing to do with being immune. There were some with djinn blood in your world, true, but there were far more who had the inborn ability to resist the Heat. Wherever that ability came from, it is not one our blood granted them."

"But you don't know why."

Now the elder's expression was almost sad. With a graceful shrug, she replied, "No. We knew that there would be some who survived, but we still do not know for sure what gave them their immunity. Perhaps it was a gift from God."

Some gift, Leila thought, *to survive this horrible disease, only to be hunted without mercy.* She said, her voice hard, "If that's the case, you'd think He would have given us some way to fight you."

"But He did," the djinn elder said. Her lips curved in an enigmatic smile. "Or rather, some of you have already figured it out. There are other survivors still, more than you might think."

"Where—?"

The djinn woman held up a hand. "Their

story is not yours, Leila. For you are Chosen and can live without fear, here in this sanctuary the man you love has provided for you. Go to him, and do not let your thoughts be troubled."

She disappeared then, and Leila blinked, still not used to the precipitous way the djinn came and went. When she opened her eyes, she saw Malik standing out by the pond, a glass of wine in each hand.

Wine sounded good. After the conversation she'd just shared with the elder, Leila thought she could use a drink. She went over to meet Malik, and smiled as he offered one of the glasses to her. "Shall we sit?" he asked, his gaze moving toward one of the iron benches arranged so you could sit and watch the solar-powered fountain in the middle of the water splash away.

This seemed like as good a suggestion as any, since the day was sunny and bright, the air warm. One would never know that Thanksgiving was coming up the next week…or at least, the day on which Thanksgiving was supposed to fall. Would the Chosen here in Bel-Air want to continue the tradition, or were they like her, wondering how much they actually had to be thankful for?

No, she told herself as she watched Malik sit down on the cast-iron bench next to her. *I have a hell of a lot to be thankful for, especially the man sitting right here. I can't let survivor's guilt taint the way I feel for him.*

"You seem troubled," he said quietly. "The house does not please you?"

"The house is wonderful," she replied, then reached over to lay her free hand on his. "You're wonderful. That's not it at all."

"I saw that Istar came to visit you."

"Is that what she's called?" It seemed to fit, with its echoes of the goddess's name. Or maybe the elder was so old, she had been the original inspiration for Ishtar. Leila paused and took a sip of the wine. A blend, but she wasn't sure of what. Pinot gris, and maybe Viognier? Whatever it might turn out to be, it was crisp and refreshing… and seemed to make her feel even guiltier for being alive to enjoy it. A breath, and Leila went on, without waiting for Malik to reply, "She told me that I did have djinn blood…and also that it didn't matter. That is, it has nothing to do with being immune."

"It was only a guess," Malik said, his tone gentle, comforting. "A logical one, but still. But at least now you know the truth."

Leila gave his fingers a small squeeze, just to let him know how much she appreciated him being there for her. It would take some time for her to adjust to the realization that her own DNA wasn't entirely human, but she'd manage. In the meantime, she wanted to hold on to what Istar had told her, that there were more survivors than she thought. Had the djinn elder been referring to the survivors in New Mexico? Maybe there was some way to reach out to them.

But then, it seemed as if Istar's words had been almost a warning. She hadn't wanted Leila to focus on those other survivors, but rather on the people who surrounded her here in Bel-Air, on the life that now lay ahead of her. This story was hers, and no other's.

"I heard from Fatima," Malik went on, his tone brightening. "Adam has been returned to her, none the worse for wear." A pause, during which he smiled and gave a small shake of his head. "Actually, it sounded as though he had quite the adventure, for Amaal gave him the run of the property, on which happened to be a small stream. Adam apparently spent most of his time fishing, as it seemed the house must have once belonged to an accomplished angler who had left his tackle behind."

This revelation made Leila chuckle, and she was glad, because she desperately needed something to lighten the mood. "Adam didn't try to get away?"

"I believe Amaal told Adam that he was many

hundreds of miles from Bel-Air, and if he tried to leave, the human-hunting djinn would come after him. Which, I fear, is only the truth. Chosen are supposed to be protected, but…."

"But Adam didn't dare take the risk."

"No, which I suppose was wise of him." Malik shifted on the bench so he faced her. His eyes sought Leila's. "As your people liked to say, no harm, no foul. He is home and safe, and—"

"And so am I," she finished for him. "Thanks to you."

He was silent for a moment. Then he set his wine glass down on one of the flagstones beneath them. "You helped as well. It was easier to confront Omar out in the open, rather than in the home he had taken for himself. Your escape attempt was well-timed."

Even though the day was warm, Leila shivered slightly. She didn't want to think about what would have happened if she hadn't managed to take the djinn off-guard with that splash of hot coffee in the face. Yes, she'd managed to get away, but if Malik hadn't come along when he did….

He seemed to sense something of her thoughts, because he took both her hands in his, then kissed each palm gently. "My love, you cannot torture yourself with thoughts of what might have come to pass. You are safe now, and we are together. What else do we need?"

What else? She thought of everyone she'd lost, of what the world had lost. Everything had changed forever, and she knew that, no matter what she did, she would never have the power to alter the past. All she had now was the future—a future with Malik in it. Malik, who loved her, who had done whatever was needed to make sure she was safe. Surely she couldn't be so arrogant as to ask for or expect anything else.

"What else do we need?" she echoed softly, her fingers wrapped tightly around his.

"Nothing. Nothing at all."

The End

Djinn Dominion will continue with Amaal's story in *Forgotten,* due out in June 2018. Sign up here for Christine Pope's mailing list so you never miss a new release!

THE WITCHES OF CANYON ROAD

(Paranormal Romance)

Hidden Gifts

Darker Paths (May 2018)

Mysterious Ways (July 2018)

———

DJINN DOMINION

(Paranormal Romance)

Stolen

Forgotten (June 2018)

Driven (August 2018)

———

THE WITCHES OF CLEOPATRA HILL*

(Paranormal Romance)

Darkangel

Darknight

Darkmoon

Sympathetic Magic

Protector

Spellbound

A Cleopatra Hill Christmas

Impractical Magic

Strange Magic

The Arrangement

Defender

Bad Blood

Deep Magic

Darktide

Books 1-3 and Books 4-6 of this series are also available in two separate omnibus editions at special boxed set prices. Chronicles of Cleopatra Hill includes the series' two "back in time" novellas, *Bad Blood* and *The Arrangement.*

———

THE DJINN WARS*

(Paranormal Romance)

Chosen

Taken

Fallen

Broken

Forsaken

Forbidden

Awoken

Illuminated

The first three books of this series are also available in
an omnibus edition at a special low price!

———

THE WATCHERS TRILOGY*

(Paranormal Romance)

Falling Dark

Dead of Night

Rising Dawn

———

THE SEDONA FILES*

(Paranormal Romance)

Bad Vibrations

Desert Hearts

Angel Fire

Star Crossed

Falling Angels

Enemy Mine

The first three books of this series are also available in an omnibus edition at a special low price!

TALES OF THE LATTER KINGDOMS*

(Fantasy Romance)

All Fall Down

Dragon Rose

Binding Spell

Ashes of Roses

One Thousand Nights

Threads of Gold

The Wolf of Harrow Hall

Moon Dance

The Song of the Thrush

Books 1-3 and Books 4-6 of this series are also available in two separate omnibus editions at special boxed set prices.

THE GAIAN CONSORTIUM SERIES*

(Science Fiction Romance)

Blood Will Tell

Breath of Life

The Gaia Gambit

The Mandala Maneuver

The Titan Trap

The Zhore Deception

* Indicates a completed series

Christine Pope has been writing stories ever since she commandeered her family's Smith-Corona typewriter back in grade school. Her work includes paranormal romance, fantasy romance, and science fiction/space opera romance. The Land of Enchantment cast its spell on her while she was researching her Djinn Wars series, and she now makes her home in Santa Fe, New Mexico.

Don't miss any of Christine's new releases—sign up for her newsletter here.

Christine Pope on the Web:
www.christinepope.com

 facebook.com/ChristinePopeAuthor

 twitter.com/ChristineJPope

pinterest.com/ChristineJPope